THE BAND
PLAYED
MURDER

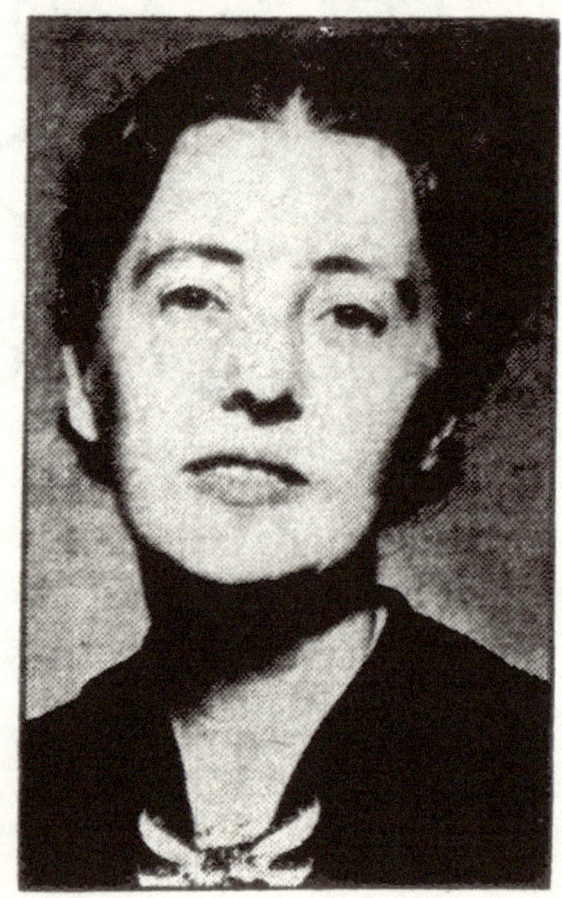

Edith Howie

THE BAND PLAYED MURDER

Edith Howie

COACHWHIP PUBLICATIONS
Greenville, Ohio

The Band Played Murder, by Edith Howie
© 2022 Coachwhip Publications edition
Introduction © Curtis Evans
Front cover: Vocalist (William P. Gottlieb/Ira and Leonore
S. Gershwin Fund Collection, Music Division, Library of
Congress)

First published 1946
Edith Howie, 1900-1979
CoachwhipBooks.com (print) / Coachwhip.com (epub)

ISBN 1-61646-528-X
ISBN-13 978-1-61646-528-5

MURDERS END IN LOVERS MEETING:
THE MYSTERIES OF EDITH HOWIE

Curtis Evans

Dear miss Howie

*I saw a picture in the family circle and liked
the looks of you. Thought I would like for you to
correspond with me. I am single not been married but would like to if I could find the rite
girl ha ha. Maybe that you. I hope it is. Please
write to me. Send picture of your self and I will
do the same. I would like to come up and see you
if that all rite with you. I have been in Dakota
a few years now and liked it all rite. How is
crops. They look good here. I am 43 years old
and have brown eyes and dark haire and weigh
175 and 6 feet tall. Write. Tell me all a bought
your self. I will cease now.*

A friend

When an August 1941 profile in the Sioux Falls *Argus-
Leader*, the leading newspaper of the Great Plains state of
South Dakota, described Edith Howie as an "unpretentious person, quiet, small-featured and trim," with auburn
hair, "deep blue eyes and . . . small, tapered . . . unusually
beautiful hands," Edith, an unmarried woman of forty-one
years who lived quietly in Sioux Falls with her parents,

5

had just published her maiden mystery novel, *Murder for Tea*, about the fatal poisoning of the town vamp at a literary luncheon. The novel had appeared in *Three Prize Murders*, a trilogy of tales which had received honorable mentions in publisher Farrar and Rinehart's second annual Mary Roberts Rinehart mystery contest, named for America's preeminent woman crime writer (one of her sons had co-founded the company); and it had been highly praised in the *New York Times Book Review* by Isaac Anderson, who pronounced it "as puzzling and as entertaining a mystery as one could desire." (The previous year Elizabeth Daly had entered her debut novel, *Unexpected Night*, in the first Mary Roberts Rinehart mystery contest, in which she, like Edith Howie the next year, was a runner-up.)

Living up to her "unpretentious" reputation, Edith Howie wryly noted to her *Argus-Leader* interviewer, Lois Thrasher (who the next year would transfer to the *Chicago Daily News*, where she became night editor in 1945), that so far her greatest putative perk of fame as an author consisted of receiving myriad marriage proposals from importunate "mail-order bachelors," like the gentleman quoted at the top of this introduction, who had eagerly espied Edith's picture in *The Family Circle*, a women's household magazine distributed for free at the once omnipresent Piggly Wiggly grocery store chain. Another of Edith's male mystery admirers rang her up at home on the telephone one night, obviously inebriated and gushingly praising her books. When he failed to make any headway with the object of his fervent devotion, he rang off, angrily admonishing her, "I guess your books aren't so good after all!" Edith, resistant to the charms of such men, remained single for the rest of her life. Yet she enjoyed an impressively full creative existence, allowing her to give rewarding expression to her twin true loves: professional writing and amateur acting.

Between 1938 and 1946 Edith wrote eight mystery novels, seven of which were published in the United States and the United Kingdom as well as other countries (there are some particularly nice Spanish-language paperback editions); and during this time as well, and for many years afterward, she was one of the leading lights in Sioux Falls' community theater, both writing plays and performing in them. After her retirement from acting in the 1970s Edith reviewed local productions for the *Argus-Leader*, publishing her final review (*The Fantasticks*) in March 1979, just two months before her death at the age of seventy-eight. Although her career as a mystery writer was a brief one, lasting less than a decade, Edith during this time established herself as an American exponent of regional mystery and became as well a pioneer of the "cozy" detective story, where the tone remains light amid larcenies and criminal mayhem fails utterly to falsify the adage "murders end in lovers meeting."

****

Edith Christy Ann Howie was born on July 12, 1900, the eldest of three children of William Henry Howie and Christy Ann McLean, natives of Ontario, Canada of Scottish derivation. Shortly after the couple's marriage on April 12, 1899, they moved to Bradley, a town of fewer than 350 souls in the northern part of the raw, decade-old state of South Dakota, where Edith entered the world. William Henry Howie was the son of Cyrus Thompson Howie, an Oxford Mills farmer and Wesleyan Methodist, while Christy McLean was the daughter of Hugh McLean, a Maxville furniture store owner, Presbyterian and freemason. For four years prior to his marriage William had been a member of Canada's Northwest Mounted Police and at the time of his nuptials he managed a cheese factory in

Maxville. He carried on this latter occupation in Bradley, also adopting his wife's faith, before moving with his
growing family in 1905 to the city of Sioux Falls, South
Dakota, the state's largest city, located on the bank of the
Sioux River in the far southeastern corner of the state,
tucked between Minnesota and Iowa. For many years there
he sold farm machinery for International Harvester Company. In this capacity he was often away on the road, plying
his vital trade among Great Plains farmers, but his family
became staunch members of Sioux Falls' First Presbyterian
Church, where Edith in the 1920s served as an organist.
"Always an organist and never a bride," self-deprecatingly
comments a character in one of Edith's later mystery novels, which was true enough in her case.

Edith's father lived a more outwardly eventful life. For
eleven months between June 1924 and April 1925, William
Howie served, at the request of his highly-placed friend,
Mayor Thomas Mckinnon, as chief of police at Sioux Falls,
which then had a population of about 30,000 individuals.
In 1925 Chief of Police Howie reported that the police
department had made 1135 arrests during the previous
year, about 4% of the population. The great majority of
these arrests were for minor violations of liquor laws and
traffic ordinances, although there were also eight cases of
burglary, seven of bootlegging, five of bank robbery, five
of prostitution, four of grand larceny and four of forgery,
as well as two rapes and an assault. Happily not a single
murder was reported that year. "Nashiona (aka Sioux Falls)
is small town Middle West and doesn't go in for murders,"
asserts the narrator of *Murder for Tea* with unintended iro-
ny. "It isn't that sort of town." Most of the other offenses
with which Chief Howie and his men had to deal, like
discharging firecrackers within city limits and bathing
outdoors in the nude (i.e., skinny-dipping), admittedly
strike one as disarmingly minor.

Hanson & Leigh Photo
Chief W. H. Howie

As Halloween approached in October 1924, Chief
Howie issued a stern reminder to the city's boisterous
youth that pranks were only tolerated on All Hallows' Eve
itself, while the commission of acts of actual damage to
people's property would most definitely be prosecuted.
Rather more seriously, Chief Howie the previous month
warned local representatives of the Ku Klux Klan that his
department was prepared to make "wholesale arrests" of
any masked persons parading through city streets. During
the Twenties, which saw a national resurgence of the Klan,
South Dakota, like other Midwestern states, was, as one
authority puts it, "plagued by cross- and circle-burnings,
tar-and-featherings, and mass rallies and parades, including one attended by nearly 8000 people," mostly with the
goal of intimidating the state's Catholic population. Perhaps it was this sort of thing which prompted Chief Howie
to resign from office after having served for less than a
year. He had been long retired from policing in 1934,
when John Dillinger and his gang dramatically robbed
Sioux Falls' Security National Bank, in the process pumping eight bullets into a local motorcycle cop.

During his short tenure the Chief had done his part
to make Sioux Falls safe for law-abiding people like his
daughter Edith, who lived a virtuous and placid life in the
city, presumably eschewing even illicit firecracker lighting
and skinny-dipping, not to mention acts of grand larceny.
In addition to her performances at the organ and piano at
public programs (she confided that she had relinquished
any hope of becoming a concert pianist on account of the
"smallness of her hands"), Edith in the 1920s was active,
along with her slightly younger sister Bessie, in the local
chapter of the Delphian Society, an international organization which promoted women's cultural education. For a
time Edith, who attended writing classes at the University
of South Dakota in Vermillion but never took a degree,

succumbed to the vogue for archaic Old English names and self-consciously styled herself "Edythe," but happily she abandoned this affectation.

During the Thirties just plain Edith Howie became active in Sioux Falls' community theater and began publishing short stories in magazines, including *Good Housekeeping*, *Ladies' Home Journal, Liberty* and the Canadian *Chatelaine*. In 1938 she completed her first mystery novel, *Treeholme House*. The novice mystery writer submitted the manuscript to Doubleday, Doran's Crime Club imprint, who snobbishly turned it down, sadly, on the grounds, Edith later wryly confided to *Argus-Leader* reporter Robert Gunsolly, that "four of the five persons murdered in the book were servants." Instead the tale appeared later that year, spiffily illustrated, in the Canadian magazine *Maclean's*.

Undaunted by her limited success at mystery writing, Edith in 1939 began simultaneously writing two new mysteries, which she entitled *Murder for Tea* and *Santa Claus Died*. She submitted the two manuscripts to Farrar and Rinehart, who accepted both works and published them within a few months of each other in 1941, *Tea* in August in its *Three Prize Murders* volume and *Santa* in December (appropriately enough), with its title altered to the rather more anodyne *Murder for Christmas*. Presumably the publisher was leery of traumatizing, with Edith's original blunt title, dewy-eyed innocents desirous of raking in their annual seasonal haul from Saint Nick.

Both *Murder for Tea* and *Murder for Christmas* are light "couples mysteries," in which a husband and wife are confronted with murder, respectively during a tea party at a literary luncheon and at a country house Christmas gathering, where, reminiscent of Ngaio Marsh's popular Seventies mystery *Tied up in Tinsel*, a man dressed up as Santa Claus is violently done to death. *Tea* takes place in Edith

Howie's fictional Great Plains city of Nashiona, an imaginative rendering of Sioux Falls, which also appears under the same name in one of Edith's later mysteries, *Cry Murder*. Conversely *Christmas* is set in rural New York State, perhaps as a sop to Plains wary editors, who once queried her having some of her characters travel twenty miles without encountering a single house. Edith worked on her first two published mystery novels in tandem, taking up one as she became stuck with the other, a process which she again employed with *Murder at Stone House* and *Murder's So Permanent*, both of which were published in 1942, and *No Face to Murder* and *The Band Played Murder*, both of which were published in 1946. *Cry Murder* appeared singly in 1944.

Once she had her characters and their milieu set firmly in her mind, Edith would begin writing, even though she claimed that typically she had no notion when she started of who her actual murderer would be. She might change her mind on that matter more than once as she wrote. All of her mysteries are brightly narrated by chatty young women, either married or well on their way to wedding their crime-busting beaux by the end of the story. While arguably not the most rigorously plotted of Golden Age mysteries, Edith's detective stories deliver the entertainment goods to likeminded readers, in the ingratiating manner of the modern "cozy" mystery.

In his reviews of Howie's mysteries in the *San Francisco Chronicle*, prominent American reviewer Anthony Boucher emphasized their amorous underpinnings: "Ross Langdon doubles as love interest and detective. . . . Good reading for the romance public. . . . (*Cry Murder*); "Randolph Garrison is more efficient as a lover than as head of homicide, but the telling and the church background . . . are pleasing." (*No Face to Murder*); "Jewel thefts, love and marihuana tie into the murders of two girl vocalists with

a big-time band. . . . Colorful, unassuming and pleasant"
(*The Band Played Murder*).

Five of Edith Howie's seven published mystery novels
are set in cities on the Great Plains, including the three
reprinted by Coachwhip (and reviewed by Boucher above):
Cry Murder, No Face to Murder, and *The Band Played Murder. Cry Murder* concerns killings and attempted killings
which take place in Nashiona among a little theater group
putting on a trial run of a play by a famed New York play-
wright (and former Nashiona native). The first murder, of
hateful diva actress Nola Powers, takes place at the Olympia Theater, for which the author likely had been inspired
by Sioux Falls' own Orpheum Theater, a beloved institu-
tion still standing today.

The Orpheum opened in 1913 and staged vaudeville
acts until 1927, when it was sold and converted into a
second-run and B-movie theater. By the time Edith wrote
Cry Murder sixteen years later, the theater had fallen into
disuse and been abandoned, but in 1954 the building was
purchased and renovated as a stage theater by the Sioux
Falls Community Playhouse, of which Edith was an important member. Mary Thorpe, the narrator and heroine
of *Cry Murder*, memorably describes the Olympia Theater
with WASPish middle-class distaste as follows:

> The Olympia was an eight hundred-seat thea-
> ter that, once in use almost exclusively for
> vaudeville and stock, had, with their passing,
> degenerated into a third-run movie house.
> . . . Cheap hotels and cheaper restaurants sur-
> rounded it and its audiences were drawn quite
> frankly from that class of people who scorned
> to pay the 'forty cents and tax' price of first-
> run theaters and were willing to wait for their
> pictures. One visit there, during my noviciate

in town, had been enough for me. The place
had been poorly lighted and smelly, the screen
a flickering disgrace. The seat to which I'd
been ushered had been broken and sagging; I
was suspicious of the probability of mice, or
their big brothers, rats; while overhead the
tireless dance of two creatures, which could
have been none other than those anomalies of
the animal kingdom, bats, had appalled me.
My first visit had been my last.

Appropriately Edith stages the most atmospheric section of her novel here, when Mary goes there to meet Nola
and encounters . . . well, read it for yourself and see! The
case ultimately is solved by Mary's love interest, handsome
private detective Ross Langdon, although not without
Mary's help. Also contributing to the case is folksy Chief
Hanover of the Nashiona police, whom Mary explains had
"been a small groceryman before he picked off the plum-
iest of Nashiona's appointive jobs." Somewhat defensively
Chief Hanover tells Mary and Ross: "[W]hile maybe you're
thinking I'm only a dumb old fogy who got the job of
police chief in Nashiona by reason of being a good friend
of the mayor's, you want to remember I've held onto that
job mainly by getting results. And results are just what I
aim to keep getting." Mary describes the Chief as a "short,
stout, ordinary-looking man in a wrinkled gray suit whose
waistcoat was crossed by an old-fashioned watch chain. He
had thinning gray hair, a somewhat straggly gray mustache
and eyes that were shrewd and sensible behind gold-rimmed
spectacles." The description matches that of Edith's father
when, at age fifty-two, he headed Sioux Falls' police force.
    The Fort Worth Star-Telegram delightedly described Cry
Murder as "a typical murder mystery, the sort everybody
enjoys," with "appealing characters and situations and an

atmosphere of eerie danger and suspense that marks the most satisfying type of mystery thrillers." In its review the *Argus-Leader* spotted similarities between Nashiona and Sioux Falls, including the fact that with the advent of the Second World War, Nashiona's population, like that of Sioux Falls, had virtually exploded. Observes Mary in the novel:

> Nashionites consider that they dwell in a metropolis, which I suppose they do—it being the largest city within the border of two sister states—but nowhere has there been normality since Pearl Harbor, and Nashiona was no exception to the rule. Close against the boundaries now sprawled the mushroom growth of the huge army school. . . . No one knew just how many soldiers were stationed there in the rows of wooden, tar-paper covered barracks but the number hovered somewhere between the twenty and thirty thousand marks. . . . the soldiers formed a little city in themselves. . . . sweethearts and wives . . . simply picked up their belongings and moved to Nashiona on the chance of finding accommodations that would enable them to spend a few more precious months with their loves ones. . . . Every apartment, every hotel, every rooming house was jammed to its roof top. Rents had risen—temporarily, for a freezing order was imminent—to unprecedented levels. Tourist homes and cabin camps . . . were being rented upon a monthly basis. At the edge of town a flourishing trailer city had sprung up overnight.
>
> It was all pretty breath-taking. . . .

In real life, Sioux Falls in 1942 became the site of the Army Air Forces Technical School, which over the course of the war trained nearly 50,000 hostilities-bound men in radio communication, Morse code, and aircraft identification. The school enabled Sioux Falls finally to recover from the lingering effects of the Great Depression, lessened the city's Plains parochialism and launched a building boom which lasted well into the 1950s, as many recruits remained there after the war, married and started families. Much of this phenomenon is captured, albeit fleetingly, in *Cry Murder*—not the least of the novel's felicities.

No Edith Howie novel appeared in 1945, but in January 1946 the author published *No Face to Murder*, which, like *Cry Murder*, is set during the war, in 1944, with wartime scarcity rather more advanced. (In *Cry Murder*, characters are still able regularly to consume waffles and grapefruit for breakfast and chocolate cakes with chocolate icing for dessert.) *Face* takes place in the Great Plains city of Dorchester rather than at Nashiona, but Dorchester, like Nashiona, sounds a lot like Sioux Falls, or possibly Sioux City, Iowa, about ninety miles south of Sioux Falls, where Edith's sister, Bessie, a bank cashier, had moved and Edith frequently visited. The novel's St. Thomas' Episcopal Cathedral seems quite a lot like Sioux City's St. Thomas' Episcopal Church, imposingly constructed in the Richardsonian Romanesque style and completed in 1892.

In the novel double slashing murders, respectively of the church caretaker and the organist, incongruously take place at St. Thomas' Episcopal Cathedral, in an opening surprisingly reminiscent of P. D. James' lauded 1986 crime novel *A Taste for Death*, where two people, a homeless man and an MP, similarly are found dead at St. Matthews' Catholic Church, their throats cut. Despite its uncharacteristically grim opening circumstances, however, *Face* ultimately bears a much greater resemblance to

Agatha Christie's *The Murder at the Vicarage*, peopled as it
is with a charming cast of principal characters, including
the young church secretary narrator, Tess King; church
dean Alec MacDonald and his wife Ruth; Bishop Walters,
who takes an interest in the case; and Randolph "Ran"
Garrison, the handsome head of the Dorchester police
department's homicide division and Tess' love interest.

Drexel Drake of the *Chicago Tribune* deemed *No Face
to Murder*, which in my view is the author's finest mystery, a "well-written yarn" with a "well-planned puzzle,"
while noted crime writer Dorothy B. Hughes in the *Albu-
querque Tribune* praised the "English atmosphere to this
Midwestern mystery," tipped off by the name of the city
in which it is located, as well as the "authenticity" of its
church setting and the "quite nice feeling to the whole
. . . along with the bite of small-town nastiness." For her
part Avis DeVoto in the *Boston Globe* gave the novel an
unqualified rave review, selecting it as her mystery of the
week. "An unusually penetrating picture of a small community, with a double murder in a church as the highlight.
Practically every member of the choir, around which the
story is built, is a suspect," DeVoto wrote. "Inspector Ran
Garrison, assisted no little by his girlfriend, who is also
the rector's secretary, and a cooking bishop come through
with all the answers, just too late."

Ten months later came *The Band Played Murder*, Edith
Howie's final published crime novel. While with *Cry Murder* and *No Face to Murder* Edith had been able to draw
heavily on her own familiarity with theater and church
milieus, with *The Band Played Murder* she had to bone
up on swing music, dance bands and "crooning" by reading back issues of *Downbeat* at the Sioux Falls Carnegie
Free Public Library. Her protagonist and narrator, Connie
Waring, another would-be concert pianist, is persuaded to
serve as a last-minute substitute singer in Gale Ullman's

—Harold Photo.

Edith Howie with her nephews Billy and Gary

band. When murder beats the band at the city of Harriston during its annual Harvest Festival, Connie, who discovers the dead body, finds herself a person of interest to both local police and the actual murderer. The devoted Edith Howie reader can be certain there will be ample love interest in the novel as well.

The Band Played Murder is another enjoyable Edith Howie mystery, pleasingly more sympathetic and informed about its subject than Ngaio Marsh's *Swing, Brother, Swing*, which appeared in print three years later. "Reading Ngaio Marsh's *Swing, Bother, Swing*," wrote crime writer and composer Edmund Crispin disgustedly in 1966. "Poor, and if she's going to try and write about jazz bands, why can't she find out something about them? 'Tympanist,' indeed." Edith did rather better in this regard than Ngaio, although like Cornell Woolrich in his notorious 1941 crime novella "Marihana," the author propagates the myth that the drug can immediately transform people into murderous maniacs. (One guesses that Edith, like the heroine of her story, had never personally tried it.) The *Lexington Herald* deemed Edith's "swinging" novel "a bang-up yarn that does not drag a paragraph throughout the whole 243 pages," while the *Knoxville Journal* avowed: "It's an unusual background and a well written story told in the first person by a girl who is as confused by life in a dance band as most readers would be."

After *Band* came silence. Edith accepted a position as a librarian at the Carnegie Library and continued working on mystery writing, but she never published another novel, criminous or otherwise. In 1951 *Argus-Leader* reporter Bob Gunsolley wrote that Edith was simultaneously working on not two, but three, mysteries, the most promising of which concerned an identical twin sister who, after awakening in bed with a choking sensation, later that morning learns that her twin was strangled during the night. Of course she sets out to find her sister's killer. Apparently Edith completed neither this novel, nor the other two which she was writing (one of which took place among a horsey set in Kentucky bluegrass country), although by her own admission she remained a "rabid mystery fan," getting first dibs on all the new mysteries at the public library.

After the deaths of her parents Edith in 1960 retired from the library and moved to Sioux City to live with her sister Bessie in a two-story, foursquare Craftsman-style house, which still stands today. She remained active in Sioux Falls little theater, for decades indulging her own "taste for death" with parts in such mysterious plays as the chiller *Night Must Fall*, the farce *Arsenic and Old Lace*, the ghostly *The Innocents* (the stage adaptation of Henry James "The Turn of the Screw") and a 1969 performance of Agatha Christie's *And Then There Were None*, arguably the most renowned murder mystery of them all, where, at nearly seventy years of age, she played coldly pious spinster Emily Brent, who memorably gets figuratively "stung" to death by a "bee."

In real life Edith Howie passed away, a decade after this performance, at the age of seventy-eight on May 1, 1979. Her younger brother, William Lawrence Howie, a photography enthusiast who four decades earlier had advised her on the properties of potassium cyanide for her first published mystery novel, had predeceased her in 1961, while her sister Bessie expired in 1996, at the age of ninety-three. "Reviewer, Thespian Here Dies," read the headline to Edith's 1979 obituary in the *Sioux City Journal*, omitting mention of her mysteries until the body of the article, in which it was briefly noted that "she had eight books and 40 short stories published. Stories by Miss Howie have been widely published in the United States, England and

Australia, and have been frequently translated for publication in Norway, Denmark and Spain."

Having noticed that copies of Edith Howie's novels were quite scarce and highly collectible, I wrote in 2012 about the author's *Murder for Christmas* at my vintage mystery blog *The Passing Tramp*, while two years later Edith was profiled in a series of articles by *Argus-Leader* features writer Jill Callison. Finally in 2022, over eighty years after the publication of her first mystery, Edith Howie's books are again back in print, as part of the remarkable ongoing reclamation of worthy crime writers from our past. Death for Edith Howie, it seems, came not as the end, but rather an intermission.

THE BAND
PLAYED
MURDER

For Lawrie and Agnes

1

What happened to me—the first part, at least—was the sort of thing that happens only in dreams, or in the movies. Many movies have made familiar the saga of the underdog who makes good; the substitute halfback who languishes on the bench through three long seasons and as many quarters, until a desperate coach puts him in, at the big game's crucial moment, to score the winning touchdown; the understudy who plays a Broadway show to a personal triumph when the star suddenly becomes ill; the singer . . .

I had a radio program on our local station, fifteen minutes every day except Saturday and Sunday. They didn't feature it—it was only a fill-in between network programs—but it gave me a little money and hence assumed, to me, a perhaps disproportionate importance.

I sang. It was ironic to contemplate that the years I'd spent in studying piano and organ had brought me, thus far, no monetary return, whereas with my voice . . .

My voice was a soprano, light, lyrical and sweet, the sort of voice that is at its best coming out of a microphone. I'd had a few lessons, more for diction and breath control than because I had any hopes of vocal greatness. Of course I had sung for years in glee clubs and choirs and choruses but I was no Lily Pons and I knew it. I didn't even care. So far as I was concerned, my voice rode along with the rest of my musical talent and that was all.

I acquired the radio program through a fluke and kept it, more because I needed the money than because there were a dozen girls at the Conservatory—girls with better voices than I possessed—who'd have given their eye-teeth to have it. But I had the inside track. I didn't stay at the dormitory; I was a little older than the other girls and community life bored me. The room I rented in town happened to be at the house of Tom Raines, the business manager of the radio station. Tom had been a musician of sorts at one time—dance band, theatre orchestra—and evenings we sometimes sang around the piano. It was as simple as that.

The station didn't expect anything highbrow from me, which was just as well because I knew my limitations. I stuck to the things with which I was reasonably sure I could get by—program stuff, popular songs, old ballads. The radio listeners seemed to like it, if the fan letters that came in proved anything. I even got a certain number of requests. If they made sense, I sang them. If not, I threw them out. Occasionally I made a little speech at the beginning of my program and explained that, while requests were welcome, the senders were please to keep in mind the fact that I was neither "torch" nor "blues" singer. The little speech always worked and for a while after it I'd get requests for Stephen Foster and Irving Berlin and *The Last Rose of Summer*.

Fifteen minutes wasn't long. I only had time for four or five songs in between the commercials, and I did my best to vary them; something old, something new, something humorous, something sad—because people love to cry—a request number with which to finish if there was time. At Christmas I sang carols and, during Holy Week, Lenten numbers, and the rest of the time I tried to keep my songs seasonable as well as pleasing. I'd had the program for two years now, a fact that spoke well for its general appeal.

The day that everything started, I was particularly well pleased with myself and my program. It was early September, I had a new and very satisfactory accompanist, and that very morning the director of the Conservatory Symphony Orchestra had invited me to be piano soloist on their fall program. I was riding high and, for that reason, I suppose, I sang a little better than usual. I liked my songs, too, that day—an old ballad to open, *The Four Maries;* one of the newest of the popular novelty numbers, *If You Wanta, Why Doncha?;* a new love song, *Love Drifted By on a Dream;* and the Brahms *Lullaby.* For a wonder the commercials were short, and I was able to get in a request, Stephen Foster's *My Old Kentucky Home.*

By the time I'd finished, there were quite a few people outside the studio, listening. That didn't bother me—I was used to it. The studio walls were of glass, and davenports and chairs had been placed in the wide hall outside. People were encouraged to come up from the street to rest and hear the programs. Today there was the usual collection of weary shoppers, wide-eyed youngsters, giggling high school girls, and one tall, youngish man in an expensive tweed suit whose dark hawk face was vaguely familiar. I had the feeling that I'd seen it somewhere before, and that, given time to put my mind to it, I could remember where.

I was a little surprised when I came out of the studio to see him still lingering in the middle distance. One of those, I thought disdainfully as he smiled and took a tentative step in my direction. There were always listeners who, for motives best known to themselves, felt impelled to accost performers. Sometimes this came out of an honest liking for what you'd done but more often, if the accoster were masculine, it was for another reason. Idly

I wondered who and what he was—traveling salesman, advance publicity agent, or just wolf on the prowl. Oh, well, I thought, secure in my disdain, I'll freeze him out.

But I didn't. I never got the chance. Before he came within speaking distance, Mary Ward, Mr. Gilbrau's secretary, touched my arm and told me that Mr. Gilbrau wanted to see me in his office right away.

Mr. Gilbrau was the owner of the radio station and hence to be obeyed. He was a tall, thin, gray man who once had been a power in financial circles and who now ran the radio station for the amusement of his declining years. He was shrewd, honest and kindly, and he had a very real respect for music and the musically talented. But he never permitted himself to mix this respect with business judgment.

About once a month he called me into his office to express his regret that he couldn't countenance the type of program I'd like to be putting on. "Piano numbers—they just don't go over," he would say sorrowfully. "Maybe now, if we had a good band for you to play with . . ." Here I always interrupted to say firmly that I didn't want to play with a band, good or bad; that that wasn't the kind of playing I wanted to do; and he would shrug his shoulders and turn down the corners of his mouth. "Well, we'll see," he'd say, "We'll see. Perhaps some day . . ."

I supposed this was going to be another of those sessions.

I told Mary "all right" but I clung firmly to her arm while I said good-by to my accompanist and arranged for next day's rehearsal. I had the idea that, with Mary for protection, the dark man might lose his courage and leave me alone.

I didn't need to worry. He let us pass, stepping out of our way with easy courtesy, but when I opened Mr. Gilbrau's door, I could feel him right on my heels.

I wanted to glare at him but, under Mr. Gilbrau's kindly regard, I didn't have the nerve.

The station owner was in the act of switching off the loud-speaker connection to his office. "Come in—come in, my dear," he said. "That was very nice—very nice indeed. I thought so. So did this gentleman. This is Mr. —"—Believe it or not, it sounded like Mr. Uh-huh—"Miss Constance Waring."

I said, "How do you do?" stiffly, but tall, dark and distinguished took it right on from there, not in the least abashed. "I did like your singing, Miss Waring. I liked it very much. So much that I was wondering if—I've already suggested it to Mr. Gilbrau—you'd be willing to sing another number or two for me?"

I looked at him blankly and sought, automatically, for an excuse. "My accompanist has gone." A swell excuse that was! Couldn't I have accompanied myself?

"I'll play for you," said Mr. Uh-huh as though that would settle it.

It did. Mr. Gilbrau stood up and rubbed his hands with pleased expectancy. "Splendid, splendid. Let me see now—Studio B should be vacant at this time. We'll go there."

What could I do? I went—like a lamb to the slaughter.

Studio B is at the end of the corridor. It is used almost entirely for rehearsal and there is no provision for prying spectators. The glass walls are heavily curtained. It contains nothing but a few straight chairs, a battered grand piano, shelves of records and some toppling piles of sheet music. As we came in, I noticed that Red Harrigan was in the control booth at the left. There was a microphone beside the piano and I suspected that it was a "live" one. I didn't ask. I simply wondered what was up.

Mr. Gilbrau went into the control booth and spoke to Harrigan. When he came out, he nodded to Mr. Uh-huh.

"All set," he reported and seated himself in one of the chairs over against the wall.

I could have ground my teeth with rage. Red Harrigan—that meant they were going to record whatever we did. What did they think they were doing? And why?

Mr. Uh-huh had drawn a straight chair to the piano and was lifting great handfuls of chords up and down the keyboard. I wondered how he could manage to play so many notes at one time and I looked at his hands. They were square, spatulate, beautifully manicured. There was a ring on the little finger of his left hand, dull gold, set with a dark, blue stone that caught, oddly, a cross of light in its depths. Memory pricked and I thought, Why, that's a star sapphire! I never saw one before. Now, who on earth is he, and why . . .

He had finished trying out the piano. He beckoned me with his chin. "Come over here."

I obeyed. I said, "Do you want me to sing into the mike?"

He said, impatiently, "Yes, of course," as though I'd asked a foolish question. "What do you want to sing?"

I got some of my own back then. "I don't," I said, "want to sing anything. This is your party, remember?"

He grunted and slashed out another great sprawling chord. "Need any music?"

"That depends."

"On what I choose? Okay. Know *Blue Skies?* Sing that."

"That's not my kind of a song," I warned him.

He shrugged. "It can be. Try it. Wait, now, I'll give you an eight-bar introduction. Take it easy and don't crowd it. And don't pay any attention to me. You've probably never sung to this sort of an accompaniment."

He was right. I hadn't. It was like nothing I'd ever heard before. Even while I concentrated on singing, I was aware of its power. It was fully rhythmic, sustained, and under the rhythm swelled an unexpected surging current of counter melody. It must be, I thought, a little like standing on the beach and raising your voice against an incoming tide. Time and tide wait for no man—neither did this music. You couldn't forget it. All you could do was surrender yourself to its drag and power and let it carry you effortlessly along.

I sang the last note. The red light on the wall blinked out. Mr. Uh-huh's hands fell from the keyboard. His fine dark eyes studied me impersonally. I couldn't tell what he was thinking.

"Not bad," he said at last. "Want to try something else? How about . . ."

I don't know how many we tried. Dozens, it seemed to me, but it couldn't have been more than four or five. One I sang the second time, after he had made certain suggestions, and for all he played the same big orchestral accompaniment.

At last, when I was beginning to get hoarse, the red light went off for good. He pushed back from the piano and stood up. He took a half turn around the room. I wasn't even curious by this time—just tired. I sagged in the piano curve and watched him without interest.

"Miss Waring," he said abruptly, "I am Gale Ullman."

"Ullman," I repeated politely. "I thought it was . . ." I did a double take then. "Ullman! Why, you're—"

He nodded. "The bandleader. Yes. My band's playing a dance engagement at the Sunset tonight—probably you've seen the advance notices. But I've run into a little trouble. Anne Kent, who's been doing my vocals, came down with an attack of—er—appendicitis last night. She's in a hospital now, for observation. I need another girl . . ."

I stiffened the jaw that was dropping in spite of myself. "Why not?"

There were tears in my eyes now, tears in my throat.
I walked over to the record shelves and stared at titles I
couldn't see. Here it was again. I'd worked all my life—
worked hard—at the piano, and now my voice, my damned
by-product voice . . .

I turned around. "I don't want to be a danceband singer," I said clearly. "I don't want to sing anywhere. Mr.
Gilbrau knows that. I wouldn't be here if it weren't for the
money he pays me. The piano's my instrument. I want to
be a concert pianist. That's what I'm working for!"

He shrugged. He was sitting now, one foot on a chair
rung, his knee drawn up and circled by his hands. "All
right, so you want to be a concert pianist. So perhaps you
can still be. How old are you, Miss Waring?"

I said it over a gulp. "Twenty-three."

"How much longer do you plan to stay here? Concert
pianists—good ones—don't burst to fame out of whistle
stops like this, you know."

It was cruel. Tears threatened again. "Of course I know
it. And I do want to get away. I will, too—some day. Only
just now . . ."

"You haven't the money? Right. Money's important to
you, you said. That's why you're singing over this station.
How much do they pay you here, if I'm not too curious?"

He *was* too curious. I stared at him, bewitched, and
Mr. Gilbrau answered. The sum sounded paltry, ridiculous, insignificant.

Again he shrugged, "You see? If you come to me, I'll
give you—" He named an amount.

It staggered me. I said, "A—a month?"

"A week. No, don't look like that. It's not out of line.
Anne got a lot more. So do most of the boys in the band.
I carry quite an overhead. Mine isn't any two-for-a-nickel
organization, Miss Waring. I've some of the best men in
the country." He flung up his head, looked at me straightly.
"Gale Ullman *always* has the best."

I said, "Then you don't want me."

His teeth showed briefly. "But I do. I'm in a spot. We're off to Chicago tomorrow. Oh, I could get someone else—perhaps. But it would take time—auditioning—and I haven't got it. We won't get in until late afternoon. That's Friday. There'd just be time to look up something for you to wear. Then, rehearsal Saturday and out Saturday night for Harriston."

"Harriston," Mr. Gilbrau mused. "Let me see, I think I've heard of Harriston."

"Sure you have. Nice little town, about thirty thousand. They put on a Harvest Festival every year. Something like a fair only with an inside show. We're playing a week's engagement there. Show every night in their Harvest Hall and a big dance Saturday night. We pick up the rest of the gang in Chicago." He looked at me. "Well, are you game?"

I threw out my hands. "I can't do it. I've never done anything like it. How do you know I wouldn't be an awful flop? And you say Gale Ullman always has the best . . ."

He laughed then. "I see I've frightened you. Sorry, I didn't mean to. Look, I've a suggestion. Why don't you come down to the Sunset tonight, sing a few choruses with the band?" I suppose he saw the horror in my face for he raised a protesting hand. "Now, wait—it won't be hard, I promise you. Not as hard as singing to that accompaniment I just played for you. I'll help you, I won't let you down. You can try it anyway, and if it goes all right, why, then"—he made a wide gesture—"you'll be set for a while. Till Anne gets back. After that, we'll see." He looked at me closely, added a last clinching argument. "Then, if you still want to go on with this concert stuff, you'll have a stake. How about it?"

"I don't know," I said. "I don't know what to do."

"Anyone you'd like to talk it over with?"

"There's no one," I said drearily. "My people are dead."

"Talk it over with me," said Mr. Gilbrau and took me firmly by the arm. We went into his office and he talked steadily for fifteen minutes. I listened but I hardly heard a word. There was something that was speaking louder than his voice, louder than anything he could say, and that was the amount of money Gale Ullman had said he'd pay me.

Eventually Mr. Gilbrau got around to that, too. "You wouldn't have much expense. Just food and lodging and you have that here. He'll take care of your traveling expenses and he'll buy the clothes you wear when you sing. You ought to be able to save quite a bit."

That did it. My resistance collapsed. I walked down the hall to the practice studio where Gale Ullman waited, smoking now. Chain-smoking, it must have been. There was a little heap of cigarette stubs on the floor.

I said, "All right, you've convinced me. I'll try it."

"Good," he said. But he didn't look too overcome with joy. Perhaps he, too, could see breakers ahead. "All right, you come down to the Sunset tonight. The dancing won't start until nine but get there a little early, will you? I want you to get the feel of the band for a few numbers. Got anything you can wear?"

"I have the dress I wore for a recital last spring," I said doubtfully. "It's long. But its yellow chiffon, sort of ingenue-ish."

He didn't smile. "That ought to do. You're a hit on the ingenue side yourself."

That was all. I was committed and, suddenly, I felt horribly let down and wobbly. In a daze, I listened to a few directions—how I was to enter the Sunset and what I was to do when I got there. Then Gale Ullman was looking at his wrist watch and it was my cue to pick up my purse—I didn't have a hat; we didn't wear hats at the Conservatory—and go.

2

I took the elevator down. It was only one flight and ordinarily I walked it, but today I couldn't trust my legs. I needed all the help outside I could get for my inside was in turmoil. I was torn, contradictorily, between an imperative urge to rush home and do things to my yellow chiffon dress and the certainty that, even if I did, it would be no use—that dresses wouldn't help. I had stepped out beyond my depth and was well on my way to being the flop of all time.

Paper crackled in my hand. Someone, perhaps Mr. Gilbrau, had given me a circular advertising the band. I stood on the street corner and read it. There were pictures—ranks of white-coated men with blurred faces; photographs of soloists—Tait Gilmore, a flashing grin above the glitter of a trumpet; a dark sultry-looking woman, Mandy Martin; a sober picture of Gale Ullman, baton in hand, hawk head dropped low; Anne Kent, a baby-faced blonde, with flowers clustered above her ears.

I drew a long breath and, for the first time, my intent seemed to crystallize. The visible neckline of Anne Kent's dress wasn't too unlike mine and, while I was no baby-faced blonde, I could do my hair like hers and get some flowers . . .

Or could I? I looked around for a clock and saw that it was two minutes of six—closing time. The nearest florist was half a block away and across the street. I dashed recklessly into traffic.

It was too near closing time for the girl in the florist shop to be interested in my demand for flowers I could wear in my hair. Languidly she pushed open the glassed show doors. They had roses—red ones, on long stiff stems—purple and white asters, bronze baby chrysanthemums and, after I'd murmured a wistful preference for yellow, calendulas. Then, when I still shook my head, she looked disparagingly at my skirt and sweater, my bobby socks and saddle shoes, and said haughtily that of course they had gardenias but they were expensive, a dollar and a half apiece. Entirely out of my class, her glance implied.

I became just as haughty as she. Recklessly I squandered half a week's income. I bought five.

Once outside, with the gardenias secure in their box, I became panicky again. Sure, buying gardenias to impress a florist's clerk was a nice gesture but one that cost a lot. And if I failed tonight I'd *need* that money.

Sobered, I looked in my change purse. Thirty-five cents—all that was left after paying for the gardenias. Could I eat on that? And what about tomorrow? Even if I were successful tonight, I could hardly expect to take off into the blue without some money in my pocket. All right, then, I'd just have to borrow—from Mr. Gilbrau perhaps. I could pay him back when I got my first check.

But all that was in the future. Why worry about it now? My immediate problem was to eat on the funds at my disposal. Could I? I did. Soup and coffee at the corner drugstore.

There was no one at home when I got there. I was thankful. I routed out the ironing board, put the iron to heat, and brought down the yellow chiffon.

I wasn't impressed with it. It was an evening dress all right, but that was about all. Fourteen ninety-five from the Campus Dress Shop. There was a tear in the hemline where one of my spike heels had stabbed. I mended that.

I was struggling to upsweep my hair when the telephone rang. It was Mr. Gilbrau. He had been worrying about me, he said in his stiff courteous way. He imagined that I must be pretty nervous by this time and he didn't like the idea of my going down to the Sunset unescorted. If I didn't object, he would like to come for me in his car.

I didn't object. So far I hadn't had time to figure out just how I was going to get down there. I thanked him gratefully and went back to my comb and my bobby pins and my five gardenias.

Now, of course, I realize that I should have gone alone. I was stepping over into a new world that night, a world in which who you were mattered not at all but only what you did and the manner in which you did it. I had no right to try to drag my background, as well, across that barrier, even though the background, in the person of Charles Albert Gilbrau, was an imposing one. The attempt marked me for what I was and would, probably, remain—the eternal amateur. I didn't know it then. I know it now.

He came early, a little after half past eight. From my point of view, it was just as well. My throat was closed up, my stomach wound tight, and I'd stared at myself and my unfamiliar hair-do until I'd lost all critical judgment.

Mr. Gilbrau thought I looked nice and said so. It helped.

He was nice, too, about lending me the money I asked to borrow. In fact he said that he'd thought I might need some and had come prepared. I asked for twenty-five dollars but he insisted on giving me fifty. He said you never knew what might happen and it was better to have too much than too little. I agreed gratefully and took it.

The Sunset Palace was a big frame building. I had been there lots of times, to dances, but always through the front way with its turnstiles and ticket windows. Tonight we made our way around the side, along a narrow path sheltered by rude trellis work. A light shone dimly over a door at the back. Mr. Gilbrau opened it and we stepped into a bare, narrow room. There were a couple of long tables, some dilapidated folding chairs and two small mirrors almost lost among the danceband posters that had been tacked against the plastered walls.

There were people in the room. How many I don't know, even now, for the numbers in Ullman's band fluctuated according to the sort of stands he was playing. There were nineteen of us on the train next morning, that I do know, but now I was only conscious of a multitude of black coats, of curious, impersonal faces, of a woman in a sheath of blazing scarlet who looked at us out of hostile, sullen eyes.

One of the faces moved out of the impersonal—Gale Ullman's. He slipped off the corner of the table on which he'd been perching and came over to us. All the while he was shaking hands with Mr. Gilbrau, he was studying me curiously, and I thought with disappointment.

It only lasted a minute. Then he swung away from us and toward the others. He said, "Boys, this is Mr. Gilbrau, the owner of the radio station here, and Miss Constance Waring. Miss Waring is going to sing a few choruses with us tonight."

That was all the introduction. It was the only one I ever got. Names and their specific faces came later, spread over a period of time and in the press of work.

No one in the group before us moved or spoke. There were a few raised eyebrows, a suppressed smile or two, quick sidewise glances that touched and passed. My own smile died unborn. I felt like a fool.

Gale Ullman had turned back to us. "Find yourselves some chairs. I'm not putting you on, Miss Waring, until after the first intermission. You'll sing three choruses—" He named them. "Sing them the way you did this afternoon and don't worry. You'll be all right. Keep your eye on Mandy. See how she does it."

He nodded and moved away. Mr. Gilbrau found me a chair and I sat down stiffly, lapsing, I hoped, into invisibility. I seemed all joints and awkward angles.

There was movement and laughter in the room, but none of it was ours. We had no part in it. It flowed around and past us, dividing as a river, nearing an island, divides of necessity and sweeps on for a little while, before once more reuniting.

Mr. Gilbrau was happy and interested. I wasn't. I was as miserable as I'd ever been in my life before, and that included my first day in kindergarten. Because, all of a sudden, white as a flash of lightning, I knew what I'd done. I should have come alone. I shouldn't have let Mr. Gilbrau bring me. He shouldn't be in this at all. And, because he was in it, my status had changed, willy-nilly. It had been plain in Gale Ullman's introduction. I wasn't his discovery now. I was Charles Gilbrau's protégée, a little singer from his radio station whom he was anxious to push, perhaps even his "girl friend." I writhed inwardly. But it was too late to do anything about it. There was only the one hope now—I'd have to sing well enough to wipe out the impression I'd so inadvertently given. I'd have to be discovered all over again, this time in my own right.

Of course there was one other way I might have settled the whole matter. I could have gone away. But my pride wouldn't let me.

I was too sunk in misery to notice when the room emptied. It just happened. Suddenly the members of the orchestra were gone and the slow insidious melody that

was Gale Ullman's signature song came filtering through
the back of the bandshell.

I was wrong. They weren't all gone. The woman in the
scarlet dress, the woman with the sullen, hostile eyes was
still there—Mandy Martin. The hostile eyes were on me. I
winced, meeting them.

She had been pulling furiously at a cigarette for some
time. Now she flung it down, crushed it under a scarlet
slipper, and undulated over to me. She was that sort of a
woman: black hair—beside it mine looked brown—that
broke upward in two great sweeping waves on either side
of a dead white part; black eyes under narrow curving
brows; olive skin with just a wash of color on high cheek-
bones; a mouth like a crushed poppy; and an expression
of hatred, hatred for me, so intense that I went cold all
over. I wanted to ask her why and I didn't dare. I simply
cowered a little closer to my chair back and waited.

She stood in front of me for a full minute, looking
me over, and, gradually, the hatred faded into something
else—contempt, perhaps—and irrationally, I was glad and
I didn't mind. Hatred—it was reasonless. I couldn't meet
it. Contempt was something else again. It was based on
lack of knowledge and I'd done nothing to merit it—not
yet. And I wasn't going to! For the second time that night,
I felt the saving prick of pride. What if I had gone into
this halfheartedly? I wasn't half-hearted now.

She had her hands on her hips and now there was inso-
lent amusement in her eyes. Perhaps she'd been reading my
mind. I wouldn't know.

"Look," she said throatily, "Gale doesn't like your hair."

I set my teeth on what I wanted to say. So he didn't
like my hair—and so who the hell was he? Gale Ullman,
orchestra leader. What did he know about hair-dos and
what were his likes and dislikes to me? A red haze, not all

of it engendered by the dress before me, wavered across my vision.

She spoke again, still with that tinge of amusement. "He says it won't do."

I opened my mouth to say that it would have to do or else, and then closed it again. I'd caught the expectancy in her eyes. I was going to do just what she thought I was. Very well, then—just for that, I wouldn't.

I said, with forced meekness, "All right, what do you think I'd better do?"

"Get it down and get rid of those damned flowers. It takes a professional to do a decent upsweep, don't you know that?"

I could hear Mr. Gilbrau making clucking sounds of distress behind me but, so far, he hadn't barged into the conversation. For little things I was thankful.

My hands wavered, up, dropped again. "I haven't a comb . . ."

She clicked her tongue in exasperation. "You'll have to use mine." She swished across and opened a square leather case. She took out a comb, one of those clear plastic ones. It was clean. I looked. She came back and watched my fumbling fingers. "Here!" she said. "Let me do that."

I didn't want her to but what could I do? Meekly I bowed my head.

Pins, combs, bobby pins lay in a little pile on the table top. My gardenias—my precious seven-dollar-and-a-half gardenias—she pushed aside with a careless, "They stink, don't they?"

Well, she "stunk" herself, if that was the way she wanted to put it—pleasantly, of Chanel Number Five. I said nothing. I couldn't. Tears were catching up with me again.

I suppose I thought she'd ruin me but, when she dragged the comb through for the last time and pushed me in the direction of the mirror, I looked much as I always had: dark brown hair swept across from a side parting; gray eyes—darker now than usual; pale skin; coral mouth—a rose, not a crushed poppy. I was a pallid imitation of what she so flamboyantly personified.

She was still frowning, dissatisfied. "Here, wait a minute," she said crossly and took up one of the despised gardenias. She anchored it firmly just above my ear and stepped back. "You'll do," she said grudgingly. "That's what he wants."

I suppose I should have been grateful. I wasn't. Nevertheless I made the attempt. "Thank you very much . . ."

She cut me off with a brusque gesture. "Save it—it wasn't my idea. I only did it to keep peace in the family."

I wondered what she meant by that and at once she told me—gratuitously, a little viciously. "Out there," she said with a wide flung hand, "I'm Mandy Martin. Back here, and the rest of the time, I'm Mrs. Ullman, Mrs. *Gale* Ullman—do you get that, Miss Big Eyes? You'd better. I don't know what your game is and I haven't found out what *his* is yet, but watch your step, that's all. I don't give up easy."

I couldn't believe what I was hearing. "There's no game to it," I said hotly. "I don't know what you're talking about. I came down here because Mr. Ullman asked me to."

I might have saved my breath. The band was playing *Blue Skies* out in front and, even as I spoke, she was leaving us. I turned and looked to where Mr. Gilbrau was happily pinning one of my gardenias to his coat lapel. "Did you hear that?" I exploded. "Did you hear what she said?"

"I heard her. A most unpleasant young woman," he said judiciously. "Don't mind, my dear, there's some mistake here. It will all come out all right, you wait and see." He had finished pinning the gardenia. Now he took my chin between his thin, dry fingers. "But she was right about the hair, you know. It's better this way, much better. You look like Constance again."

How could I tell him that that was just the thing I didn't want—to look like myself, not tonight.

Blue Skies ended. Mandy Martin came back. She didn't speak to me, nor I to her. The next number was a waltz and she didn't sing a vocal. The next, *I Never Told My Baby*, was well under way and she had already started for the door; when it dawned on me that I'd had orders to watch her and I hadn't been doing it. I jumped to my feet and trailed along behind.

Not very far—just to the door, from which vantage point I watched her jealously. Every movement, every facial expression. She walked out to the microphone on the last half of the first chorus. She smiled at Ullman, she smiled at the dancers. At the exact moment they began the second chorus, she started to sing. She didn't try for any effects—I heard her records so I knew what she could do—she simply sang the words to the hard-driving rhythm of the band. When they went into the third chorus, she walked off. That was all there was to it.

A new confidence filled me. Why, there wasn't anything to *that!* If that was all and she could do it, so could I.

And, for a wonder, I did. The intermission came and went. I wasn't nervous any more. I waited for the moment—my moment—with a sort of fierce exultation. I'd show her. I'd show them all.

The band was playing *Day Dreams*. It was time to go. I shook out my skirt, touched my curls, flung up my head and walked out.

I did everything exactly the way I wanted to. By some miracle of detachment, I seemed to have the power to stand off and watch myself. I walked out to the microphone. I moved it a little. I smiled at Gale Ullman, expressionless, before his band. He showed his teeth at me. I smiled at the dancers, or, rather, at their blurred faces. I caught Gale Ullman's almost imperceptible signal. At the right moment I began to sing.

My voice sounded good—even to myself. I sang in strict time, concentrating upon getting the words across. When the chorus was done, I walked off. Gale Ullman made a circle of thumb and forefinger and the band crashed in fortissimo.

But the dancers wouldn't let them finish. Few were even dancing. They were clapping their hands. There were a few foot stamps. Somebody called, "Connie—we want Connie!" Others took it up. I thought, Oh, a lot of them must hear my radio program. And of course there are kids here from the college . . .

Mr. Gilbrau was one wide smile, Mandy Martin a black glower. Out in the dance hall the noise died to silence. The band began to play the chorus of *Day Dreams* as they had played it for me a few seconds before.

Mandy Martin grabbed my arm and fairly flung me toward the door. "Go on!" she commanded. "He wants you to sing it again!" As I moved forward, she spoke venomously. "Did that claque cost you much?"

I did it all over. Only this time I picked up the chorus as I walked out, and finished it, and then sang it all over again. There was more applause and then they let me go.

It was the same with my other two numbers. People I knew danced close to where I stood and called out nice things to me. It was very pleasant. No matter how it would be in other places, I was by way of being a success in my home town.

I haven't any idea what time the dance ended. I only sang the three times and when they were done I sat and waited. Every time I looked in Mr. Gilbrau's direction, he beamed at me. I was afraid to look at Mandy Martin.

The band played *Good Night, Dear*. There was a final squall of saxophones and it was all over. I heard feet going away, feet that came near. Gale Ullman was in the doorway. I stood up. Once more my knees were shaking.

They didn't need to be. He walked over, smiling a little. He took one of my discarded gardenias from the table,
sniffed at it. "Nice," he said, "nice," and I had time to
wonder if that was the reason Mandy Martin didn't like
them before he spoke again, "That was all right—swell.
What were you worrying about? The train goes at eight
forty-five tomorrow. Can you make it?"

I nodded. It was all I could do; my voice seemed to
have gone elsewhere.

"We get into Chicago about three. Then we'll see about
your clothes." There was a commotion at the door and he
turned his head. Someone was calling, "Mr. Ullman—Mr.
Ullman!" He said, "Yes, what is it?"

It was the manager of the dance hall. He had a yellow
envelope in his hand. "This just came for you, Mr. Ullman. 'Fraid it's important. They don't deliver much any
more . . ."

Gale Ullman took it, ran a finger under the envelope
flap. When he crumpled the message and looked up, his
hands were shaking.

"Mandy," he said, "Mandy, for God's sake, listen to this!
It's from that doctor. Anne's run away from him—left the
hospital without leaving a trace. He wants to know what
he's to do. How can I tell him? It was all wrong from the
start, I knew it. I never should have let him take her—"

"Nonsense!" She snatched the telegram, flattened it.
"You had to do something—the girl was dangerous. If you
think I wanted her running around loose . . . And you
don't need to worry—he'll find her. He'll have to. Come
on, we'll call him. He'd better get the police . . ."

They were gone. They had forgotten me. I seethed with
questions but there was no one to answer them. Mr. Gilbrau came with my long cream-colored cape and laid it
about my shoulders. We went home.

3

Even at eight o'clock in the morning, the station was crowded. People were going places—soldiers and sailors, shoppers and businessmen. Gale Ullman's band, complete with instruments and baggage, sprawled over the benches in one corner. I walked that way, stood a little back and to one side.

A face detached itself from the other faces, moved in my direction—a little man, scarcely up to my ear, with sandy hair, snub nose and a wide cheerful grin. He said, "I'm Shorty Sims, business manager for the outfit. You Constance Waring?"

I said I was and he took a list from his pocket and marked something on it. "Okay, you're the last. Stick around. The train's on time."

I stuck around. I was tired—I'd been up all night, packing and explaining things to the Raineses—and I wanted to sit down. But there were no seats visible and, after a minute or two, I walked over to the combination newsstand and lunch counter. Some of the band were there, drinking coffee and dunking doughnuts. I envied them but, again, there were no vacant places, so I bought two magazines, a morning paper, and, remembering what I'd heard about travel conditions, a candy bar.

The train came in with a rush and a roar. Bags and instrument cases were snatched up. The band, herded by little Sims, surged forward. I followed.

They were all in the car and settled before I managed to push my way through. There was a vacant double seat. I sank into it, suitcase at my feet, glad to rest and conscious of a taut, breathless expectancy. Whether I would or no, I was off. This was adventure and I was committed to it.

The members of the Ullman band were experienced travelers. Overcoats came off, were rolled and thrust into the racks above. Seats were let down to their fullest extent. Many slept. A few read papers or magazines. One or two wandered off to the diner in search of coffee. Across from me, a sardonic-lipped youth drew music paper from a bulging portfolio and, with a fountain, pen, began to trace an intricate pattern of dots along the staves. A blond boy directly in front worked at a crossword puzzle, demanding help from all and sundry. His seatmate snored loudly, a thin wrist across his eyes.

No one paid the slightest attention to me. To all intents and purposes, I might have been invisible and that suited me. I needed all the time I could get for orientation.

Midway in the morning, Shorty Sims dropped down beside me. I closed my magazine, kept a finger in it. I wanted it plain that I asked for nothing . . .

I needn't have bothered. He only wanted to tell me that there would be an hour stopover at noon before we caught the main-line train into Chicago. Plenty of time to get something to eat in the station restaurant. We'd be in Chicago by three o'clock.

Chicago! It was something like standing on a cliff edge, sheer and stark, with nothing beyond. Here I was all right, trailing along, but what would happen in Chicago? Would they separate? And where would I go?

I asked.

Shorty Sims wrinkled his infinitesimal nose. He was a nice little man, not young, engaging with friendliness. "Ullman told me to fix you up at the same hotel as the boys." He named a hotel. I'd never heard of it. "He'll get in touch with you there."

I looked thoughtfully at the visible members of the band. "Where is Mr. Ullman?"

Sims frowned as though he didn't like the question. "They're driving in. Took some of the band stuff with them. Ought to be there before we are."

He put one hand on the seat arm preparatory to rising. I stopped him. "Did they find Miss Kent?"

He glared at me. "What do you know about Anne Kent?"

I shrank back a little. "Nothing. I was there when they it got the wire, that's all. I knew they were worried."

The glare vanished. "Yeah. They were worried all right." He picked industriously at a thumb nail, did his best to keep it casual. "No, they didn't find her."

I said, "I don't see how anyone could get away from a hospital. Somebody must have been terribly careless. Especially when she was waiting for an operation. I thought they gave you sedatives . . ."

"Operation?" He was scowling again. "Anne wasn't down for any operation. Where'd you get that idea?"

I wasn't sure. No, I *was* sure! Gale Ullman himself had told me. I decided to play it cagey. "Something I heard, I suppose," I said vaguely. "I thought appendicitis . . ."

"No, it wasn't appendicitis." He gave me a side glance. "It was a mental hospital. Anne was off her head,"

"That's a lie!" It was the blond boy who'd been occupied with the crossword puzzle book. He had turned in his seat and was glaring at us over its back. "Anne wasn't any crazier than you are and you know it! Maybe just at the last but . . . What the hell are you trying to put over?

More of Ullman's dirty work? You know damn well it was
Mandy—"

"You shut up, Dick!" Shorty Sims had gone so white
that the freckles stood out in brown polka dots across
his nose. "You leave Mandy out of it! She's got troubles
enough without you guys . . ." He caught himself, looked
at me. "All ancient history, Miss Waring. Nothing to do
with you."

I hoped it hadn't but I wasn't so sure. I didn't care much
for the bits and pieces of information I was accumulating.
Anne Kent was a mental case. Anne Kent was dangerous.
The wire had said so. Dangerous to whom? To Ullman?
To Mandy Martin? Or, conceivably—since it I was who'd
taken her place with the band—to me?

To me? I gave a little start impossible to control. This
thing had potentialities I had almost overlooked. Anne
was not only a mental case and dangerous. She was free
of whatever restraint they—who were they? The Ullmans
or other authorities?—had put upon her. I had the uneasy
crawling sensation that, had I been secure at home, would
have sent me peering under beds and into dark closets. But
there were no dark closets here.

Shorty Sims had heaved himself to his feet and now
stood, lurching to the train's movement. "Anything you
want to know . . ." he said and I managed to smile. There
were plenty of things I wanted to know but I had an idea
this was neither the time nor the place to ask them. Later
on, perhaps, when I saw the Ullmans again.

Sims had gone forward to his own seat but the blond
boy, Dick, still leaned across the back of his. He had heavy
dark eyebrows that contrasted oddly with his light hair,
eyes whose iris showed as a slender ring of gray about en-
larged pupils, and a prominent Adam's apple. He appeared
very young.

He said, "Look, Anne was a nice kid. He wouldn't tell you—too far under Gale's thumb. He's Gale's man, see? Anne wasn't crazy. Don't let them tell you that. Anyway she wasn't, not at first. She just fell too hard for Gale and Mandy found it out and raised a row. Then Gale got fed up like he does and Anne, poor kid, couldn't see that it was over. She started—oh, I don't know—drinking, maybe, or drugs. Two nights ago she blew her top, pulled a knife on Gale. So they got hold of some quack doctor and rushed her off. Oh, what the hell! Nothing to do with you, he says! Don't kid yourself. It happened to Anne. It could damn well happen to you!"

Consoling thought. During the rest of the trip I sat and alternately shivered and tried to figure an out for myself. There didn't seem to be one. I had agreed to come. Even though, professionally, I might have no wish to enter this particular branch of music, still my word was my word and long lines of shadowy ancestors rose up to demand that I keep it good. In addition there was the fifty dollars I'd borrowed from Charles Gilbrau. That would have to be repaid, how I wasn't certain. The sensible thing would be to go on with this, at least until the Harvest Festival was over. Then, knowing the lay of the land, I'd be in a better position to make a decision.

Of course, forewarned is forearmed, and God knows I'd been warned. I had Anne Kent's example before me. I didn't need to "fall for" Gale Ullman. I didn't need to fall for anyone. I'd keep myself to myself. I'd play it safe.

It was a nice idea and oddly comforting. How was I to know it would be impossible to carry out?

But, for a little while, I held to it. During the noon hour stopover, I ate alone, at one end of the long station restaurant. When the Chicago train came in, I dragged my own bags on, again sat alone.

The two-hour trip seemed to pass on wings. We were in the big echoing station, being herded toward taxicabs that I took us to the towering Loop hotel. There was a room for me. I suspected it had been originally for Anne Kent but that didn't matter. The room was pleasant, chintz-hung. When I shut the door it was mine, all mine, and no one could get at me. It was sanctuary.

Like fun it was; I'd forgotten the telephone. I'd hardly taken off my hat and coat before it rang peremptorily. It was Mandy Martin Ullman. Would I meet her at a Michigan Avenue dress shop right away? I said I would, shrugged back into my coat, and called a taxi for surety in arrival.

It didn't take long to buy the dresses. Mandy knew just what she wanted and what I wanted didn't count. There were two of them—both chiffon, one blush rose and the other deep ivory. Save for the niceties of cut and fit, they might have come from the same dress shop as my despised yellow. Both were bouffant, with demurely puffed sleeves and almost blatantly modest neck lines. I was disappointed. It seemed there was to be no glamour build-up for me.

We bought silver slippers, silken wreaths of rosebuds for my hair. Evidently I was to be trusted with no more gardenias. Then Mandy flung a coat of matched leopardskins about her shoulders and dismissed me. There'd be a one o'clock rehearsal tomorrow—she told me where. The dresses would be sent to the hotel and, in the meantime, I'd better see about getting my hair done. My hair was naturally curly but she seemed to feel a hairdresser could do more with it than I. I didn't even have the spirit to protest.

I spent a quiet evening. Submerged in the crowds that filled the hotel, I gained welcome anonymity. I didn't see any of the band but that wasn't surprising. I wasn't sure I'd recognize them anyway. So far as I was concerned, it was too early for them to have individuality.

Chicago was sunny and bright as I walked the few blocks to the rehearsal hall. It was a big, bare room with a little raised platform at one end upon which Shorty Sims and the bitter-lipped youth I'd noticed in the train were arranging chairs.

I was the first one there. I would be.

They acknowledged my presence—Sims with a hearty "Hi!" and the other with sidelong disdain. Later on, when I was to know more about Morris Levinsky, I was to pity him, to like and trust him. He was brilliant, frustrated, as out of place, with his background of Juilliard and Paris Conservatory, as myself in this galaxy.

The others straggled in. Having nothing special to do, I amused myself by watching them and trying to guess who they were and what they played. Tait Gilmore was easy enough, because of his beautiful golden horn, but his was the only name I knew. The blond boy, Dick, who'd sat in front of me on the train played a guitar and sang vocals in a husky baritone that throbbed with synthetic emotion. A redheaded stringbean slapped at a string bass and a roly-poly with three chins settled himself among a bewildering muddle of drums. A tall, dark youngster in uniform, the wings of a pilot on his breast, assembled a clarinet and began to play torrid runs in the upper register. At the piano, a good-looking boy in horn-rimmed glasses chatted with a bald trombonist who occasionally lifted his instrument to throw out a raucous "ha ha" as period to some of the more frenzied squawlings of the clarinet. It was all very noisy and to me, the novice, bewildering.

The Ullmans arrived. Mandy, still in leopardskins, shot one sharp glance in my direction—to pass on my hair, I suspected—and then crossed to the piano. She stood some music sheets on the rack, spoke to the boyish pianist, one hand familiarly upon his shoulder. He nodded, tried a phrase, nodded again. Apparently satisfied, she sat down, well across the room. Gale Ullman brought his stick sharply down upon the music stand before him. The rehearsal had begun.

I learned a great deal that day. I was to learn more in the days to come. As with most musicians trained in the classical tradition, I had only an immense contempt for the danceband, the theatre, the "union" musicians. This contempt, perhaps distaste is a truer word, was either instinctive or consciously implanted. From our earliest days, we had been warned away from jazz, told that its playing would ruin or distort our approach to the classics. A definite line was drawn, across which, on our peril, we must not step. Now, fascinated, I perceived that such line and warning were unnecessary. We could not, either by inclination or training, make the transition. No symphony musician with whom I'd yet come in contact was capable of rising at his leader's nod—as Tait Gilmore was doing— and improvising a solo that was, so far as I could tell, melodically true to mood and tempo, rhythmically and harmoniously correct. Nor was it possible to imagine his fellow players providing an accompaniment to such a solo on the spur of the moment without the assistance of written notes. It just couldn't be done. No, the line was there, rigid and inflexible, but I had a hunch it was uncrossable only from the one side.

The rehearsal continued. They went over numbers that were to be used for the Harvest Festival. Mandy Martin sang some of the choruses; the blond boy—his full name was Dick Travis, the Travis pronounced with a long ā— sang others. Two or three, dripping sentimentality, were earmarked for me.

Gale Ullman spoke briefly of the composition of the show. The other acts would join us in Harriston. There would be two dance teams, an M.C. of national reputation, a juggling act, a magician, wire artists, a bicycle troupe—

the usual hodgepodge. The band would provide novelty numbers and background music. The quartet would sing and the sextette, Ullman's "band within a band," would play hot numbers.

There was some grumbling. It was evident such an engagement was not to the taste of the band. What they wanted, I never did find out. When insurrection briefly reared its head, Ullman put it down with a firm hand, but the spirit of rebellion, barely to be discerned, remained.

I wasn't even sure it *was* there. When, during a cigarette intermission, Shorty Sims came over to my corner to speak of trains and tickets, I asked him. "Is it always like this?" I said.

His light little eyes narrowed. "What do you mean, always like this?"

I made a gesture. "You know, they pull one way. Mr. Ullman pulls another. Why?"

He said, "Hunh!" and left it like that for a moment. "Lots of prima donnas in that outfit."

"You don't need to tell me." He didn't. Wherever four or five musicians are gathered together . . . "I'm not just curious. I want to know. Because I like knowing what I'm getting into. It's—safer."

He said, "Uh-huh." Once more his light little eyes examined me. "Okay. Put it this way. Gale's made his name with one kind of music, the gang likes to play another."

I hastily thought over all I'd ever heard about jazz. "You mean that they want to play swing?"

"Hot jazz," he corrected. "Gale plays a modified swing but these fellows want it hot. Most of them are 'hot' men, like Gilmore. They don't want a big orchestra—they like a small combo—and they don't want to be tied down to black and white stuff. Their idea of how to play a tune is, well, to kick it around."

"I see," I said. I think I almost did. I'm not stupid. I applied the acid test. "Why do they stay?"

Shorty Sims said, "Huh! Why do you suppose? Money. Gale pays big. You can't hardly make a living off hot jazz—not yet. These guys are the best in their line. Know how we bill Gilmore? As the greatest living trumpet player. Well, he is—of the white ones. That's why Gale wants him. He likes having the greatest living trumpeter playing in his band and taking his orders."

"And how does Mr. Gilmore feel about it?"

"He hates Gale's guts. But he can't figure any way of getting out. He's married—got a couple of kids. He needs the money Gale pays him. He can't quit."

I looked at him soberly. "Which side are you on?"

"Me?" His smile flashed suddenly. "Lady, I don't have a side. I stay strictly in the middle and most of the time it keeps me scrabbling so I don't fall down the crack." He patted my shoulder in comradely fashion and was gone.

The rehearsal dragged on. When, finally, the band was dismissed, Gale Ullman's nod kept me. The piano player, too, remained, and for another hour we ran over my numbers. Gale Ullman was patient, considerate, long suffering. It was hard not to succumb, whole-heartedly, to his charm. But I worked at it. So far as I could see, I had to. I knew too little—or too much.

When he was satisfied, at last, there was barely time to get back to the hotel and make the train. I rushed, conscious of the evening dresses that, unpacked, still spilled froth over my bed. There was a huge dress box that had come with them. They'd have to go in that. Bother! More luggage to carry. I had enough as it was.

The clerk gave me my key at the desk. As I was turning away, he spoke. "By the way, Miss Waring, a young lady called to see you a few minutes ago. She said she might

wait but"—he peered short-sightedly about the lobby—"I
don't believe she did."

I thanked him. I was halfway to the elevator before I
remembered that I didn't know anyone in Chicago, certainly no woman. Unless it were Mandy Martin . . .

I retraced my steps. "This young lady," I said. "Do you
remember anything about her?"

Reflectively the clerk tapped a penholder tip against
his teeth. "She was about your height, I'd guess. Well-
dressed. Pretty—very pretty. Lots of blond hair. She wore
dark glasses . . . I'm sorry. That's really all I can tell you."

"She gave no name?"

"Naturally not." The clerk's glance was a rebuke. "You
were not in."

I didn't really need the name. I didn't think I did. Blond
hair, dark glasses . . . There was only one person, so far
as I knew, that such a description might fit and that was
Anne Kent—Anne Kent who'd sung with the band, who'd
attacked Gale Ullman with a knife, who'd been confined
to a mental hospital and who'd escaped.

What could she want of me?

4

Harriston was a pretty little town. It sprawled flatly on the prairie, an oasis centered in cornfields. Its streets were wide and tree-shaded, its pleasant homes separated by stretches of smooth, grassy lawn. Fall flowers burned in gardens, riots of raw color, gold and red and purple. Over fences and arbors morning glories dropped bells of heaven's blue.

The broad main street of the town had been converted into a carnival midway. The six or seven blocks stretching from the railroad station to the great squatting bulk of the Harvest Hall were lined with gay booths, with rides and concessions, shooting, galleries and fortunetellers' tents, bingo stands and popcorn machines. In great open tents, women from church aids served chicken dinners. Children darted about, sticky with spun sugar candy. Ice cream vendors and soft drink stands did land office business. It was all very gay and exciting.

Lucky for me that it was, I thought. All in all, I expected to spend a good deal of time upon that midway, and not from choice. My hotel room was dreary. No chintz-hung splendors here. You took what you could get and liked it. The beds were iron, the bath a mere cubicle that substituted a shower for a tub. Worst of all, it was a double room and I shared it with—of all people!—Mandy Martin. Save for sleeping, I determined early to give the hotel a wide berth.

It was that determination that sent me forth that very first Sunday afternoon. We'd arrived at Harriston about noon. After registering, unpacking and finding something to eat, I had nothing to do and a long afternoon in prospect. Staying in the hotel room was out of the question—Mandy Martin had elected to catch up on some of her lost sleep there. As yet, little stirred on the midway. A few booths were being set up but none was open. I considered a movie but I'd seen all but one of the shows the theatres offered and that I decided to save until later. There'd still be the evening to get through. I would take a walk—a long one.

No sooner thought of than done. Why not? It was a beautiful warm afternoon. I wouldn't plan to go anyplace in particular, just choose a street and follow it until it merged with the open country. It was a thing I'd done many times before. Hiking was rather a fad at the Conservatory. The very nature of music keeps its devotees physically confined and precious hands and fingers must be guarded against too strenuous sport. But walking was safe enough. Besides healthily tiring you, it tended to blow mental cobwebs away and God knew I had plenty at the moment that could do with a little ventilation. I decided to change to walking shoes and be on my way.

The lobby of the Marvin Hotel was crowded. The hotel wasn't large and Festival time was taxing its facilities to the utmost. Someone had told me that the rooms of the entire fourth floor had been turned into dormitories. It was there that the band was quartered.

I saw a few of the members of the band lounging in the chairs at the window end of the lobby. Later on, when I wanted to remember who they were, I couldn't. How should I? I didn't even know their names for a certainty. They were simply Joe and George and Buddy and Art. I was only sure of the one thing—that Tait Gilmore was not there.

But Gale Ullman was. I was ringing for the elevator when he detached himself from a group near the desk and came over to me.

"Whither away, pretty maid?"

I started to say whither I was away and then, abruptly, remembered my determination to play it safe. I said I hadn't made up my mind.

"Know anybody in town?" I shook my head. "Tough." He had one of those soft, "poor-little-girl" voices. "Sunday afternoon and nothing to do. I can't even break the monotony by offering you a drink. All the bars are closed."

I said hastily that that was perfectly all right, I didn't want a drink.

He wasn't to be stopped. "Sometimes it helps. I've got a pint upstairs but I can't take you *there*. They've got us in barracks. Still," his eyes narrowed, "you've got a room . . ."

I decided it was time to assert myself. Good grief, had my first estimate of the man been the right one? Was he really no more than a wolf on the prowl?

"Oh, you couldn't come *there*," I said firmly. "Mandy, your wife, is there."

"Mandy!" His eyebrows shot upwards. "Sorry—but she's not. She's gone off in the car—got some cousins who live about twenty miles east of here. I gave her the keys myself."

The elevator came just then. I stepped inside. "She told me," I said through the grille, "that she was going to sleep all afternoon."

Our room was on the third floor toward the back. I checked the number on the door, inserted my key.

Mandy was there, lying on her bed, a blue comforter pulled high to her chin. The window shades were down. So were the windows. The room was hot, stuffy, heavy with perfume. Discarded clothing lay where she'd stepped out of it. Her eyes were closed.

I dislike a messy room, especially if I have to live in it. I tiptoed around, picking up things—handmade satin underwear, ornate with lace; wisps of stockings; shoes that were little more than soles suspended from narrow straps. The beige wool dress and jacket I hung in the narrow closet where my own things were neatly aligned.

Acting as lady's maid made me mad but apparently I had no choice. I could sacrifice my pride and pick up after her or I could live in the midst of clutter. Only one thing brightened the darkness—it would be only for the week. After that I'd see to it that I had a room to myself.

The bathroom was worse, if possible. Lumps of bath towels made wet islands on the floor. She'd used mine as well as her own, darn her, I thought grimly. A fat cake of pink soap was melting in the puddle under the shower. Dusting powder snowed over it all.

I closed that door with emphasis. The maids could just clean that up, not I—not if it never was cleaned. And when I got back, I'd see that I got fresh towels . . .

Closing the door had wakened Mandy. She was sitting up and glaring at me. The blue comforter had slipped down and I thought, Good heavens, I don't believe she has a stitch of clothing on . . . .

She said acidly, "Do you have to make all that noise? I told you I wanted to sleep!"

I tied the laces of my old saddle shoes. "Don't worry, you can sleep all you want to. I'm going."

She had hunched the comforter up again and was lying back but her eyes weren't closed. They were fixed on me with peculiar intensity.

"Where?"

"I don't think it's any of your business, but I'm going for a walk."

"A walk!" she repeated and laughed unpleasantly. "Walking—poor Gale! So he's reduced to that. He must have it bad! Well, you don't get the car—*or* the keys—if he walks until his legs drop off! You can tell him that for me."

I was so mad I fairly sizzled. "You've got it wrong," I said. "I'm walking—but I'm walking alone. Your husband is definitely not invited!"

She laughed again, only this time it was a giggle. "Does he know that?"

For answer I slammed the door so hard the hinges rattled. While I was locking it again, I thought she called something to me. It sounded like, "Tell Gale to come up here." I didn't answer. If she wanted Gale so darn bad, let her call the desk, have him paged. If she thought I was going to add messenger service to my other accomplishments, she thought wrong.

I had my finger tip on the elevator bell when I had another idea. Perhaps, if I wanted to go walking alone, returning to the lobby wasn't the smartest thing in the world. Maybe Mandy Martin knew her husband better than I did. Suppose he decided to come along? What could I do?

I took the elevator only to the second floor. There must be some other way down. Elevators got out of order and hotels had fire regulations to consider. If I could find the stairway . . .

I couldn't. I wandered up and down a few halls without seeing any door that looked as though it might be the one I wanted. One turn brought me out on the mezzanine. I walked over to the railing and looked down. My hunch was right. Gale Ullman still lounged near the elevator door. I moved away—fast.

I started down the hall again, another hall. This time I met a gray-haired woman in the black dress and white apron of a hotel housekeeper. She had towels over her arm and was inserting a pass key into a door lock. Her eyebrows went up slightly when I told her what I wanted but she pointed to a door that would bring me down near the kitchen. I thanked her.

The stairway was steep and narrow. It led straight downwards into a strong odor of Brussels sprouts. At its foot, there was a short hall with a door through which I saw daylight. Opposite the stairs another door led into the kitchens. I saw a white-coated chef cutting steaks at a table. He looked up for a moment, stared curiously, his knife poised. I kept on going.

I came out into a cobbled alley. Untidy backs of bricked buildings, each with its loading dock, lined it. It was narrow and, out of the sunlight, dark and a little frightening. My steps echoed along its emptiness.

I reached the street, turned to my right. I didn't know in what direction I was going and I didn't care. Directions didn't matter. I meant to keep on this street until was out in the country. Then I'd *walk*. I was in the mood for walking.

The street I'd chosen lasted only a dozen blocks. Then a rough bridge crossed a turgid brown stream, its surface already thick with fallen leaves. Beyond the bridge, a road, gray and soft with dust, lifted over a little hill. I crossed the bridge, took the road winding. The road was narrow. Weeds grew to its very edges. Sunflowers nodded above it; daisies, asters, and even a few late plumes of goldenrod clustered in fence corners. Beside outcroppings of pinkish granite, sumac blazed royally and in swampy hollows cattails rustled. The air was filled with infinitesimal hummings, plain to the ear now that all other sound was stilled. I began to feel better.

The road led over gentle hills, down into pleasant valleys. A few farm driveways straggled from it. In fenced meadows, cows and sheep fed placidly without raising their heads. No car passed me. I saw no one.

I had been walking perhaps an hour when I saw the man sitting at the side of the road, and for a moment the sight gave me a nasty qualm. Horrible things happened sometimes on lonely roads . . .

Resolutely I pulled myself together. What was the matter with me? He was probably no more than a farm hand who'd stopped to rest for a minute. Perhaps he lived along here somewhere. People did—they must. These fields and sheep and cattle belonged to someone. For all he knew I might belong here, too. I might be someone's hired girl. I had a suspicion I didn't look too well. My shoes were gray with dust, my carefully styled hair was windblown and the edge of my tweed skirt studded with burrs. Of course, a hired girl probably wouldn't be carrying a draggled bunch of field flowers . . .

Hastily I cast it aside.

It wasn't a hired man. It was Johnny Davis, the piano player with the band. He was as surprised to see me as I was to see him. Without the horn-rimmed spectacles, his eyes were very blue. He was hatless and the wind had roughened his dark hair into loose waves. More than ever, he looked like any college boy, temporarily fugitive from any college campus.

He said, "Hi! You're a long way from home. Sit down and take a breather. I thought I was the only one in this outfit who knew how to use his legs."

I said that I'd always liked to walk and sat down on the other end of the pinkish granite ledge. It was warm with sun and suddenly I realized that I was tired and that it was good to rest.

He had a couple of apples and he pushed one over. We sat there and ate them and talked. Silly, inconsequential talk. Completely disarming. I forgot all my mental reservations. He told me of his early days on a farm, about college where he'd played with pick-up orchestras for

66

local dances, about finally deciding to get away and strike out for himself, about engagements with minor orchestras, about meeting Gale Ullman. He was twenty-eight and he'd been with Ullman for five years. I countered with a vignette of my own past and my hopes for the future.

He wasn't much impressed. He looked at my hands and said they were pretty small for concert work, but he was sympathetic and helpful about my wanting a piano for practice. There was a music store in Harriston. He thought they had a piano salon. They'd probably be glad to let me practice there.

Shadows lengthened. The air turned chill. Johnny Davis cast a considering eye at the sun, then put out a hand and pulled me to my feet. "Come on, time to be getting back."

The walk into town seemed very short now that I wasn't walking it alone. We crossed the narrow bridge, once more had pavement under our feet. It was half dark now. There were lights in the houses along the street. Neon brightened the front of a sandwich shop.

Johnny Davis nodded at it. "Let's go in—get something to eat. I'm starving."

So was I. The place was small, clean. There were booths, and we took one at the back. I left for the washroom to cleanse fingers that were sticky from wildflower stems. When I came back, Johnny was fingering the juke box controls.

"Here's one of ours," he said. "Want to hear it?"

I didn't, particularly, but I nodded and he inserted a nickel. Music began to throb through the room. It was an old record—old for popular music, that is—*Long Ago and Far Away*. Halfway through, a soprano voice began to sing—a sweet voice, light and rather fragile, with an engaging little catch of breathlessness in it.

The music died. I looked at Johnny Davis. "That," I said accusingly, "wasn't Mandy Martin."

He didn't look up from the forks he was pushing around. "Nope. That was Anne, Anne Kent."

I took my courage in both hands. "I wish you'd tell me about her."

"About Anne?" He looked at me then. "Why?"

I shrugged. "Why not? I've taken her place. Naturally I'm curious."

He shook a cigarette from his. pack, offered one to me. "Nothing to tell," he said when he had them going. "She was just a nice kid. Everybody liked her."

"What happened to her?"

Smoke veiled his eyes. His face was tightening, shutting me out as all the faces did when I mentioned her name. "Happened to her? What makes you think anything happened to her?"

"Don't be silly," I said. "I'm not just thinking—I know. Listen to me, when Gale Ullman came to the radio station that day, he said she was in the hospital for an operation. Appendicitis. That night at the dance hall, he got a wire from some doctor saying she'd escaped from the hospital. You don't 'escape' from hospitals, especially if you have appendicitis. In the morning, Mr. Sims told me that she didn't have appendicitis—she'd been in a home for mental cases. That blond boy, Dick Travis, says she tried to kill Gale Ullman, that that was why they'd put her there. Yesterday, in Chicago, she came to see me."

"*Who* came to see you?" He'd forgotten his cigarette. A great blob of ash dropped in his shirt front. He brushed it off impatiently.

"Anne Kent."

"I don't believe you. Did you talk to her?"

I shook my head. "Then what makes you think it was she?"

"It had to be." I told him what the hotel clerk had said, about not knowing anyone in Chicago. "I didn't see her.

I wish I had. She was in trouble. Perhaps I could have helped."

He crushed out his cigarette. "All right, I'll tell you. It's not much. Anne looked like an angel but she didn't have an ounce of real brains. Singing with the band was too much for her. She couldn't take it. She went completely off her head over Gale and for a while it looked serious. But Mandy wanted Gale for herself and she . . . Well, I never did know just how she worked it but a week ago she and Gale were married."

"Only a week ago?" My voice sounded shrill. "Why, I thought . . ."

He grinned. "Not the accepted kind of newlyweds, are they? Well, it was a pretty bad shock to Anne. She'd always drunk some but now she went all out. A couple of nights she couldn't even appear. Then, last Wednesday—we were playing over at Inwood Lake—she came down but she was pretty drunk. And ugly. She sang a couple of times but she was rotten, hardly able to stand up. During one of the intermissions, Gale talked to her and tried to send her back to the hotel. She didn't want to go but maybe if Mandy'd stayed out of it . . . Only she didn't. I don't know what she said to Anne but—there was an open clasp knife on the table; Shorty or someone had been sharpening a pencil. Anne grabbed it and went for Gale. There were a lot of us there—we saw it. Well, somebody had to do something and Gale knew this doctor—he runs a sort of rest home. They came and got her." He spread his hands. "Next day we moved on. That's all."

I was outraged. "How can it be all? What about her? Did you really go off and leave her there?"

"What else was there to do? We knew Gale would see to it. He's always decent about things like that."

"I see," I said, heavily sarcastic. "And now that she's escaped, I suppose he feels his responsibility is ended."

"How do I know what he feels? What's the good in talking about it anyway? There's nothing you or I can do."

Things didn't go so well after that. I think we were both relieved when our dinners were eaten and we could go back to the hotel.

He left me at the door, making some excuse about getting cigarettes. I had a few qualms myself about going in in my disheveled state. Luckily the lobby was still crowded and no one noticed me.

The third-floor halls were quiet. My feet made no sound on the thick carpets. I found my room, inserted my key in its door.

The room was still dark, Mandy Martin still a lump in the farther bed. I sniffed disapproval of the thick atmosphere to which something new, sweetish and unpleasant, had been added. I switched on the lights. She didn't move.

The room was a mess. It had been bad enough before I left but now . . . What in the world had she been doing? When I went for my walk, I had left everything straightened. Now confusion really reigned. Her bags were open, empty, their contents strewn about the floor. The drawers of her wardrobe trunk dripped finery. Shoes lay supine. Dresses, ripped from their hangers, lay where they'd been flung or had fallen.

I was so mad I fairly ached. If she thought that every time I came in . . .

I said, "Mandy!" and I wasn't quiet about it.

There was no answer.

I thought, Okay, if that's the way she wants it, she can just go ahead and sleep. For me, I was sticky and dirty and I meant to have a bath.

I was completely undressed, wrapped in a robe of toweling, before I remembered the last-seen state of the bathroom. Well, I wasn't responsible for that and I wasn't going to clean it up. Mandy could do it and she could just do it now! I went over to the bed and grabbed her shoulder and shook it.

The shoulder didn't feel right. Even through the comforter's folds, I knew that. She seemed to be tipping toward me. The comforter slipped off in my hands. I saw blood, thick and coagulated, blood on white skin, on the bed; the inside of the comforter was purple with it. There was a hole in her throat, toward the side . . .

I screamed, then.

5

No one heard me. The scream seemed to cut the silence like a knife.

No, not like a knife. Not knives—not knives ever. There'd been too many knives . . .

I was backing away now; my hand over my mouth, away from the bed, as far as I could go. My shoulder struck against the wall. I'd reached the room's limit. I stood there shivering.

Her eyes were closed. You'd think she was asleep. If it weren't for the blood—and the hole in her throat where the knife had gone in . . .

This wouldn't do. Something had to be done and *I* had to do it. Get hold of yourself, Connie Waring.

I turned around, stared hard at the wall. It was easier that way. Nothing to see but blue-scrolled wallpaper. All right, think it out. Take your time. You'd come into your room—yours and hers—you'd turned on the light, decided to take a bath, touched her shoulder—and screamed.

Screamed and no one had heard you. How did you know? Because, hearing a scream, people came to investigate. No one had come so they hadn't heard. *Quod erat demonstrandum*. Consider it proved.

But people would have to come and quickly. I myself I would have to call them. The hotel manager, the police, Gale Ullman . . .

It came to me like a dash of cold water that I couldn't call them as I was now, naked under turkish toweling. I'd have to dress.

No one had ever dressed so quickly. The clothes I'd taken off I'd thrown on my bed. I snatched at them, crammed them on—the dusty saddle shoes, the skirt edged with burrs, the sweater, backwards, but I didn't know it then, the jacket . . .

I was ready. There was nothing to do now but walk to the telephone. I walked to it. When the desk answered, I was surprised to hear how clear and steady my voice sounded. I asked for the manager.

I got him. I said, "This is Constance Waring in Room 320. Will you come up, please? Miss Martin, who shared the room with me, has been murdered."

I heard a gasp, the severing of the connection. I replaced the handset, went to stand at the door, my back to the bed. On second thought, I opened the door and went out into the hall.

The hall was still quiet. I heard the elevator coming up, the clang as its door opened. Feet came, running almost. There were three of them—the manager, the desk clerk, a nondescript creature who turned out to be a detective attached to the local police station and who had been loaned to the hotel for the Festival season.

The manager was a small man. He had a shining bald head completely encircled by a narrow fringe of dark hair. He had a blob of mustache and pale eyes that popped now behind thick lenses. He was moving so fast his breath came in asthmatic grunts. His name was Lewis.

He caught at my arm. "Miss Waring? I—I hope I misunderstood you just now over the telephone—"

"You didn't," I said flatly. "She's dead. Look in there if you don't believe me."

They surged past me. I heard the door open, a voice—
the manager's—say, "Good God!" and another, flatter
voice, "She's dead, all right. Hang on to the girl. I'll call
the station."

"The girl!" *I* was the girl. "Hang on to her." Did
that mean that they thought I would run away? I turned
indignantly to face the little manager who was mopping
at his collar with a green-bordered handkerchief. Over his
shoulder I saw the desk clerk, green as the handkerchief
but in his own right. The detective was at the telephone.

Mr. Lewis said, "Miss Waring, this is a terrible—a horrible thing! And to have it happen now, of all times, at the
very beginning of Festival Week with the hotel full to its
doors . . ." Words failed him. He diverted the handkerchief to his moisture-bedewed brow. "I have no idea what
the owners—this hotel is owned by a Minneapolis chain,
you know—I can't imagine what they will say."

"It won't make a damn bit of difference what they
say." It was the detective, who'd abandoned the telephone
and was now leaning against the door frame. His little
eyes were going over me in hard jabs. "That is, supposing
they're where they ought to be."

Mr. Lewis wrung his hands. "Of course they're not here.
How could they be? The head office is in Minneapolis. I
expect I'd better telephone Mr. Rogers at once. He may
want to come here himself—"

"Oh, skip it!" the detective snapped and thrust along
finger at me. "You—who're you?"

I drew myself up. "Constance Waring."

"And her?"

"Mandy Martin. She—we both are—were—vocalists
with Gale Ullman's band."

"Ullman, huh? That his band that's playing for the Festival? Yeah. Well, that kinda narrows it down, don't it?"

"Does it?" It sounded stupid but I couldn't help it. This wasn't real—it couldn't be—standing here, answering questions . . . Surely it was a dream. I'd wake up. Please God, let it be soon.

His little eyes were hard. "Figure it out yourself. All strangers here, ain't you?"

Were we? I didn't know. It seemed reasonable. I said nothing.

"Go on, spill it. What's your story? How'd you happen to find her?"

"This is my room. We—we shared it."

"Well?"

I drew a long breath. I needed it. "I'd been out for a walk—a long walk in the country. She was alive when I left."

"Sure of that?"

"Of course I'm sure. She talked to me."

"Huh!" It sounded like disbelief and I hurried on. "When I came back, she was still lying there on the bed. I thought she was asleep. But when I touched her shoulder, I knew. So I called the desk—"

"Now, wait a minute. We talked to the elevator girl coming up. You put that call in at eight-twenty. She says she brought you up a good fifteen minutes before that. What were you doing all those fifteen minutes before you got around to calling the desk?"

If it wasn't red I was seeing, it was a good deep shade of pink. I said, "Will you tell me why I should answer your questions? Who are you anyway? When the proper authorities come here—"

"Lady, I'm the proper authorities." He showed yellow teeth in a gloating smile and turned back his coat lapel to reveal a silvered badge. "Detective Burns. Dee-tailed from the station to look after this hotel during Festival Week. That authority enough for you?"

I wanted to say it wasn't. I wanted to say that I didn't think he'd done a very good job of watching, when people could get murdered. I said, "When the police get here—"

Mr. Lewis wailed. "The police! They'll be coming through the lobby! There'll be a scandal, I know there will! People will see them, they'll be frightened—"

"Shut up!" Detective Burns rounded on him. "I thought of that. Told them to come up the back way, nice and quiet. You"—he pointed to the desk clerk who had recovered somewhat from his unnatural greenness but not sufficiently to contribute conversation—"you go meet them, bring them up. Not you, you stay here. I'm going to need you."

Mr. Lewis, deflated, subsided and the desk clerk, after a questioning glance at the authority *he* recognized, scurried away.

Detective Burns came back to me. "Now, you—get going with your story. And you better make it good. Maybe we can get this finished up—*before* the police come."

It was red now, a bright glowing scarlet. "This is ridiculous! Suppose it did take me a little while before I called downstairs? What difference did it make? She was dead long before I touched her . . ."

"Yeah." He leered at me. "I guess that's right. Blood pretty sticky—drying. Must have been dead quite a while. But maybe you wanted to look around a little, make sure everything was cleared up—"

I had reached boiling point. "I did not clear up the room. You ought to know that if you took the trouble to look around! And I did *not* kill her," I emphasized the words. "You might as well realize that right now. And moreover I am *not* going to answer any more questions, not until—"

He looked pained. "Lady, that's just dumb foolishness. Sure, they all say it but what's the good? If you didn't kill her, you don't need a lawyer. If you did, no lawyer's going to get you out of it. See?"

I didn't. "I don't want a lawyer." That was a lie. "I don't need one." Another lie? "What I was going to say was this: until you get Gale Ullman here!"

His eyebrows shot up. "Ullman? Why him? What's he got to do with it?"

I was on top for the moment. It felt good. "I don't know. Perhaps nothing. Perhaps quite a lot. He's my boss, and her husband."

"What the hell! What's she doing sleeping here with you if—"

Mr. Lewis explained that. "We were so crowded. And there are twenty-three in the band, besides the other acts for the show. They haven't come in yet but they'll be here tonight. We could really only spare the one room. We fitted up dormitories on the fourth floor—"

Burns didn't let him finish. "Okay. You know Ullman? Go get him."

Mr. Lewis fluttered away. The detective's eye upon me was more tolerant. "Have it your way. The husband's always a better bet in a murder. Unless, of course, you and the husband . . ."

I didn't answer that. I didn't feel the necessity.

There were heavy footsteps in the hall—a lot of them. Burns said, "Here they come!" He sounded relieved. I didn't know whether I was or not.

There were six of them. The one with the little black bag was a doctor—he had to be. There was another, laden with a photographer's paraphernalia. There were three blue-coated patrolmen. A tall gray-haired man with a military bearing and a mouth like a snapping turtle's.

The desk clerk did the honors. "Miss Waring, this is Chief Bradley." He indicated the gray-haired man. "Miss Waring found the body, Chief. This is her—room."

The chief said, "I see. Come on, Doc!" and pushed past me. I could hear their voices, low-toned, as they clustered about the bed. Then footsteps again—back to me.

"Was she like this when you found her, Miss Waring?"

I didn't turn my head. I couldn't. "No. She was covered. The comforter was up to her chin. I pulled it down—when I tried to awaken her."

He said, "Um-m" on a long-drawn note. "All right, Doc?"

The round little doctor bustled up. "Tell you more after I've done the PM. Right now my guess is she's been dead five or six hours. Put it somewhere between two and three o'clock. Near as I can come."

I chimed in. "She was alive at two-thirty, when I left for my walk. I talked to her then."

"All right, all right." The doctor glowered at me. "That'd fit. Can't tell the time of death within a second or two, young lady. No one can. Don't care what they tell you in books."

Chief Bradley said, "Huh!" I suspected he'd heard all that before. "All right, boys. The doc's through and you can take over. You know what I want—photographs, finger-prints, all the usual. When you're done, phone Fisher to get over here for the body."

The mouse-like desk clerk intervened. "They'll be quiet, won't they, Chief? Mr. Lewis is very much upset. And couldn't this door be closed? If any of our guests should come along— The hotel is so full, with the hunting season opening and—"

"You can't sit on a murder!" the chief barked, but he reached back and pulled the door to. I made certain that I was on the hallside.

He looked at me as though, for a moment, he'd forgotten my existence. "I've got to talk to you." He looked at the desk clerk. "Got another room somewhere?"

The desk clerk wrung his hands, literally. "Not a room. Everything is filled. We're turning away people." His face brightened. "There's the banquet room, off the mezzanine. But our guests will see—"

"Your guests are going to see and hear a lot," the chief said grimly. "Maybe they'll have to answer questions, too. All right, that'll do. Take her down, Murphy. You"—he nodded to the desk clerk—"go along. When you've landed them, you can go down the back and wait for Fisher. I'll be along as quick as I can."

The chief was right. The people on the mezzanine did see. They didn't hear anything because there was nothing to hear. Oddly enough, our passing caused no excitement. The glances cast our way showed curiosity, that was all. Murphy's blue uniform was unmistakably police. I might have been a thief caught red-handed.

The banquet room was medium large. Units of tables were piled, one upon the other, in the corners. Chairs made spidery clusters. The walls were maniac with black and scarlet scrawls upon pale cream.

The desk clerk fussed about, turning switches. Wall lights bloomed to amber. He pushed chairs into a compact circle before vanishing. Murphy slumped down. I didn't. I found a dilapidated pack of cigarettes in my pocket, lit one, walked about. It was warm in the banquet room—too warm. I slipped out of my jacket.

It was perhaps ten minutes before the chief arrived. He'd removed his hat but his eyes were still granite hard, his mouth a tight line. I thought, I'll have trouble with him. I did. I went over my story again and again while Murphy took notes and the chief tap-tapped irritatingly with a pencil. I'd gone for a walk in the country—why? Because I was cramped, I wanted exercise. We'd been traveling all night. I didn't know anyone here. There was nothing to do. Besides; I liked to walk . . .

The chief's glance found that incredible. "Which road did you take?"

"I don't know." It was the third time I'd said it. "It was the street that runs along the side of the hotel. I walked straight along until it ended. There was a bridge and then just open country. It wasn't a highway, there was no traffic."

"Umm. And you started on this walk—what time?"

"I've told you and told you. About two-thirty."

"Two-thirty's about the time the doc says she died."

That touched me on the raw. "He couldn't tell exactly. He said so. He said any time between two and three o'clock."

"That'd suit you better, wouldn't it?"

"*No* time suits me. It's just that, well, she was alive when I left. Listen! There must be guests in the rooms next to ours. We were talking. Someone might have heard us."

"Talking, were you? Loud enough to be heard?"

I saw the trap yawning. "Not too loudly. It was just that I, well, I slammed the door as I went out. She—Mandy —called something to me. I heard her through the door. Someone else might have, too."

"We'll check it. So you slammed the door, did you? Why?"

"I don't know."

"Have a fight?"

"Certainly not. I don't fight. It was simply that she said something I didn't like. I shut the door a little hard, that's all."

"What did she say?"

"It doesn't matter. It wasn't anything. Not important enough to make me want to kill her."

"We'll come back to that later. Okay. Anybody see you start on this walk?"

"I don't think so. How could they?"

"I'm asking the questions, Miss Waring. Take the elevator down?"

"No. That is, I took the elevator to the second floor. I walked down from there."

"You took the main stairs?"

"I saw a—a housekeeper or maid. She told me how to get to the service stairs."

"Why the service stairs? Why not go through the lobby?"

"I didn't want to. I—I wasn't dressed—"

He surveyed me. "You look all right, as good as the rest of them. Come, Miss Waring. That won't do. We want a better reason than that."

"All right." I let him have it. "I wanted to be alone on my walk. I was afraid, if I went down through the lobby, that I'd see someone I knew."

"Yet you just stated that you knew no one in Harriston."

"I don't—I mean, not in Harriston. But there are—the members of the band. I didn't want to see any of them."

"Any one of them in particular?"

Oh, what was the use? It was all going to come out, one way or the other. I drew a long breath.

"Yes. The leader of the band—my boss, Gale Ullman."

"And her husband." It wasn't a question so much as a statement of fact.

"Yes. You see, I'd seen him after dinner when I—when I was going up to my room. He wanted to come up with me—he said he'd give me a drink. I told him Mandy was up there—he'd thought she'd gone off with the car to visit relatives. I got away from him then but I was afraid, if I came back down through the lobby . . ." I gestured with my hands. "That's why I stopped at the second floor. And when I looked down into the lobby from the mezzanine, I saw him. He was still standing over near the elevator. I was afraid he might be waiting for me, so I—met the maid in the hall and asked her . . ."

"I see." I wasn't sure but I thought some of the steel had gone from his voice. "Don't care much for Ullman, do you?"

"I don't like him well enough to drink with him in my room," I said. "Why, I hardly know him! Or Mandy, either. That's why it seems so silly for you to think I could have killed her. You don't kill a person you've only known three days—at least I don't!"

"Three days! Wait a minute! What are you talking about? What's this three-day angle?"

"I've only been with the band three days," I said and then went on with the rest of it—the Conservatory and Mr. Gilbrau and the radio station program; singing at the Palace; going into Chicago with the band; the train trip here.

He listened patiently. When I was done, he got to his feet and walked the length of the banquet room, back again.

"Miss Waring," he said slowly, "I'm inclined to believe your story. It sounds straight to me. The part of it that can be checked will be. If it's true you've only been with the band three days—"

"It is true!" I said. "Oh, it is! Ask any of them, they'll tell you!"

"I told you I was inclined to believe you, and I would— if it weren't for just one thing: that long walk of yours— alone—out into the country. Think of it my way for just a moment, Miss Waring. A trafficless road—you told us that—a bridge over a river, weed-grown ditches, fields, swampy lowlands—a hundred places where you could hide a knife, a knife that you didn't want to have found again."

6

I sat and gaped at him. "But haven't you got the knife?"

"Was the knife there? Did you see it?"

I shook my head. "I don't know. I didn't look. There was so much blood, I just supposed—"

"It wasn't there," he said flatly. "If it had been left in the wound, there wouldn't have been so much blood. The big artery was severed. She literally bled to death."

I said, "But wouldn't she have screamed? Couldn't she have gotten help—"

"This is the way we think it was done. She was asleep or dozing. The murderer came into the room. If she heard him, probably she thought it was you and didn't even open her eyes."

"But how would he get in?" I asked. "He'd have to have a key. I locked the door when I went out, I know I did. Well, then, where would he get one? Can't you find out? I have mine—I didn't turn it in at the desk because I didn't go out through the lobby."

"What are you trying to do—get yourself hanged?" There was a thin hint of a smile on the chief's lips. "All right, you've got your key. Let's see it."

I pulled it out of my pocket—just a key, silvered, a leather tab hanging from it that read *Room 320, Hotel Marvin*. I looked at it. I said, "I think I see."

"This is an old hotel, Miss Waring, and the locks have never been changed. Almost any kind of a key could be substituted for that one. Certainly a skeleton key—"

I regarded it with distaste. "Then anyone could get into my room and—and murder me?"

"If they wanted to, yes. Probably the keys of many of these rooms are interchangeable."

I tossed the meaningless symbol of privacy to the floor. "If Gale Ullman thinks I'm going to *stay* in this hotel after this, he's crazy," I began.

He stopped me. "Not so fast, Miss Waring, if you please. I was telling you how we think this murder was committed . . ."

I wasn't sure I wanted to know, now. I said, "All right. But—"

He went on, unheeding. "Once inside the room, he went over to the bed—possibly she was asleep—jerked the comforter over her face and held it over her mouth and nose with one hand while he plunged the knife into the hollow below her ear. Then he drew out the knife again, and waited."

My lips were stiff. "Then, you mean she not only bled to death—she was smothered. She couldn't struggle or cry out—"

"No. It wouldn't even take very long. With that artery pumping out blood and the loss of air, it must have been over very quickly."

Now even my face felt stiff, unmanageable. "With all that blood wouldn't the murderer have gotten some on him?"

"We think he did. Miss Waring," the question came sharply, "did you look in your bathroom?"

I seemed to be choking with a nameless fear. The bathroom! What did the bathroom have to do with it? "When I went up, you mean? No, I didn't."

"Someone had taken a shower there. The floor was wet. So were the towels."

"Oh!" I breathed easier. "But it was like that before two-thirty. Mandy wasn't very neat and she'd taken a shower and used all the towels—mine, too."

"I'm afraid," said Chief Bradley grimly, "someone else also took a shower. Those towels show faint stains—blood-stains. If the murderer stripped before committing the crime . . ." He was looking at me again with that gimlet glance. "Miss Waring, do you always wear your sweater back to front?"

I gasped, looked down. He was right. Now I was aware that the neck of my sweater was choking me in front yet behind it yawned below my shoulder blades. The elbow bulges were on the wrong side of the sleeves. Two years— four years ago, girls had worn sweaters this way but not any more. This wasn't even the right kind of a sweater . . .

"Was it like that when you went on your walk?"

"No." I flung out my hands. Even this poor secret was going to come out. "Oh, I might as well tell you. When I came in, I was warm and dusty. I wanted a shower. I even undressed. Then I remembered what the bathroom was like when Mandy'd finished with it. And I was mad. You see, Mandy wasn't very neat. She took off her things and left them wherever they fell. I'd straightened the room once, before I left for my walk. Then, when I came back . . . Well, you saw what it was like—"

He put up his hand. "Wait a minute. You say the room was neat and orderly when you left it?"

"It was. I'd hung up her dress, put her underwear away. But I wasn't going to keep on doing it. I thought she'd deliberately thrown her things around again to be mean, because she didn't like me very well . . ."

"It didn't occur to you the room might have been searched?"

I let out my breath slowly. "No, it didn't. Searched by her murderer, you mean?"

"Obviously."

"But why? What would he be looking for?"

"I don't know—yet. Perhaps her husband can tell us."

"Were my things—disturbed?"

"Not so far as we saw. I'll tell you better later."

"If you'll let me look . . ."

"All in good time, Miss Waring. Now, let's go back a little. You said you first discovered that Miss Martin was dead when you put your hand on her shoulder to waken her. Had you tried to waken her before that?"

"I spoke to her when I first came into the room and saw what it looked like. She didn't answer. And I wanted that shower. But, after I was undressed, I remembered about the bathroom and I tried to waken her—to clear it up. Then, after I knew she was dead . . . well, I couldn't call the desk or the police until I'd dressed. So I put my clothes on again. I was upset and I hurried. I suppose that's why . . ." I gestured toward the sweater.

"That explains the fifteen-minute lag in time?"

"Yes. I undressed first and then I—tried to waken her. Then I had to dress again. I was all in pieces. It took a while."

"You make it all sound very simple and logical, Miss Waring."

"Because it's true." I didn't like what I saw in his eyes. "You don't really think I did it, do you? She was bigger than I, heavier. I couldn't hold her down and smother her."

"Perhaps not. But you could have disposed of the knife."

I was staring at him in horror. "But that would make me an—an accomplice!"

"Exactly!"

"But who could I possibly be an accomplice to?" That sounded ridiculous and I went on. "Outside of the murderer, I mean. I told you I didn't *know* these people. Most of them—why, I'm not even sure of their names! Do you think I'd listen if one of them walked up to me and said, 'Here, I've just murdered Mandy Martin. Do away with this knife, will you?'"

"It doesn't sound sensible," Chief Bradley admitted, "not unless you had a reason. Well, we'll see what develops."

"What" developed right then with the door of the banquet room bursting open and Gale Ullman, a little disheveled, his tie awry, rushing in. He was followed closely by the puffing hotel manager.

The band leader was furious. He looked at me as though he didn't see me. He glared at Chief Bradley, said, "What the hell is all this and who are you and why was I dragged out of a poker game just when I was holding the first decent hand I'd had all evening? What—"

The chief eyed him calmly. "My name's Bradley—Chief of Police for Harriston." There was the brief flash of a badge and then it was back in his pocket. He studied Ullman, his face impenetrable.

"So what?" Ullman flung at him. "So you're the Chief of Police? What's that got to do with it? Why haul me in? Is a friendly game of poker a crime in this God-forsaken town?" His eyes, questing, discovered me and he stiffened, "Connie! What are you doing here?" He saw Murphy. "More police! Good God, what is all this?"

Mr. Lewis was fairly dancing under the chief's accusing eye. "I didn't tell him, I didn't tell him! I didn't know whether you wanted me to or not! And I didn't want a scene. I was afraid of upsetting him—"

"Upsetting *me!*" Ullman shouted. "Good God, you're more upset than I am! Will you tell me what I've got to be upset about? What—"

"Just a minute, Mr. Ullman," Chief Bradley said. "Maybe Lewis knew what he was doing at that. Now, if you don't mind answering a few questions—where have you been this afternoon and evening?"

"I thought you might have gathered that." Ullman's eyes were bright and angry. He lit a cigarette with fingers that shook a little. "I've been playing poker across the street in mine host's rival hostel—in Room 204, to make it definite—with some of my own boys and a couple of traveling salesmen to say nothing of a gentleman who said his name was Rogers and who claimed that he was the Mayor of this burg! Now, want to make something out of that?"

"Umm," the chief said. "No. What time did this game start?"

"Look," Ullman said, "will you please tell me—"

I couldn't stand any more. I went over to stand beside him. "Gale"—it was the first time I'd called him that—"what they're trying to tell you is that Mandy's dead. Somebody killed her this afternoon—up in our room."

"Mandy—dead!" He sounded dazed. The cigarette dropped to the floor. A little curl of smoke rose whitely and his foot moved automatically to crush it out. "You mean—Connie, my God, is that straight? She's dead? Mandy's dead?"

"Murdered, Mr. Ullman." The chief scowled at me. "Miss Waring, will you keep out of this? She was stabbed in the throat."

"I—see." It came on a long dragged out note. But it wasn't the truth. You knew he didn't see—he didn't see at all. "I'm sorry, gentlemen, but I'm afraid I'll have to ask you . . . Thanks." Murphy had pushed a chair forward. He sagged upon it, drew a handkerchief from his pocket and touched his lips. "It's rather a—shock. It's hard to believe. She was so—*so* alive." He shook his head.

One part of my mind stood back and viewed him coldly. He was putting on a good show but that was all it was—a show. He was saying the things he thought we'd expect him to say, doing the things he thought we'd expect him to do. Well, it wasn't getting over—not with me. I didn't believe in either his words or his actions. They were just a little too—too good.

I looked at Chief Bradley but I couldn't tell what he was thinking. He had nodded slightly to Murphy, who took up his pencil again, and now was saying quietly, "She was your wife, Mr. Ullman?"

"My wife—yes. We were married a week—no, eight days ago. Perhaps that's why I—I can't believe it—that she's dead . . ." He dropped elbows to knees, hid his face in his hands. "I'm sorry." His voice was muffled. "I'll have to ask you to pardon me . . ."

Somebody should have been making comforting noises. Maybe that was my role. If it was, I muffed it. We just stood there, stupid, silent, looking at him.

Suddenly, bewilderingly, he was on his feet again. "Take me to her! I don't believe it. It can't be true. Let me see her . . . perhaps there's been a mistake—"

"There's been no mistake." The chief was pushing him down into the chair again. "Just take it easy, Mr. Ullman. It's her, all right. Miss Waring told us that. And you couldn't see her now anyway. There's things that have to be done. Later on you can see her. Just now I'd like you to answer a few questions."

"I'll answer them, of course," Gale Ullman said. He sounded completely broken now—and I didn't believe that either! "But first, won't you tell me what—happened? I—think I have a—a right to know . . ."

The chief told him. Gale Ullman listened quietly, head down, gaze bent on his folded hands. When the story was done, he looked up. "Thank you," he said simply. "It still sounds incredible but probably I'll come to realize it. But who'd want to kill her? That's what I don't understand. Who—"

"That," said the chief acidly, "is what we want to find out. Now about those questions—"

"Oh, yes, the questions—certainly." Gale Ullman leaned his head to the chair back, closed his eyes. "I'll be glad to answer them."

Maybe yes and maybe no, I thought. Brother, you don't know what you're letting yourself in for. I hadn't worried about answering questions once myself. Now I was as wary as a cat on a strange doorstep.

Chief Bradley began innocuously enough. "When was the last time you saw Miss Martin"—he didn't like that; changed it—"your wife."

"We had dinner together."

"She appear all right to you then?"

"What do you mean?" Gale Ullman's eyes flew open. "Chief Bradley, you don't mean that there's a question as to how she died? You're not hinting at suicide?"

"There's no question of suicide," the chiefs said with finality. "If you'll just answer my questions, Mr. Ullman. I've a reason for asking them. Now, was she the same as she usually was at dinner?"

"I think so." The blue in the star sapphire ring smoldered as he drew his hand across his eyes. "She asked me for the car keys—I drove my own car down here from Chicago. Mandy had some distant cousins who live about twenty miles from here, in Somerset. She wanted to drive over and see them so I gave her the keys."

"Then, so far as you knew, she'd gone to visit these cousins?"

"Well, no." He was being careful—oh, so careful. His glance barely brushed me, moved past. "I was more or less sure she hadn't. You see, I met Miss Waring at the elevator. She told me she understood from Mandy that she was planning to rest all afternoon. It puzzled me a little— yes—but . . ." He shrugged. "I didn't check on it."

Again the cat-like pounce. It was growing familiar now. "Why not? Weren't you curious as to why she'd changed her plans? She might have been ill."

"Not ill—not Mandy." He shook his head. "You simply didn't connect illness with her. As to the reason I didn't look her up, well, the whole set-up was a little unusual, Chief. My wife's room was also Miss Waring's. Unless I was sure Miss Waring was out of the room—and I didn't see her come down again—I didn't feel at liberty to go up." He had something there. Of course he hadn't seen me come down again. How could he? But it also proved what I'd told the chief: that Ullman had been on the lookout for me.

It also proved something else and it took a moment or two for me to grasp it. It proved that Gale Ullman, for one, could scarcely have been Mandy's murderer. Because, unless he had some way of making certain I'd come down, he'd hardly have dared go up to that room on such an errand. Of course if he'd telephoned . . .

The chief had thought of that, too. But, to the question, Gale Ullman shook his head.

"No, I didn't. What difference does it make?" Suddenly he seemed to realize what difference it made. He sat up. "Look here! I don't know for sure what you're getting at but I don't like it. Sure she was my wife but you don't think I killed her, do you? *Do* you?"

Chief Bradley chose to ignore that. He glanced at his notes. "You were in the lobby, then, when Miss Waring went through. What did you do for, say, the next hour?"

"That being the critical time?" Angrily Gale Ullman jerked out a cigarette, lit it. "Don't you think if I were your murderer I'd have a nice little alibi all cooked up? Well, I haven't. I can tell you where I was—what I did— but I haven't any way of proving it and I suppose that's what you want. All right, I was in the lobby. How long? I don't know. Maybe fifteen minutes, maybe half an hour. I wasn't clock watching. After that I walked down the street to that barn you call the Harvest Hall. I wanted to look it over. Only nobody was there and I couldn't get in. I walked back—the other side of the street, this time. I stopped in some place, had a coke, killed a little time talking to one of the carnival men. Then I came up as far as the hotel across the street. Dropped in to see what it was like. That's where I ran into Tait and Joe. They were waiting for a couple of traveling men who wanted to get up a little game. I said I'd sit in. When the other fellows arrived, they had the mayor with them. We've been playing ever since." He stood up, ground the cigarette under his shoe. "Well, that's it. Help you any?"

"Can't say it does," the chief said phlegmatically. "You neither. What time'd this game start?"

Ullman shrugged. "After four, I guess. Perhaps four-thirty. How do I know?"

"According to Doc, your wife was killed between two o'clock and three." The chief appeared to be thinking out loud. "Miss Waring came down about two-thirty, she says. That narrows it some. Puts the time between two-thirty and three unless Miss Waring's lying and your wife was dead when she—"

"Wha-at?" Mouth open, Gale Ullman looked at me. I shrugged. I was getting philosophical about being accused of lying. "Is that why you've got Connie down here? You've been grilling her! You don't think she killed Mandy, do you?"

"I don't know who killed her—yet," the chief said equably. "And nobody's been grilling Miss Waring, as you call it. She's been asked to answer a few questions, that's all."

"Yeah, I've had a sample of those questions," Ullman flung at him. He crossed over to me, put his arm tight about my unwilling shoulders. "Darling, this is all wrong—

you know that? You don't have to answer a single question unless a lawyer's present. I'll get one. You—"

I squirmed around, put my two hands against his chest and pushed. Three clear feet of space yawned between us.

"Don't be ridiculous!" I said coldly. "Chief Bradley's not a *fool.*" I emphasized that. "He doesn't really think I killed Mandy, at least I don't think he does. He only thinks I might have been an—an accomplice."

His arms were down again. "I don't get it, I'm afraid. What sort of an accomplice?"

The chief cleared his throat but I hurried on, lest he stop me. I said, "You see, they haven't got the knife. He thinks that, well, because I took a walk this afternoon, that someone might have given me the knife and I went walking to—to get rid of it."

What Gale Ullman said about the chief wasn't nice. "What kind of a knife was it? Or don't you know that?"

"Oh, yes, we know," Chief Bradley drawled. "Got a pretty good idea anyway. It was just a common garden kind of knife—pointed, sharp on one side. Might have been a kitchen knife. Might even be a big clasp knife. Can't tell exactly—not now."

Ullman said he didn't think that was much help—nobody'd be apt to carry a knife around with him. The chief said not unless the murder were planned in advance and Gale said that didn't prove anything—you could always buy a knife if you felt a murder urge come on. The chief said, "Not on Sunday, not in this town," and that seemed to settle that.

But the chief still had a question, the sixty-four dollar one. "Miss Martin was pretty careful to make you think she was going out of town. And then she didn't go. Looks almost as if she might have been expecting a visitor she didn't want you to know anything about. Got any ideas about that?"

I said, "Up in our room? But she wasn't dressed!" and Gale Ullman said, "Look here! I don't know what you're getting at but I don't like it," and the chief said, "Umm. Well, we'll see. Looks like somebody went over the room pretty careful looking for something. Looks like she had something somebody wanted pretty bad. Maybe he got it—maybe not. The whole room was searched—trunks and grips upset. You know what it could be?"

Gale shook his head. He looked bewildered.

"She have any jewelry—valuables—money?"

"Nothing to speak of. Her jewelry was costume stuff. She didn't even have an engagement ring—just the wedding band."

The chief said that was still on her finger and there was money in her purse. "Could have been it wasn't robbery. She have any papers she kept careful? Or letters?"

But that Gale didn't know. He was a little haughty about it. "If you think I'd search my wife's possessions. . ."

The chief said, "All right, all right. It was just an idea."

I stopped listening then. There were things I wanted to say myself—I wanted to tell the chief about Mandy being jealous and about her calling to me to tell me to send Gale upstairs when I was leaving—but I could do that later. Just now something else was bothering me; something about that knife. "A big clasp knife," the chief had said. Somewhere, back in my brain, I had heard about a clasp knife. Wait a minute! I had it. It was a clasp knife with which Anne Kent had attacked Gale Ullman. To whom had it belonged? Had whoever told me said? I couldn't remember. But that didn't matter. With the information to his hand Chief Bradley could surely dig it out.

I started to tell him. I got out three words, not enough to damn anyone. I said, "I've just remembered—"

And then stopped. There was a commotion at the door. We all turned that way. The door opened and Johnny Davis was inside.

He was breathing quickly and he didn't look at anyone but me.

He didn't stop with looking. He came over, caught me in his arms. My nose jammed against his fountain pen clip. He said, "Connie, I just heard. What are they doing to you, darling?"

It was the second time within ten minutes. I was so mad I fairly sizzled. I tried to struggle but the push tactics didn't work this time. He had too good a hold. I said, "Let go, you idiot! Let go—" and wasn't heard because my mouth was all mixed up with tweed.

He was whispering in my ear. "Shut up and listen! This is important. Have you told them anything about Anne?"

I managed to wag my head negatively. I said, "No. But I was just going to—"

His embrace became a shake.

"No—no, you mustn't. Not now. She's here—Anne. I talked to her. She's got to see you—talk to you before they know. I told her I'd fix it. Okay?"

Unless I wanted to form part of a Laocoon group forever I thought I'd better say okay, too.

I said it.

7

I'd forgotten we had an audience but the audience was there, interested and angry. Gale Ullman said, "Well, well! Where'd you drop from? This is Johnny Davis, Chief—my piano."

Chief Bradley didn't waste any time on the amenities. He said, "How'd you get in here?"

Johnny Davis grinned. "It wasn't your man's fault, Chief. He was otherwise engaged for the moment. You don't think you can coop up twenty guys in a room and not have things happen, do you? I slipped out. Wanted to make sure Connie was all right. Now that I've seen her"— he made an amiable gesture—"well, I'll go back."

He turned toward the door again but the chief stopped him. The chief was madder than I was. His mouth was so tight it made an indented line. "Oh, so now you'll go back, will you? Just like that! Well, know what I've a notion to do? I've a good mind to throw the book at you—breaking and entering, assaulting a policeman in the course of his duty—"

"You couldn't make it stick," Johnny Davis said. His smile was jaunty as he moved to the door.

"Murphy, you go along. See that he gets there," the chief ordered. He was still angry when he turned his attention to me. "You want to tell me what that fellow said to you?"

It was one of those questions, plain as black and white. I said, "No."

He said, "I didn't think so. Okay. You two stay here. I'll be back."

We weren't to stay alone. Murphy was at the door, his back solidly blocking the opening. He was talking to someone in the hall, his voice a murmur. I found a chair as far away as possible. Gale Ullman followed me, offered cigarettes.

"Nice fellow, Davis," he said casually.

I said I supposed he was but I was wary. Probably he, too, was curious as to what Johnny Davis had said to me. He might even hope that, where the chief's bludgeon methods had failed, he, by guile . . . I said, "Gale, I'm sorry. That's not much to say after what's happened but it's true."

Smoke swirled between us. I tried to see his eyes and failed. He said, "You found her, didn't you? Perhaps I should be the one to say I'm sorry."

I didn't want to think about it. I said, "Gale, who could have—"

He didn't let me finish. "I don't know."

"Someone in the band?"

"I suppose so." He was dully acquiescent. "We're a little world of our own. Too much to hope that an outsider killed her."

It was narrowing things again. I didn't like it. I said, "But who—which one—"

He cut me off. "How do I know? Any one of them—or you—or me. Mandy wasn't so lovable, was she? She was pretty much of a bitch . . . Oh, hell, I don't want to talk about it! I've got to think fast. When this breaks for the papers, it's going to be swell publicity for the band. Maybe . . ." His voice trailed off.

I thought, Well, there's another reason the murderer couldn't be Gale Ullman. It's his band. It has a big reputation.

He wouldn't do anything to hurt it. He wouldn't do anything that would make for bad publicity.

I came out of my dreaming to find his eyes on me. He said, "Seen much of Davis, Connie?"

I thought, Well, of all the nerve! I said, "No. You're forgetting it's only three days since you hired me. I learned his name for the first time this afternoon, on my walk. He was out walking, too, and we came in together. That's all." I thought, Now make something of that, if you can.

He did. He said, after a moment, "Oh, well, Johnny's all right, I guess. But I don't think I'd be taking any more walks for a while, Connie, until this is cleared up."

I looked my question. He went on slowly, "How do you know how far this—killer is willing to go? He might think Mandy'd told you something or given you the thing, whatever it was, that she had on him." He was watching me carefully.

I said, "But she didn't! She didn't tell me anything! We hardly spoke. And what do you mean—whatever she had on him?"

He leaned closer, spoke softly so that those others near the door wouldn't hear. "Mandy had something on everyone—she always did. That was the way she worked, the way she held her job with the band—the way she got me to marry her . . . Hell!" He bit that off. "Sorry, I didn't mean to let that slip but it happens to be true. Take it from me, she knew what she wanted and she got it—or she knew the reason why. She—she was a devil. There's going to be a lot of people drawing free breaths now that she's gone."

I was repelled. Maybe it was all true enough but it seemed to me this was hardly the time or the place to reveal it. Nor was I the person to whom to tell it. I said, "Will the police find out all that?"

He shrugged. "I won't tell them, if that's what you mean. But they're going to have to dig up a motive, aren't they?"

"I've been wondering," I said. "Anne Kent . . . Do you think—"

"So you know that story, too?"

"Some of it," I said cautiously. "I know that she and Mandy quarreled, that she went after you with a knife."

"Not me." He shook his head. "It was Mandy she went for. Naturally I—got in the way. Look!" He pushed up his coat sleeve to show a new-healed scar. "That's the souvenir I got out of it."

I was beginning to get one of those sinking-down feelings. All this time I'd believed Anne Kent to be sinned against, not sinning. Now I wasn't so sure. She'd attempted murder once; now the murder she'd attempted was an accomplished fact. It was just a little too—too something. Perhaps coincidental was the word. Either Anne Kent had followed through or someone else was using her murderous attack as a smoke screen to cover his own acts. Either way I didn't like it.

He was watching me. He said, "I wouldn't think about Anne Kent if I were you, Connie. I wouldn't bring her into it. Anne wouldn't kill anyone—not even Mandy. She was a nice kid, quite a bit like you. That night—well, she was a little crazy. She'd been drinking a lot. Ever since she knew that Mandy and I . . . Oh, hell, I might as well go all the way, Connie. There was a time when Anne and I thought we'd be married. That was before Mandy put the screws on me. I—oh, skip it. What does it matter now? Anne didn't kill her. I'd swear to that."

Would he? You could swear to a lot of things—be willing to swear—and yet that wouldn't make them true. I said, "But the wire said she was dangerous—that the police—"

He shook his head. "No. It was Mandy who said that. The wire just said she'd slipped away and that they didn't know where she'd gone. It was just a rest home. They had no authority to restrain her in any way. I only wanted her there for a little while until she got back on her feet. I couldn't help feeling that some of it was my fault."

Two versions of the same story—no, three—and none agreed. Perhaps, after I'd met Anne Kent, and had her version, I'd know the truth. I said, "Do you know where she is?"

"No." His voice sounded dreary. "I wish I did."

I debated whether to tell him, decided against it. If she'd wanted him to know . . . I moved to another subject.

"What will happen now? Does the show go on anyway?"

"The show always goes on," Gale Ullman said bitterly. "Didn't you ever hear that? You can be sick in body and soul and heart, you may have lost the thing you call dearest in this world, you may spend your days weeping in a darkened room. But when night comes and the lights go up on the stage, you're there, cavorting and grimacing for the crowd. That's show business." His voice broke out of all control. "For God's sake, let me alone, can't you? How do I know what's going to happen? How do I know?"

I was silent, awed and a little frightened. One thing I was sure of—the agony in him was not for Mandy's death, not for the band nor what might happen to it or to him. It was for Anne Kent.

I began to wonder what she was like, this girl who so far was little more than a name and a pictured face to me. I thought he must have loved her very much. It was odd that I put it in the past tense.

I was glad when Murphy turned toward us again and Chief Bradley came back. The chief was alone and his mouth was tighter than ever.

Gale Ullman roused to glare at him and bark. "How much longer do you mean to keep us here? Don't you understand I've things to do—wires to send?"

"You can go right now," the chief snapped. "You, too, Miss Waring. You understand, no leaving town. Stick around. You'll be wanted."

Gale Ullman was on his feet, his good humor apparently restored. He said, "Thanks, Chief," and was halfway to the door when I stopped him. . . .

I said, "Where—do either of you know—have any idea what I'm going to do? Because I can't sleep in that room! What's more I won't!"

There was a vacuum of silence. Then the chief spoke hastily. Of course I couldn't sleep there. Anyway the room was locked, he wanted it that way. Gale Ullman said, "Good Lord! And I can't even offer you my bed. Perhaps Lewis . . ."

But the hotel manager, summoned, had nothing to suggest. The hotel was not only crowded, it was overflowing. The desk was turning away people every hour. "There's not even a place I can set up a cot for you. Unless one of our guests—and that I doubt very much!—would consent to share her room . . ."

I doubted it, too. I tried to imagine what I'd say if I were invited to sleep in the same room with a murder suspect; I presumed I came into that category for the present, at least. Imagination failed. I said I didn't believe that would work.

Mr. Lewis agreed. He said feebly that of course the hotel might call a few tourist homes. One of them might have a room although he doubted it very much. But he could try . . .

Chief Bradley considered his watch and shook his head. Three o'clock. Nobody, even if she happened to have a room, was going to welcome being disturbed at this hour. "No," he said, "that's no good. There's nothing for it—she'd better come along with me."

My heart did an elevator hop, up and down. "To jail?"

"No." He pierced me with a gimlet eye. "My house. I'll phone my wife. We have an extra room."

I wondered wildly how his wife was going to like being awakened at three o'clock in the morning to take in an evacuee. I thought that he must be very sure of himself— or of her. . . .

I said, "You're very kind but really . . . Couldn't I just sit up in the lobby? It's almost morning." Mr. Lewis's face expressed such shocked propriety that I hurried on. "You see, I haven't a nightgown, or a toothbrush. Everything I have with me is—is up there."

Paying no attention to Mr. Lewis, who was twittering excitedly that there was an open-all-night drugstore on the corner, the chief informed me that I didn't need to worry—his wife could supply whatever I needed. Of course, if I insisted, I could go up myself and get what I wanted. Murphy could go with me.

The idea of the now scarlet Murphy helping me to pick out nightwear was too much. I began to giggle first and then to laugh. The laughter went beyond control, became hysteria . . .

Someone had me by the shoulder—Gale Ullman. He was shaking me. "Stop it, Connie. Stop it, I say! You're all right, you're all right, I tell you. Here, somebody get her some water!"

But water didn't help. I continued to sputter weakly while I was being conveyed by the ubiquitous Murphy— the chief wasn't ready to come yet—to the Bradley house.

It was a comfortable, wide-porched frame house, white painted. Lights were bright over the lower floor. The door was opened by a plump, little woman wrapped in a blue chenille robe.

She acknowledged delivery. "Thank you, Charles. Now, come in, my dear. Fred just called me. You poor child! You've had a horrible experience but, never mind, it's all over now. As soon as you've had a good night's sleep, you'll feel better."

I was never going to feel better. I knew that. "I haven't any nightgown and I'm filthy dirty and my clothes are all on ba-ackwards," I wept. "And I want to go home. I want to go home!"

But I had no home to go to—only the Conservatory. That was the most terrible thing of all.

She didn't pay any attention to the tears that slithered steadily down my cheeks. She dunked me in hot water, shrouded me in linen, voluminous as a tent, brought me sandwiches and warm milk once I was safely in bed. When the milk was gone, she drew the covers close under my chin.

"Now, go to sleep, my dear. Everything will be all right in the morning. Fred will find out all about it. Fred's a very smart man—you just leave it to him!"

I wanted to say that Fred, that very smart man, thought I'd had something to do with the murder but I couldn't. My eyelids were too heavy. Unwillingly, I slept.

Not peacefully. There were dreams. Endlessly I pursued a will o' the wisp with the face of Anne Kent through swamps and bayous where dark moss dripped from old gnarled trees and quivering quicksands sucked at my flying feet. The scene changed. I was pursuer no longer; I was the pursued. I stood, pressed tight against a tree trunk, waiting, and all about me, shoulder-high, jungle grasses waved. The grasses parted. Something came through, something that walked like a man, that had a man's shape. I couldn't see its face—that was hidden. All I could see were the hands that weren't hands at all, but claws. They were reaching for me. One of them dragged at my shoulder . . .

There was no claw on my shoulder. Bright sun poured through ruffled white curtains to riot among the wreaths of roses festooned upon pale cream wallpaper. Mrs. Bradley was shaking me. She stopped as soon as she was sure my eyes were open, retreated to the far side of the room. Her eyes were shocked blue marbles. She said, "Miss Waring, I'm sorry to have to wake you but Fred's downstairs. He wants to see you—right away."

She didn't wait for my reply. She scurried away.

Something's happened, I thought, as dressed hurriedly. She's changed. I'm neither "my dear" nor "poor child" this morning. Perhaps Fred hadn't told her all of it last night. But she hadn't needed to go away so fast. It was almost as though she were *afraid* of me.

I went downstairs—straight narrow stairs whose treads were silenced by gray carpeting. Chief Bradley was waiting for me in the parlor; I'm sure it would have been called a parlor. Bead and eucalyptus portieres separated its tidy-covered plush from the hall. I stood between swaying strands, said, "Good morning."

He didn't reply to my greeting. There was no warmth, no kindness in his eyes. He gestured toward the leather Gladstone at his feet. He said, "Is this your bag, Miss Waring?"

I knelt beside it, reaching for the tag, although I knew. Of course it was mine. Old, its Russian leather scarred from travel. It had been my father's. I said, "Yes, it's mine."

His voice was harsh. "You identify it, then. Will you look through its contents?"

I wanted to ask why. I wanted to say that I didn't need to—that I knew every garment it contained by heart. I didn't. I touched the catches. The bag wasn't locked, it opened wide. Nightgowns, pajamas, underwear, stockings, all lay revealed in orderly layers. But not as I had left them. There's something about the packing you do your-self, there's a way of putting things together that's unmis-takable. I looked up at Chief Bradley. "Someone's been at this," I said accusingly. "It's not the way I left it."

He only said, "Go on, unpack it."

I did. Even if I hadn't known from looking at it, the lower layer would have told me. My hands were shaking as I lifted garments, shook them out, unrolled stockings, opened boxes of trinkets, unscrewed jars in which cream lay molded, unblemished save for my finger marks.

One side was done. There was nothing there, nothing that wasn't my own and as it should be. I removed the contents of the pockets—hairnets, combs, clamps to hold a wave in place, hobby pins, hairpins, Mother's silver-backed brush and mirror.

Again I looked at the chief. "There's nothing here. What do you want? What do you expect me to find?"

He said, "Go on."

I threw over the dividing flap. There was less in this side, bigger things—a satin robe, mules to match, two sweaters, a blouse; down at the very bottom, a big thick bath towel that Mrs. Raines had given me last Christmas. I remembered packing it, thinking that sometime, somewhere, I might need it. Well, I'd needed yesterday but I'd forgotten it was there. I thought, I could have had my shower after all, if I hadn't forgotten. Would that have made things better—or worse? Taking a shower wouldn't alter the fact that Mandy was there—dead—in the bed.

The towel was heavy, heavier than I'd remembered. It wasn't folded, not the way I'd left it. It was wadded together. I took the ends to shake it out . . .

Something clattered to the floor, something with a wooden handle, steel that should have been bright but was, instead, inexplicably dulled. There were rusty stains on the towel . . .

I reached toward that thing on the floor but a hand caught my wrist, held it.

"Don't touch it!" Chief Bradley said sharply. "Well, Miss Waring, that's the knife that killed Mandy Martin. It was found among your things. What have you got to say about it?"

8

I didn't have anything to say. What was the use? Whatever I said, he probably wouldn't believe me. I remained standing there, the knife on the floor at my feet, the towel, with its ugly stains, dangling from my hands.

Chief Bradley didn't like it. He wanted me to talk—so he could talk me down, I suppose. He pointed a long finger.

"Miss Waring, that is your bag. We found the knife wrapped in your own towel. We—"

"How do I know you didn't put it there?" I asked dully. "I certainly didn't. I hadn't even touched that bag. Opened it, yes, but not unpacked it. I didn't need to—there was nothing in it that would crush."

"Now, now." It was a new voice, fat and oily. It emanated from a round little man who now, cigar in hand, strolled into the center of the scene. "No accusations, young lady. Planting evidence—that's not the way the police work. They want to find a murderer, not create one." He flashed me a gold-toothed smile. "My name is Goodwin, Miss Waring. I'm the D.A. here."

I didn't care if he was the angel Gabriel. I said, "You men don't give me credit for having *any* brains, do you? If I'd killed Mandy, do you think I'd have wrapped the knife in my own towel and put it into my own suitcase? Don't you think I'd have been smart enough to take it with me—

because I *did* go on that walk, you know—and get rid of it there?"

"Unless," said the District Attorney, "you were smart enough to foresee that very thing and—shall we say?—forestall it?"

Nice going, Connie. First you were afraid they'd think you were dumb. Now you don't want them to think you are smart.

I appealed to the chief. "You don't think that, do you? Someone put it there—he must have—the murderer. Don't you see? It was my room. The knife would be just one more bit of evidence against me. Why, it isn't even sensible! It's crude. It's a slip."

"Might be, at that," the chief admitted grudgingly.

I was encouraged. I rushed ahead. "Why, you're doing just exactly what he wants you to do—suspect me! While he"—What *was* he doing, for heaven's sake? Inspiration came!—"while he establishes his own alibi!"

The chief shrugged. "Nobody," he pointed out, "has got an alibi, so far's I can find out—not even you."

Not so good. "Then there's the key," I said. "Anyone could have gotten in—"

"No," Chief Bradley said. "Maybe that's what I thought last night but I know better now. There's only three other keys in the whole hotel that will unlock that door—barring pass keys—and, if the hotel help aren't lying, and I don't see why they should be, the pass keys were just where they ought to be."

I said, "I'm afraid I don't understand."

"It's like this," the chief said. "The locks come in sets—the keys go with the room numbers. That is, your room was 320. Well, the keys for Rooms 220, 420 and 520 would open it—none of the others. Likewise 319 would open 219, 419 and 519, but not 218. No," he said as I started to protest, "skeleton keys are out. We tried some. They didn't work so well. Maybe if you got hold of just the right kind. . . . But that would take a lot of premeditated planning and a lot of advance knowledge about these locks that I don't think the murderer had."

"But how would he know about the keys fitting the same room numbers? I wouldn't."

"Maybe he ran across it before. Lots of small hotels are like that."

The band, I thought, someone in the band. Theirs must be a history of small hotels. One of them might know. I said, "Who are in those rooms—220 and 420 and 520? Can't you tell from that?"

"Some. 220's a traveling salesman—rubber goods. He reserved it by mail two weeks ago and didn't check in until ten-thirty after the Milwaukee pulled in. He's out. 520's been rented for three years to an old fellow about eighty— used to be night clerk here at the hotel. Now he's retired on pension but he can't seem to get hotel life out of his system. I've marked *him* off, too."

"And 420?" I held my breath.

"420's one of the rooms turned into dormitories. Whole floor's like that—fixed up with bunk beds to accommodate the show that's coming in. 420's got six in it, all members of your band. Want to know who they are?" He counted on his fingers. "Davis, Ullman, Sims, Gilmore, Levinsky, Travis. Know them?"

"I know who they are," I said carefully. "Gale Ullman and Shorty Sims—he's the business manager—I know, of course. Johnny Davis—he's the one I met out walking." I saw the reminiscent gleam in the chief's eye—no doubt he was remembering Johnny's fervent embrace—and hurried on. "I've talked to Travis once. Morris Levinsky was at rehearsal early when I was. I've never spoken a word to Tait Gilmore."

"Huh!" The chief didn't like believing that. "What's wrong with him? Don't fraternize easy?"

"I don't know." I was getting angry again. Careful, Connie. You'll play right into their hands. "I told you I've only been with the band a few days."

"You told me." The chief studied the floor for a minute. "How'd it happen you joined them?"

That was easy. I relaxed a little. "I told you—they needed a singer in a hurry. Ullman heard me sing at the radio station. I could use the money he offered. That's all."

"What happened to the other girl?"

"Other girl?" I repeated stupidly. But I wasn't stupid. I knew what he meant.

"The girl whose place you took. You said they needed a singer in a hurry. Sounds as though somebody'd failed them."

I said, "Oh. Oh, well, she was ill. She couldn't go on with them. That was why . . ." I let my voice trail off.

"Know her name?"

"Anne Kent." There, it was said. I breathed a mental apology to Johnny Davis but—why should I protect her? She was nothing to me. Besides, when you were asked a direct question, what could you do but answer it? I comforted myself by thinking, Well, you haven't told him anything, nothing he couldn't have found out easily from some other source . . . .

He didn't seem over-interested. His questions sounded perfunctory. "You wouldn't know if this Anne Kent and Miss Martin—Mrs. Ullman—got along together?"

I shook my head. "No, I wouldn't know. I—"

"Yes, I know. You told me. You only just joined the band. Seems to me you make considerable of a point about that, Miss Waring. Don't want me to forget it, maybe. Makes me wonder if it isn't a bit unusual for a big man like Ullman to pick a singer out of a small town radio station. Makes me wonder about his *reason.*"

Wordless, I stared at him.

"You and Mrs. Ullman got along all right, didn't you? She wasn't jealous of you, was she?"

"I think perhaps she was," I said slowly. I wanted to be scrupulously honest. "Just a little. She had no reason to be, but I think she wanted very much to be Mrs. Gale Ullman, I think she was a little afraid of me—afraid she might have reason to be jealous."

"Making up to you, was he?"

"Gale Ullman? No, I don't think so. There are some men who think they have to be—oh, extra nice to girls. You heard him call me 'darling.' That doesn't mean anything—not from people of his world. They all do it." It seemed to me that what I was saying wasn't very smart but I couldn't help it. I struggled on. "You can't remember a person's name, perhaps. The simplest, thing, the easiest, is just to say 'dear' or 'darling' and let it go at that. It's a—a term of address."

But the chief wasn't to be sidetracked. "But you said you were afraid she might be going to be jealous. What did you mean by that?"

"Oh, good heavens!" I said. "I told you Gale Ullman tried to make a date with me that afternoon. I think she suspected that he would. She accused me of intending to go out with him. That's why I used the back stairs. Haven't you checked on a single thing I've told you?"

"Oh, yes, we've checked," the chief said somberly. "We talked to the elevator boy, found the housekeeper, Mrs. Garrett, who told you where to find the service stairs. Woman in the room next to you seems to have heard a lot. Walls in these old buildings are pretty thin—"

"Then if she heard, she must know that Mandy was alive when I left the room!" I said triumphantly. "I slammed the door, and Mandy called to me—"

"She heard it." The chief's voice was grim. "Everything tallies the way you said. Mrs. Tracy—that's 318—says she heard the two of you talking loud and then the door. She says Miss Martin called to you to send 'Gale' up to the room. Ullman says he never got that message."

"How could he?" I was exasperated. "I didn't want to see him. That's why I went down the service stairs."

It fell flat. The chief said nothing. I waited. Still he was silent. At last, meekly, I spoke. "Didn't she hear anything at all, after I left?"

"She says not. Says she went to sleep."

I considered that, shrugged. "Well, I suppose the murderer was quiet. Doesn't that let me out?"

"Why should it? You could have come back."

"But I didn't!" I said. "I didn't kill her! I went straight down those service stairs and out. Why, one of the chefs saw me! He was cutting meat. Didn't you ask him?"

"He saw you, all right. Says he did. Trouble is, a second or so after he saw you, he was called to the telephone over in the pantry. Left his meat and his knives. When he came back, one of his knives was gone. He thinks maybe this is it." He flicked a delicate finger toward the knife in question.

I said, "But—but you mean you think I only pretended to go out, that I really slipped into the kitchen and took one of his knives and went back up the stairs . . ." Words failed me,

"Could have been," the chief said.

I went on as though he hadn't spoken. "And undressed, and killed Mandy Martin, and took a shower to wash off the blood, and dressed again, and *then* went for a walk . . ."

The chief gave a noncommittal shrug. "I didn't say that was how it was. I said it was the way it could have been."

"And I'm saying it wasn't that way at all! Listen! Why don't you ask Johnny Davis where it was he met me? You know what time I told you I left the hotel: Couldn't you tell from that? I mean, it would take so long to walk a certain distance. And all the rest of it—dressing and undressing and taking a shower—that would take time, too. If the times weren't right . . ."

Chief Bradley was looking at me with more favor. "We might do that," he conceded. "Won't hurt to see what Davis says. Of course you could have hitched a ride."

"I didn't," I said flatly. "There were no cars on that road."

"Guess we can check that easy enough. If the road's the one I think, it comes to a dead end fifteen miles out. Nobody uses it but the people who own farms along there." I was still staring at the knife. I said, "What makes the chief think that's his knife? It looks like any butcher knife to me."

The chief shrugged. "Says he can't be sure, says it looks the same. Does. Same kind of handle, same shape of blade as the rest. All bought over to Olson's Hardware Store. Olson's still have a few."

I drew a long breath. Was there hope of a sort in that last? "We came into town at noon yesterday. Perhaps—"

He destroyed the hope. "Nope. Sunday. Store was closed. Watt Olson's a deacon at the Methodist Church."

"No burglary?"

"No burglary." It was final. I looked down at my fingers, lacing and interlacing in my lap. "Then someone else must have come down those stairs after me and taken the knife."

He pounced. "You see anyone?"

"No."

He looked pleased. "I didn't think so."

I broke then. "I didn't! I tell you, I didn't—"

"Now, now. No need to get excited. Maybe you didn't kill her—sounds reasonable. But maybe you could have taken that knife and given it to someone else . . ."

It was too much, I began to cry, ugly raw sobs that shook me out of sanity and beyond control. Chief Bradley and District Attorney Goodwin stood awkwardly, silent, uncomfortable.

Vengeance struck—in the person of Mrs. Bradley. White curls bobbing, blue eyes flashing, she bore down on us. Her arms came about me, held me tightly; my face crushed against her shoulder. Her voice shook with anger.

"You two, you get out of here! Haven't you any sense? Pestering this child, when she's not had one bite of breakfast! Haven't you any eyes? Can't you tell she didn't kill anyone—she couldn't! You and your knives! You get out of here—quick!"

They got. But not until the District Attorney had warned me, unnecessarily, about leaving town. The front door closed on the mumble of their talk. I heard the chief's disgusted, "Women!"

Mrs. Bradley dried my tears with a firm hand. She led me to a spotless kitchen, installed me at a shining white table, produced bacon, toast, marmalade, superlative coffee, before she plumped down into another chair. She splashed cream into her coffee, added sugar, stirred the mixture vigorously. Oddly enough, her first word was the antithesis of her husband's last.

"Men! They make me sick! Always pestering around, badgering the wrong people! Mighty high and mighty Fred can be over the Gestapo! I wonder what he calls such goings on? Gestapo indeed!"

I shook my head. "I know it looks bad. And they have their duty to do—"

"Duty!" It was a snort. "I'd 'duty' them. Why aren't they out after the murderer instead of lounging around here where nobody wants them?"

I took another sip of coffee. "Well, I think that's what they're trying to do—find the murderer." I wanted to be fair. "Most of the evidence seems to point my way."

"Huh!" That disposed of that. "You didn't kill her, did you?"

"No."

"And you don't know who did?"

"No." I qualified that. "At least, I don't think I do."

"Well, then." She sat back triumphantly, "Wasting their time—I knew it! You're not the only one in that band are you? Lots of the others may have better reasons for killing that woman than you have. What about the husband? Seems as though he . . ."

"I don't know," I said. I was in two minds about Gale Ullman. "I can't tell. He seems—very nice."

She gave a satisfied nod. "It's him, you mark my words! When a woman's murdered and she leaves a husband, the husband's always got more reason for killing her than anyone else. Same way with women. Most wives have cause for killing their husbands sometime during their married lives. That they don't always give in to it doesn't mean it isn't *there*. No, sir—I'd watch that man!"

I was done with eating. I swallowed the last mouthful of coffee, pushed my cup away. "That's your husband's job. I'm not doing any watching. I don't care whether I see Gale Ullman again or not—or any of the rest of them either. I'm sick of them all. I wish I'd never come with the band. I wish I was back in Ogden City singing at the radio station . . ."

I was teetering on the edge of tears again. The telephone saved me. Mrs. Bradley answered but it was for me. It was Gale Ullman, the man I didn't want to see again.

He sounded brisk and business-like.

"Connie? Get down as fast as you can to the Harvest Hall. We've a hell of a lot to do."

As I sought my coat, flung it about my shoulders, I reflected dreamily on the immeasurable gulf that separates wishing from reality. I might wish forever to be out of the band, but so long as I accepted Gale Ullman's money, I was under his orders and subject to whatever whip he chose to crack.

9

There was fine confusion in the Harvest Hall, nor was it all of the bands contriving. The wide lobby—foyer, whatever you wanted to call it—was crammed with small booths that offered everything from vegetable graters to Indian beadwork. Crepe paper lay in straggles on the floor. The noise of hammers rose staccato over the sound of tuning band instruments.

From the perfume booth, an exhibitor rushed at me with an atomizer of perfume. The spray struck me in the eye. Furious, I pushed through swing doors into a wide auditorium. Rows of temporary chairs covered basketball court markings. The vast stage, framed in maroon velvet, shoved forward into a curving apron. A man in overalls tested the sound system. Alternately his voice whispered and boomed.

Dimly, around the handkerchief with which I was dabbing at my blinded eye, I saw Johnny Davis hurrying toward me.

He stopped, sniffed. "Whew! What's the idea? Some stink!"

I glared at him. "Go away! Chief Bradley wants to talk to you and it's not going to look well if we're seen talking together."

He grinned. "Relax. He's talked. Wanted to know how far out it was I met you yesterday. I had to guess it— I don't carry a pedometer. I made it two miles, told him about the granite ledge we sat on, remember? He said I could show him where it was, so for this afternoon, I've got a date. Look, Connie." He thrust his hand into his pocket to jingle some coins, lowered his voice. "About Anne . . ."

My eye only smarted now. I put the handkerchief away. "What about her?"

It was his turn to glare. "I don't like the way you said that. What have you got your knife into her for?"

I felt my face go white. "Don't say that." It was the best I could do, a pallid whisper of my usual voice.

He showed his puzzlement. "What did I say? Oh, the knife. Good night, Connie! Don't you go off half-cocked. I didn't mean anything."

"Better not say it then." My color was coming back. I felt better. "I'm sensitive about knives right now."

"That's nonsense!" he said hotly, "Nobody thinks you killed Mandy. Don't be a dope!"

I made myself smile. "All right, maybe I am a dope. I wouldn't know. But at least two people have the idea."

He frowned. "Bradley, you mean? That small town fat-head! I wouldn't worry about *him!* I'll bet he never had a murder to play with before. Listen, Connie, we haven't much time . . ."

But I wasn't listening. How could I? Tumult was all about me. A line of chorus girls—tiny things made taller by towering pompadours and clad, for the most part, in the scantest of playsuits—were trying a few kicks under the eye of a sardonic young man who leaned against the proscenium arch. Up on the stage, Tait Gilmore raised his trumpet in a wavering "Wah wah!" A shirt-sleeved Gale Ullman stood in close conference with Morris Levinsky, a fat double-chinned man who sported a small mustache, and a prim, spinsterish woman with eyeglasses and a three-year-old suit.

Beside me, Johnny Davis said plaintively, "Connie . . ."

I turned back. "They're really going on with the show! I didn't believe it. I don't see how they can."

Johnny's snub nose crinkled. "Sure, they're going on. What do you think? They had meetings all last night but you know what they're like in these small time burgs when they hear the tinkle of the cash register. They called in everybody—newspapermen, radio, chamber of commerce, town fathers—and decided to soft pedal the murders, give out only that Mandy died suddenly, for the good of the town. Meanwhile the police are supposed to ferret around and solve the murder under cover. Like it?"

I said, "No. Still, I suppose it's better than if they wanted to cash in on the notoriety. But how can Gale—"

Johnny Davis sniffed. "If you think that bird's wasting any tears . . . Connie, listen, will you? I've only a minute. Anne Kent wants to talk to you. You see, she was at the hotel yesterday. She saw Mandy—"

"She *what?*" My voice rose to audibility.

He sent a hasty glance around. "Pipe down, will you? Somebody might hear. Look, Connie, you don't need to be afraid. She didn't have anything to do with killing Mandy. I'll swear to that."

They were all so sure, so sure that Anne Kent couldn't be the murderer. How did they know? Anyone could be a murderer, given the right provocation. Even I . . .

I said, "I don't like it. What's she hiding for? If she wants to see me, why can't she come to the hotel?" Suddenly I remembered that I "didn't live there any more." I amended it. "Or to Bradley's."

"She's afraid." The earnestness of his tone compelled belief. "She doesn't want any of the gang to see her or know she's here. I think she's scared stiff."

"I'm scared myself," I pointed out. "We'll be a nice couple. What does she think we can do together—hold hands and shiver?" A new thought came to me. "Why me, anyway? If she's so darned afraid, why doesn't she tell you her troubles? You know her."

He shrugged. "Nobody tells me anything. I'm just good old Johnny, Ullman's piano. Look, Connie, I don't know what it's all about, but she says it's important. Give her a break, can't you?"

All right, I'd give her a break. Reluctantly, I said, "Where's she staying?"

"I don't know. She didn't tell me. She said she wanted to meet you some place out of the way. Remember that joint we had dinner at last night? She said that was okay. She said between four-thirty and five. Nobody is apt to be around there then."

"Are you coming?"

He shook his head. "Not invited. It's you she wants to see. Look, Connie, it's still broad daylight then. You don't need to be afraid."

I considered it. Broad daylight and a public place—no, I didn't think I needed to be afraid. I said, "What if some-one—the police—sees us? They could be watching me."

"You'll have to take that chance. But I don't think you need to worry. They're small town cops; probably they'll never think of it. You can keep an eye out, can't you?"

I had an instant's vision of myself keeping an eye out, skipping nimbly over backyard fences to put the police off my trail. It was ludicrous. I laughed and, with laughter, fear went out. I said, "All right, I'll go. Today?"

He said, "That's right. Thanks a lot, Connie. I don't know what it's all about but . . . I'll tell her."

I had a new idea. "I don't like this secrecy angle. If she sees you, why not me? Why can't be with you when you tell her?"

"I haven't seen her." His voice snapped it. "She tele-phones me. She's going to call again—down here—at one."

I said, "Oh. Well, why can't *I* talk to her then? I'd feel better—really I would—if I could just hear her voice—be sure . . ."

His glance withered me.

"Now you are a dope! You want the whole gang won-dering who you know well enough in this town for him to be calling you? With me it's different. It could always be a doll"—he winked at me—"I'd picked up last night."

I had nothing with which to counter that. I only nod-ded and turned away. Gale Ullman was calling for me.

I don't know how long that rehearsal took. Hours, it seemed to me. It didn't make sense from beginning to end. I hoped it did to Gale Ullman and the stage manager and the representatives of the Harvest Festival Committee. So far as I was concerned, it was chaos, pure and unadulter-ated. Maybe they had a show, but I doubted it.

Time flickered by. Actors came and went. The pony chorus were put through their paces. Johnny Davis got his phone call. As he passed me, on his way back to the piano, his left eyelid drooped a little. I nodded in reply. That was all.

There were new numbers for me, three of them. I was lucky—Dick Travis had half a dozen. I sang them, how well I didn't know. I was an automaton, standing, sitting, open-ing my mouth in obedience to Gale Ullman's lifted hand.

During the brief intermission we were allowed, I didn't lack for company. One by one, the members of the band sought my corner. They proffered cigarettes, were affable about going out for coffee. They didn't fool me. I knew why. I was "in the know," might possess information they didn't have. I said as little as possible.

Even the redoubtable Tait Gilmore approached. Clev-erer than the rest, he brought his bribes with him—two paper-wrapped hot dogs, a bottle of Coca-Cola from the vending machine at the door.

Too bad I didn't recognize danger when I saw it. But the sight of food brought hunger to memory. Once accepted, there was no reason why he shouldn't sit down beside me.

The hot dogs were gooey with sauce, pungent with mustard. He shrugged off my offer to share them. He'd had his, he told me. He sat there, holding the bottle, handing it to me when I wanted a drink.

It was the first time I'd had a really good look at him. He was younger than I'd thought, twenty-eight at most, thin and nervous. His hair was sandy, high-grown at the temples. His eyes were gray, set in darkish circles. Beside his mouth, a nerve twitched in continuous unease. His smile was lopsided. When he said I'd had a rough introduction to the band, I thought he was trying to be friendly.

Muffled by hot dog, I said it hadn't been exactly pleasant.

"Police bothering you, huh?"

I caught a straight look at his eyes. Something in them repelled me. I said, "Well, what do you think?"

He said he supposed they were. It was reasonable. "Your room and all. What I can't figure out is why anybody'd want to kill poor old Mandy."

I had nothing to confide, I said if there were reasons, he should be in a better position to know them than I.

He agreed. He said most of the fellows got along pretty well with her. They had to. Once a bandleader's wife got down on you, you might as well start framing your *At Liberty* notice. And Mandy had Gale under her thumb, all right, all right. Look at the way she put the skids under Anne Kent . . .

If I'd had any sense, I'd have let it go at that. But I didn't. I played the wide-eyed innocent "Anne Kent? Oh, wasn't she the girl who . . ."

"Yeah, you took her place."

The Coca-Cola bottle was empty now. He swung it between his hands, looking down at his feet.

Even then, I couldn't let well enough alone. "I didn't know that Mandy was responsible for Anne Kent leaving."

"Lord, yes. Mandy never liked competition and she'd come out on top with the marriage lines in her fist. But she hated Anne, and she was afraid of her. Result—Anne left us."

The hot dogs were a memory now. I wadded the paper napkins, held them in my hand. "Wasn't it a little more than that? I mean, if anyone had come at me with a knife . . ."

"Who told you that?" His eyes stabbed at me. "Gale?"

"Among others. Why? Isn't it true?"

"True enough. I saw it happen. But, somehow, I thought there was more to it than showed on the surface. They said Anne was drunk. Maybe she was but she didn't act drunk to me. I wondered if she wasn't hopped up, if maybe someone'd slipped her a stick of tea."

"A stick of tea," I repeated uncomprehendingly, "What's that?"

"Marihuana." His eyes were laughing at me now. "Don't you know anything at all, baby?"

I ignored the "baby." "You think that someone got her to smoke marihuana and that's why—"

He shrugged. "Could be. It's pretty unpredictable stuff. Gale said she was drunk, and he ought to know, but I've seen Anne liquored up before. She didn't get mad—she got maudlin, silly sentimental, sorry for herself. That's why I started thinking . . ." His voice trailed off.

I felt sick to my stomach. "But who would have—marihuana? I know there was a lot of publicity about it some years ago but I thought it had all died out."

"It can be had"—he was laughing at me again—"even out here in the sticks. Like to try it?"

I shuddered. "No." Then curiosity triumphed over the shudders. "What are you trying to tell me? That you think someone persuaded her to smoke marihuana in the hope that it would send her into a murderous rage?"

He looked away. "I'm not trying to tell you anything. Any conclusions you draw are your own. But marihuana *does* incite murderous rage in some people. Maybe it's an idea."

I said, "But that would mean that someone in the band wanted to get rid of Mandy and deliberately . . ." Words failed me; I sat silent, my mouth a little open.

"Yeah. And then when his little scheme failed, he had to take action himself." His slender hand made a quick stabbing motion. You could almost believe that it held a knife, was thrusting it home through soft flesh.

I shrank back from him. "I don't believe it, I can't! That would mean that one of these people—one of the band . . ." I couldn't go on.

His gaze softened. "Listen, kid, you haven't been around much, have you? You look at us and what do you see? Pretty average-looking bunch, aren't we? But don't forget we come from all over—different parts of the country, different homes; different levels of society. We weren't picked for what we were—only for what we can do. Jimmy Moss can't write much more than his name—know that? Sure, on the surface, he looks the same as the rest, but down underneath—well, what can you tell of a fellow's background just by looking? Even as a member of Ullman's band, he's still got his own private existence, his private hells. Just belonging to a band won't make him over."

I drew a long breath. "Are you warning me to be careful? Is that what you mean?"

There was no laughter in his eyes now. "Could be. Let me tell you something, sister. Not all the boys in the band are nice, tame little playmates. Funny things go on in bands. Take Ortman's. During the war, we all played the military circuit—you know the line, helping raise the morale of soldiers. Well, Ortman's played one of the big Air Force camps at—" He named the place. "Next day when the bands went on, the tram man and the arranger weren't with them. Because why? Because some fool soldier took it into his head to look through the tram man's portfolio and got curious as to why he had music paper all messed up with maps of camps and estimates of war strength. Sure, he'd been vouched for—he was supposed to be all right— but he was selling out to the other side just the same. No, kid, you watch your step. You don't want to end up like Mandy did—or Anne."

"Mandy's out of it," I said slowly. "And as for Anne— couldn't I warn her?" I stopped in confusion, ready to bite my tongue out.

He didn't notice my slip—not right away. "How could you warn her?" he grumbled. "And why? If she knows anything, she's probably lying low. She'd have sense enough not to come here."

Suddenly he stopped, looked full at me. I was scarlet. Guilt sat all over me. "Or wait," he said softly. "I could be wrong. Maybe she *is* here. There was a girl on the street this morning . . . Of course that's it—she's here! Hot damn! Wait until Gale knows that!"

"Wait until Gale knows what?" Gale's own voice said sourly and I jumped up, reprieved, to face a compact little trio—Ullman and Shorty Sims and Dick Travis. "What the devil do you two think you're doing—sitting out a dance? I've yelled at you twice."

Tait Gilmore hadn't moved. The pop bottle still swung between his fingers. His eyes were open and candid but there was deliberate malice in his soft whispering voice.

"We were talking—talking, that's all, about Anne Kent. Funny thing, Gale—I'm pretty sure I saw her on the street this morning."

There was a brittle little silence. Shorty Sims shot me a reproachful glance, Dick Travis gaped, but Gale Ullman stood perfectly still, staring before him. His eyes were fixed. He stood as though he were looking at something and didn't like what he saw.

"Not Anne!" he said. "But that's nonsense. She wouldn't come here."

"No-o?" There was an upward drag to it I didn't like. "Well, you ought to know. But just the same I think she's here. That girl on the street this morning—she looked like Anne. From the back, of course. I didn't see her face. Same hair, same coat; same funny little red hat. Remember that hat, Gale?"

"Yes." Gale Ullman said dully. "I remember the hat. But it wasn't here. She couldn't be here."

He stood a moment longer, still with a sort of restrained motion, before he shook his shoulders back and turned away.

"Come on, let's get to work. There's still two acts to set . . ."

10

It was almost half past three before I was free to depart from the Harvest Hall. I left then—but fast. I had no wish to be cornered by Johnny Davis, not that I thought there was much danger in view of the date he was supposed to have with Chief Bradley.

It was one of those sweet fall days that come to the middle west in early autumn, warm enough so that you scarcely needed a coat. The midway, from which all wheeled traffic was barred, was gay with bunting. People, farmers many of them, in town for the day, strolled aimlessly up one side of the street, down the other. Children darted about under foot, nickels and dimes clutched in their fists. At the board tables of the church booths, the weary-footed drank coffee and consumed sandwiches and cuts of homemade pies. The strident cries of barkers, more perfunctory now than they would be later in the day, rose at intervals.

Grateful for the anonymity given by crowds, I merged with them. I thought, This is luck. No one will notice me here. Nor would they. I was simply one more stranger among the other unknown.

The tide of traffic was passing up the street. I went with it, purposely. I had about three-quarters of an hour before it would be time to start for my rendezvous with Anne Kent. Smells of coffee from the open booths tempted me, but I told myself sternly to wait—the food was fair at the little restaurant. We'd have to have some excuse for our coming. I'd order a dinner there.

Meanwhile—what? Shopping? I shrugged that off. What was there to shop for even if I had the money to spare? There was the hotel—I could go and sit in the lobby—but that was scarcely the location for one who wanted to remain unseen. Still, there was the show tonight . . . I'd have to do something about my clothes.

I might be invisible upon the streets but in the hotel lobby I stuck out like a sore thumb. The desk clerk stiffened as I approached. Detective Burns' gaze smoldered upon my back. The elevator boy's head thrust fearfully around his grilled cage.

I asked for Mr. Lewis, my voice loud in the sudden silence. He was in his office. The desk clerk motioned me that way.

Neither was Mr. Lewis glad to see me. He jumped to his feet, careful to keep the desk between us.

"Miss Waring! We didn't expect you! I'm very sorry, but you understand, of course, that your room is still unavailable. It has been sealed by the police—"

I made a calming gesture. "I understand. But my clothes—I'll need them for the show tonight. What about them?"

He looked relieved. "But that has been taken care of. Mr. Ullman—I believe with the permission of the police—had them removed to your dressing room at the Hall."

I might have known. I thanked him, turned away. At the swing door of the lobby, I met Gale Ullman face to face. I would have ducked if it had been possible. It wasn't. He saw me, put out his hand.

"Connie! Good. I wanted to talk to you."

I stole a look at the lobby clock—a half hour at most before I had to go. "I'm in rather a hurry . . ."

"That's all right. It won't take long. Let's go in here."

"In here" was the coffee shop. Silvered tables for four up and down a center aisle, booths along the edges. We took a booth, ordered—coffee and a sandwich for him, just coffee for me.

The waitress came and went. Gale Ullman lit a cigarette, sighed. "I'm all in. What with the police last night and the damned civic committee scared to death for fear they'd lose a nickel, it's been hell!"

There wasn't anything to say. I sipped my coffee, waited.

"I didn't kill Mandy," he went on. "What makes them think I'd deliberately sabotage my own show? God knows I've always tried to give value insofar as I was able."

Talk of the show made me think. I thanked him for rescuing my dresses. He waved my thanks away. "You had to have them. Even that lunkhead Bradley could figure that out."

I protested that. "I don't think he's a lunkhead. Has he told you about—did you know he'd found the knife?"

He hadn't. He listened without comment until I was done. He said, "Whoever he is, he's being just a little too smart. I wish I knew who it was. I'd . . ." He was silent, brooding.

"I don't know," I said. "I think getting rid of the knife like that—right at the scene of the crime—was clever. It saved disposing of it later. But I think, too, it was just one too many leads in my direction. There just isn't any sense in the idea that I'd kill her!"

"No. There were others who had a lot more reason." He broke a sandwich in half, laid it down. "Connie, who do you think *did* kill her?"

I gave up all pretense of drinking my coffee. "How do I know? I don't know any of you well enough . . ."

"You don't, do you? Not even me. Well, I suppose you've heard Bradley's key theory?"

"That it was one of you in Room 420? Yes, I've heard it."

"Believe in it?"

"I don't know. I don't know what I believe."

"Morrie or Shorty Sims or Dick Travis. Or Tait or Johnny or—me. Take your choice."

I wasn't having any choice. I was thinking. "Well, it would almost have to be one of them. What I mean is, the murderer would have had to have a key. The door was locked when I left."

"Sure of that?"

"Of course I'm sure. I remember locking it. And it was locked when I came back."

Gale Ullman rubbed his hand across his eyes. "The murderer could have done that," he said. "Lord, what a mess!"

"It won't always be a mess," I said. "Sooner or later someone will talk. They always do. If the police can't make anything of how it was done, they'll start looking for a motive and once they do . . ."

"They'll get an earful," Gale agreed grimly. "Maybe— or again, maybe not. I've an idea Mandy's little games were kept strictly à deux. Lord knows I only fell over one or two of them by accident. If there were enough, and if the pressure got too high, somebody'll break and go looking for a scapegoat. And then"—the star sapphire in his ring flashed with the gesture—"then the fat will be in the fire for sure."

"What do you mean?"

He looked at me soberly. "I mean Anne Kent."

There she was again. Like King Charles' head, she kept reappearing. I said, "But—"

"Oh, I know, you don't know the story. But all the rest of them do and if someone needs to save his own skin badly enough, he'll remember Anne—and fast. She had the best motive for getting rid of Mandy. If they could prove that she was here, in Harriston . . ."

Perhaps that was a lead. If it was, I didn't respond. I just sat there. Because, if Johnny Davis was right, Anne was here. In a very short while I would be seeing her.

"That's why I hope to God Tait didn't know what he was talking about. If she's here . . . You see, Connie, Anne and I were to have been married this fall. She was a sweet kid and she—loved me. She made no secret of it. We—I think we could have been happy. If it hadn't been for Mandy . . ."

I don't know why but, all of a sudden, panic came over me. I didn't want to hear the rest of that story. I began to scrabble my possessions together—purse, gloves, cigarettes. He didn't like it. He leaned across the table, his eyes narrowing. "What do you think you're doing?"

"I'm sorry," I was a little breathless. "I've really got to go. I have an appointment and it's getting late." That was true. The hands of the wall clock seemed to be leaping forward.

His hand shot out, caught my wrist. "You can't go now. You've got to listen . . ."

I pulled free. "Please. I don't think I want to hear. I'd rather not . . ."

"You're going to listen. Someone's got to. I can't go to Bradley with this yarn." His mouth twisted bitterly. "Someone's going to believe me and that someone's *you*." Abruptly the hardness went out of his voice. "What's the matter? You're going to hear it from the others sooner or later. Don't you want to get it straight?"

I said all right. There was nothing else to do. Two of the waitresses were whispering and looking in our direction. A bellboy who'd been calling "Mr. Davis—Mr. Davis" had halted and was peering at us. Absently I thought, Why, that's Johnny he means. I wondered if I should tell him where Johnny was and then decided against it. I hoped Gale wasn't going to take too long . . .

"Mandy spoiled it for Anne and me," he was saying. "At first she hadn't paid much attention, probably didn't believe it was serious. Then Anne started wearing my ring. Mandy hated Anne anyway and this was too much to take—marrying me would put Anne on top of her. It's easy for a leader's wife to put the skids under members of the band whom she dislikes. Anne didn't like her any too well and she knew it." He paused for a second. "Well, we were playing at the Rose Room in Frisco. One night we threw a party after the show. It was Tait's birthday and we made it a pretty good affair—with a cake and candles and a hell of a lot to drink. Anne didn't stay long. She said she had a headache and begged off. The party went on all night. When I woke up in the morning, I was in Mandy's room, in Mandy's bed. I felt badly about it but Mandy was a good sport. She said we'd all drunk too much, that Anne need never know. She promised not to tell. She kept that promise."

I felt sick, revolted, "But you said Anne . . ."

"Wait. We went right on, Anne and I. Mandy didn't seem to notice or care. She had her own interests. And then, about six weeks after that party, she got me alone. She said she was going to have a baby and that it would be mine.

"I tried not to believe it. She swore it was true. She threatened scandal if I didn't marry her, a lawsuit. There was nothing I could do—she had plenty of newspaper friends. We were married."

"Without telling Anne?"

"I couldn't tell her. There wasn't time. There wasn't any way I could explain a thing like that. She wouldn't have understood. Afterwards I was sorry I hadn't tried. Mandy threw it at her that night, in front of them all. Rushed in all splattered over with orchids and that damn leopardskin coat—it was my wedding gift . . ."

I tried to imagine what it had been like. Mandy, triumphant in her furs and flowers, and Anne, soft and sweet and defenseless, not understanding what had happened, helpless to hurt. I said, "And then she began drinking?"

"She began drinking. What else was there for the poor kid to do? She'd always been careful—she didn't take liquor well and she knew it—but now she didn't care. You know how it ended. Mandy taunted her, once too often. She grabbed a knife and . . ." He made a quick gesture with, one hand.

It was a heaven-sent opportunity to find out something I'd wanted to know. "Whose knife was it?"

"Whose knife?" He looked at me blankly, "What difference does it make? It was Shorty Sims' clasp knife, but I've an idea someone else had borrowed it, I don't remember who."

A lot of help that was. Once more I reached for my gloves, began to draw them on.

"Tait Gilmore," I said casually, "thinks that someone wanted Anne to—to kill Mandy. Maybe that's why he borrowed the knife and had it so handy."

Gale Ullman's face flushed darkly. "What are you talking about?"

I smoothed a finger of my glove with care. "He thinks perhaps someone might have given her marihuana to smoke in the hope that it would send her into a murderous rage. It does do that to some people, doesn't it?"

There was no answer. I stole a look at him. The dark anger still clouded his face. The chords of his neck seemed to have swollen. But his voice, when he spoke, was quiet—too quiet. "I won't stand for marihuana smoking—the boys know it. If I thought what you say is true, and I could find out *who*—" His hands clenched. I could see the hard line of the tendons along their backs. "I'd kill him with my own hands!"

"And a lot of good that would do!" I said scathingly. "No, but, Gale, honestly, don't you think you ought to tell Bradley this—what you've told me? It might help."

"I do not! Can't you see what it would do to Anne? It would put her right on the spot. And if they could prove that she'd been here, in Harriston . . ." He was silent for a moment, fingers tapping restlessly. Then he said softly, "She is here, isn't she, Connie? Tait wasn't lying when he said he'd seen her. Have you seen her?"

I said, "I haven't seen her, Gale," and it was true.

He sighed. "I suppose not. It's queer, though, that she hasn't come to me."

"No," I said "she wouldn't come to you—not if she had any pride. Why should she? She'd trusted you once."

I suppose it hurt. He winced. "And I failed her? You're probably right. But just the same . . ."

This could go on endlessly. I looked over my shoulder at the clock. It was twenty-three minutes past four. I had exactly seven minutes to walk goodness knows how many blocks to that little restaurant and Anne Kent.

I stood up. From that vantage point, looking down at him, I had an instant's impulse to tell him, to say, "I'm going to see Anne Kent in a few minutes. Come with me— you, can see her, too."

I didn't. Instead I said, "Gale, I've really got to go. I'm sorry, I'd like to stay . . ."

He waved me away. "That's all right. Here comes Shorty now—with another load of grief by the look of him."

I escaped. I was out on the street, being buffeted by the carnival crowd, larger now as the day lengthened. I didn't take the street I'd taken before. I walked north, to the first street that paralleled it. I was being careful—why I didn't know. From what I'd heard, about half the band already knew Anne Kent was in town. Presumably the other half would soon. Yet, because I'd promised . . .

No one was following me, so far as I could tell. I had the streets to myself. That was the way I wanted it to be.

Three blocks from downtown I crossed over to the original street. How many blocks still? I didn't know. I was going to be late, however. My watch showed just past half-past four.

I was breathless when I came up the cement steps of the little restaurant, but the breathlessness wasn't all from hurrying. Part of it was excitement. I was about to see a wraith, a name, a picture, become flesh, I wondered what she'd be like—Anne Kent.

She wasn't there. Save for two fat women idling over tea and pastry at one of the center tables, the place was empty. I walked its length, past the booths, to make certain.

Puzzled and a little angry, I chose a booth that would let me face the door. What was the matter? Hadn't she come, or hadn't she waited? I wasn't so late, really. Five minutes, that was all.

A waitress splashed a glass of water in front of me, proffered a menu.

"I'm expecting a friend," I said. "I'll order later."

She was halfway across the room when it occurred to me to ask her. I called her back.

"I'm a little late—meeting my friend. I wonder if she was here before I came—a girl with blond hair, not very tall. She might be wearing dark glasses and"—What was the color of the hat Tait had noticed? I remembered—"and a small red hat." I brought it out triumphantly.

Her face remained blank. She shifted her gum. "Nobody's been in the last hour but them." She nodded toward the fat women. "Too much going on downtown, I guess."

I said all right, that I'd wait. I waited—until well after five o'clock when the place began to fill up with dinner seekers and it looked as though booths would be at a premium. Then I ordered.

I wasn't just a little angry now. I was mad clear through. Just wait until I saw Johnny Davis! Sending me off like this on a wild goose chase . . .

11

I'd hate to have been the one who wrote the review of the show that night. It wasn't nervousness that blurred my senses either. What I had to do didn't compare with playing the simplest piano number on one of the Conservatory programs. There I'd been on my own—but strictly. Here I had an abiding faith that Gale Ullman and the band would cover any errors I might make.

I found my dresses hung neatly in the dressing room. The dressing arrangements at the Harvest Hall were of the simplest. Apparently more basketball teams played there than shows, for, below stage, there was only one private dressing room and the rest of the space was divided into two large rooms, one for the men, one for the women. Across the hall were shower rooms. It was rather rough accommodation although there were mirrors along one side of the room and lights and broad shelves that could be utilized for make-up boxes.

The dressing rooms were in a state of pandemonium when I arrived. The entire feminine personnel of the other acts was present and most of them were dressed. The only mirror space left for me was at the far end where members of the pony ballet were rouging lips and beading incredible eyelashes. Beside their costumes, of towering headdresses and brief patches of sequins, my own decorous chiffons were as innocuous as skimmed milk. The knife throwers assistant wore silver lamé; even the bicyclist, in blue satin trousers, was more glamorous than I. I thought, Rosebuds in my hair—oh, gosh! but I left them in. I didn't know what else to do.

Voices all around me chattered shrilly. I had no one with whom to chatter. I sat off in one corner on a hard wooden chair.

I tired of that presently, slipped out into the corridor. That was a mistake. I would have retreated but it was too late. Johnny Davis had been watching for me.

He stepped on his cigarette, maneuvered me into a corner. His voice was low, conspiratorial.

"Well, did you see her?"

"I did not!" A sense of my own wrongs came flooding back. "I went to the restaurant and waited and waited—until after five. She never came."

He scowled. "Sure it was the right restaurant?"

"Of course I'm sure. She wasn't there."

"Maybe she got there before you did and couldn't wait."

"She didn't. I asked the waitress. She said nobody'd been in—there was too much going on downtown."

He pulled at his lip. "I don't understand it. It was her idea. She was the one who wanted to see you."

"Johnny," I said, "how do you know it was really Anne Kent who telephoned you?"

"Of course it was Anne. I know her voice." He looked at me with suspicion. "What are you getting at?"

"I've been thinking," I said. "I had a lot of time to think while I was waiting in the restaurant. Suppose the murderer just wants you—and me—to think she's here in Harriston, as a—a sort of smoke screen for himself?"

"It was Anne's voice," he said stubbornly. "Anyway, what good would it do him—just having people think she's here?"

"Plenty," I said. It was a subject on which I'd spent considerable thought. "Everybody knows she and Mandy hated one another—everybody in the band, I mean. They all know why. Well, now Mandy's dead, murdered. Wouldn't it be to the murderer's advantage to have Anne Kent known to be in Harriston, calling people on the telephone—"

"Yes, I see." He sounded a little dazed. "But that voice—it was Anne, all right. I'd swear to it."

"Perhaps it was and perhaps it wasn't. It could have been an—an auricular illusion. Now, wait! I know what I'm talking about. She said she was Anne Kent and if you wanted badly enough to believe her . . . It *was* a woman's voice, I suppose?"

"It was," he said grimly. "No doubt about that."

"Did her voice sound as usual? The way you expected it to?"

"How do I know? Anne didn't make a habit of calling me on the phone. I don't think I ever talked to her before. The voice was low and, well, sort of tense. I thought she was excited. But, look here, Connie, it was a woman. That means that, if you're right, he got someone to telephone for him."

"That wouldn't be too hard," I said. "There's a type of small town girl to whom a member of a dance band is pretty glamorous. He could tell her he wanted to play a joke on you. She wouldn't think anything of it."

"No," he said. "I guess she wouldn't—you're right. Damn it, I still think it was Anne! But if it wasn't, there's not going to be any way to find out *who* it was."

"Hardly," I said. "It could be anyone—a clerk somewhere or a waitress, even one of the town girls he picked up. It could even have been a different girl each time."

"There were only the two calls," he said slowly. "The first one came through to the hotel. I'd gone up to our

room after I left you. It must have been about eight. Anyway it was just before the police herded us downstairs.
She said she was in town and didn't want any of the gang
to know. That was reasonable enough. I asked her how she
was and she said fine. Then she said she'd like to see you
and talk to you but she didn't want any of the rest of them
to know about it. I said I'd fix it up and she said okay,
she'd call me Monday noon. That was when she made this
restaurant date. I wanted her to let me come, too, but she
said no, she didn't want to see anyone, not even me. Hell!
That's the one thing that makes me believe perhaps you're
right. But why drag you into it?"

"To add veracity," I said slowly. "I could testify that I'd
had a date with her and you don't make dates with people
who aren't there. I wonder . . . You know what I think's
going to happen? I think the fact that those telephone
calls were made is going to come out, somehow. Perhaps
the murderer meant that they would. That I'd talk or you
would—tell the police, I mean. That would set them off
on a hunt for Anne."

"But if she wasn't there—"

"They'd have to prove it. And you'd talked to her—and
I'd had a date with her. Even if they were never able to
find her . . . And once they started asking questions, the
fact that she'd tried to stab Mandy once would be bound to
come out. The police would *have* to look for her. Of course,
if they found her some place a long way from here and she
had a perfectly good alibi, she'd be out of it. But it would
waste plenty of time and time counts in a murder case."

"Yeah, we'll be out of here by the end of the week—we
hope," Johnny said inelegantly. "She said something—in
that first call—about having been to the hotel that afternoon. I didn't think anything of it then. That was before I
knew Mandy'd been killed. That could have been another
trick, huh?"

"Of course," I said, feeling superior in my wisdom. "It would put her on the scene, right smack in the middle of murder. Johnny, I bet you threw an awful monkey wrench into the murderer's machine when you didn't tell that! He'd probably counted on nobody's noticing her . . ."

I stopped. I had a horrible sinking feeling. When I spoke again, it was without volition, the words tumbling over one another. "Oh, Johnny, it would be swell if it were that way, but it's not! We're wrong—all wrong. Because Anne Kent *is* here. Tait Gilmore saw her!"

"Wha-at?" Johnny's voice rose to such a squawk that the women's dressing-room door opened and a blondined head thrust out. I scowled at it and it withdrew. "Have you gone clean crazy? If you knew all the time, what was the idea of feeding me that stuff about the murderer faking those calls?"

"Just wishful thinking, I guess," I said meekly. "I'm sorry. I'd forgotten, that's all. Everything seems so muddled when I try to think it out. And it happens so fast . . ."

"Yeah, I know." He lit another cigarette, took several deep drags. "You say Tait's sure he saw her? Anyone else hear that, besides you?"

I thought back. "Gale was there," I said reluctantly. "And Dick and—yes, Shorty Sims. But they mightn't have believed him—Tait, I mean. If I hadn't known about those telephone calls, I wouldn't. I'd have thought he was teasing Gale. He said it that way."

"Huh!" He didn't seem impressed. He threw the cigarette down, stamped on it. "You tell them anything?"

I shook my head. "No," I said. "No, I didn't. But Gale believed it. He told me so later. He asked me if I'd seen her. He said, if I did, to beg her to see him."

"God!" He took a short turn away from me, came back. "Somehow or other I've got to see her—warn her."

"Warn her!" It was my voices turn to do nip-ups. "Do you mean you think she's in danger?"

"Well, what do you think? Maybe we were half right on this, Connie. Maybe we've fallen over the truth of this thing without intending to. Maybe Anne is part of the murderer's scheme and he got her here—how I don't know. But if he did and anything happens to her—if she's found dead some place and it looks as though she committed suicide, for example—it's going to wind up the case fast. You'll see. It'll be damn convenient for the murderer, whoever he is!"

I felt sick inside. "Johnny, we'll have to find her."

"How?" It came like a dash of cold water and it silenced me. "Of course," he went on slowly, "it could be she's one factor the murderer hadn't figured on. But if it's true and she's here—and he finds out—then she's going to be a swell out for him, even if he has to kill her to make it good."

I shuddered. I said, "I think we ought to go to the police, and tell them about it, don't you? They could find her and protect her, if she's here—"

"Nothing doing! If we go to Bradley, we land her right in the soup."

"And if we don't and anything happens to her, we'll land in it ourselves. You don't need to think Gale will keep still—"

"He can't talk if he hasn't anything to talk about. You said you hadn't told him—well, then. No, Connie, I think we'd better let it ride. If Anne calls me again, I'll try and I talk sense to her—get her out of town."

You'd better talk sense to yourself, I thought wryly as I left him. Even now I wasn't too convinced of Anne Kents presence in Harriston. A telephone call wasn't conclusive evidence and she certainly hadn't kept that restaurant date. To balance it, of course, there was Tait Gilmore's testimony. Tait had seen her—or said he had. If you could believe him . . .

A thought struck me, not a nice one. It had been somewhere after one o'clock when Tait made his revelation. The rehearsal was over about half-past three. My date with Anne had been for half-past four. Had there been time, during that interval, for the murderer to have searched Anne out and silenced her? I didn't know. If he had, it implied incredible luck on his part and certainly previous knowledge of her whereabouts. Of course, in that case, appearances would seem to let Gale Ullman out; most of the hour in question he had spent in my company. Unless—and other leaders had employed like tactics—he had simply used himself to divert my attention while someone else, delegated, had taken care of the more delicate problem. Certainly he had been in no hurry to let me go—not until Shorty Sims had appeared. Suppose Shorty had been the delegate. He was business manager for the band. He was accustomed to carrying out Gale's orders. What if his appearance in the coffee shop had been a signal that all was well, that the problem of Anne had been dealt with and it would now be safe to let me go—on to a rendezvous they both knew would never be kept?

I had worked myself up to near panic by the time I reopened the door to the dressing room where sudden silence greeted me. I knew what it meant—that they'd been discussing Mandy and me, with entire freedom since I'd not been present to halt their tongues. Now, walking to the mirror in that silence, I found myself wondering what had been said. Little, I suspected, that I'd not already heard. News of Mandy's death had, of course, run through the morning's rehearsal like wildfire. The Harriston paper had been discreet in referring to it. *Mandy Martin, wife of the well-known bandleader, Gale Ullman, was found dead Sunday evening in her room at the Marvin Hotel.*

And, as it was written, so it was being accepted. Murder, so far as I knew, was not being mentioned. The mystery that surrounded her death, faint as it was, was taking form under the looser terminology of "suicide." Perhaps, I thought, it was just as well. Truth, as it always did, would come out soon enough.

Conversation resumed around me. But I was glad when the show started and the dressing room cleared.

I think the Festival audience enjoyed the show. All people enjoy drama and here it was, plenty of it, raw for them to savor. Tragedy had struck but the show went on. Gale, the bereaved husband, received an ovation to which, pale, composed, unsmiling, he responded with the slightest of bows. The orchestra's customary white coats had been laid aside. Tonight they sat somber in black. I wondered angrily if I, too, should have put on a semblance of mourning. For that was all it was—a semblance. I thought, Damn it, it's nothing but an act! He's just doing what he thinks they expect him to. Can't they see . . .

Waiting to go on, I was conscious of a great and weary contempt for such an audience. Later on, listening to the applause, my mood became kindlier. After all, why should they be blamed? They had no access to the truth. All they knew was what they read—and heard. And I'd an idea the Festival Committee was taking care that there'd be little hearing, at least until the box office totals equaled expenses. They'd see that there was no untoward publicity.

But, I wondered bitterly, would even the knowledge that Mandy's death was murder make any difference? Would it not serve to increase, rather than decrease, the crowds in attendance? The American people have a prodigious appetite for excitement. Wouldn't the fact that the Festival this year housed a murderer, free as yet and capable of causing other deaths, serve only as a fillip to that appetite? A few might be frightened off, yes, but wouldn't the greater number be drawn to attendance in the fear of missing some greater excitement? Gale was the sorrowing husband now and, as such, worthy of consideration. They had come to see him. But wouldn't they come with equal willingness to see a murderer, or a man suspected of murder? I knew dam well they would. I was pretty certain that the Festival Committee was passing up an unprecedented opportunity for balancing their budget.

The show was over by ten o'clock. I had intended to go out to Bradley's and go to bed. I might have managed it, too, if the zipper on the side of my dress hadn't stuck. It took a little time to get it free and I was adjusting my hat when the message came from Gale. He wanted to see me before I left.

I was afraid not to obey the summons. It might have been something to do with my singing. So I waited, yawning a little, leaning against the table near the stage door.

When he came, he wore coat and soft hat. He put his hand under my elbow and propelled me forward.

I said, "What—where are you going?"

"We," he corrected gently. "I want you with me tonight, Connie. I want you to help me find Anne Kent."

I was speechless for a second. "But how do you know you can find her?" I asked feebly. "How do you know she's here?"

He made a gesture of anger. "You heard Tait. He saw her. I talked to him again tonight before I went and shook some sense out of Johnny Davis. He and Anne were—friends. If she were in trouble, I thought she'd go to him. He told me what he knew—about the telephone calls and the appointment she made with you and didn't keep. If she were alive and able, she'd have kept that appointment, Connie. I know Anne. That's why I'm afraid—afraid for her. If she's in Harriston, I've got to find her. I've got to find her tonight."

I swallowed hard. There was an urgency in his tone that I didn't understand. "But how do you think you'll find her?"

"I don't know," he said hopelessly. "We can only try. She's not at the hotels, I made certain of that. I've a list here of all the known rooming houses and tourist homes and cabin camps around Harriston. I thought we'd try them."

"A list!" I said. "Where'd you get that?"

"From Bradley." His glance rebuked my surprise. "Oh, I didn't tell him the whole story. I told him I'd heard a rumor that a girl who used to be with my band a year ago was here in town and that, if I could find her, I might be able to use her temporarily until I got hold of somebody else. Bradley's a good Chamber of Commerce man and a patriotic Harristonian. Anything to help the show. He handed over the list without a question."

Dream on in peace, I thought scornfully. If you think you've fooled Fred Bradley with that transparency of lies . . .

Aloud I said, "But what do you expect me to do?"

"I want you along. She may not want to see me—probably doesn't or she'd have gotten in touch with me before this. And, supposedly, she does want to see you . . ."

We were out of the alleyway now, into the side street where Gale's car was parked. Earlier, when I'd come down to the Harvest Hall, the skies had been overcast, heavy with clouds that hinted of coming rain. But the rain had not materialized. The clouds were gone. Now the moon rode high; its rays revealed the long, cream-colored length of Gale's roadster. I made one last attempt to get out of going.

"She doesn't know me. She's probably never even seen me. If it's reassurance you want, why don't you take someone with you whom she does know and trust? She trusted Johnny. Why not take him?"

"Because"—he had the car door shut now and me safely inside—"I don't know that I trust Johnny so damn much myself!"

Nor am I sure, I thought drearily, that I trust you, brother.

The starter whirred and caught. Short of a scene—screaming, kicking, fighting—I was committed. And I didn't want to make a scene.

12

It was one of those hopeless-seeming undertakings. Gale had the map the chief had drawn. It showed straight lines for avenues; the lines that crossed them were the streets. These were numbered. Circles marked the approximate locations of houses. I was glad that Harriston wasn't any larger.

"The whole thing is just plain silly," I said after we'd pored over the map for a while. "I don't suppose the women who run boarding houses here are any different from those in other towns. What makes you think they'll tell you anything? One look at that car and they'll think 'white slaver' and that'll be the end."

"I know," Gale said meekly. "That's why I brought you along."

I might have known. "We'll have to think up a story," I said, "something plausible."

"You think," he told me. "My brain's a muddle."

So, in the end, it was I who fumbled up unfamiliar steps, searched for doorbells whose installers had hidden them, with malice, I suspected. We had a flashlight but, after being chased by two indignant householders whose street numbers we were inspecting, we used it sparingly. Almost every place owned a dog and the dog, invariably, was running free and disliked night callers. After I'd been

driven back to the car by a couple of these canine defend-
ers, Gale convoyed me to the door. Once the doorbell was
located and rung, he retreated to the car where he waited,
a second line of attack or defense.

I would ring the bell of a house where perhaps only a
dim light burned. Eventually the door would open a crack.

A head adorned with a silk hairnet would protrude,
eyes survey me fishily. Usually a hand clutched at a be-
draggled bathrobe under a wattled chin. A voice composed
of vinegar and suspicion would say, "Yes?" or "What do
you want?"

It was time to put on my best smile. "I understand you
rent rooms."

"Not now. I'm full up."

The door would start to close. Sometimes I could insert
my toe if I were quick enough.

"Oh, I don't want a room. I have one. I'm staying at
Bradley's."

That was inspiration. Sometimes it worked, sometimes
it didn't.

"Bradley's? I don't think I know them."

"Oh, you must! He's the Chief of Police here."

"Oh, *that* Bradley—hmm. I didn't know she rented
rooms. Not that she'd need to, with the town paying him
a good salary—"

I kept on being as charming as I knew how to be. I
worked hard at it. "I don't think she does—usually. This
was really just a favor to me. The town is so crowded . . ."

"Yes, I guess so. I could have had some extras myself
if it wasn't I was filled up with my regulars." Suspicion
would flare again. "Well, if it wasn't a room, what did you
want?"

Now was the time. I'd draw a long breath, begin. "I'm
trying to find a girl—a young lady. I don't know her name.
You see, we met in a restaurant and she—" Make it good,

Connie. I made it good. "Well, I didn't have any change
with me—I'd left my purse in my room—and she was kind
enough to pay for my dinner. I'd like to repay her."

It didn't go over. Beady, hostile eyes, with or without
spectacles, would examine me. "Huh! You don't even know
her name! What's a dinner cost downtown? It's so long
since I ate away from home I forget. Seventy-five cents—a
dollar? Sakes alive! And for maybe a dollar you get me but
of my warm bed . . ."

The door would be definitely closing now. I'd be desperate. "You don't understand. It's not only the money.
I—I liked her. She was nice. We had a lot in common. It
was fun talking to her. I'd like to find her again. You see,
I'm a stranger in town. I'm lonely. I can tell you what
she looked like. She isn't very tall—about my size, slender. She's very pretty with a lot of lovely blond hair—real
blond hair—not touched up. She had a red hat . . ."

"What's she do?"

"I don't think she does anything. She didn't say. I rather
got the impression she was a stranger here, too. Perhaps
here for the Festival."

"Oh, a transient. Well, I don't rent to transients. I have
my regular roomers—most of them have been with me for
years. Mrs. Ward, over on Second has some schoolteachers
who are new this fall. You think she could have been a
schoolteacher?"

"I don't know. I hardly think so."

"Well, she's not here, that's certain. Now, take your
foot out of my door, young lady, and let me go to bed."

It wasn't always like that, of course, but that was the
general pattern. Some few tried to be helpful. One or two
didn't even give me time to tell my story—or insert my
foot in the doors crack. Discouraged, I would repair to the
car and Gale.

"It's no use. My story isn't good enough."

"Then you'd better make it better."

"How? Honestly, Gale, we aren't getting anywhere, doing it this way. Besides, it's late—it's almost eleven. People in small towns go to bed early. They resent being wakened. Most of these places have just one light in the hall—left for the roomers, I suppose."

"I can't help it. Being wakened isn't going to kill them for once." He'd started the car by this time. "Where's the next?"

"Two blocks farther on," I sighed. "You know, even if we're lucky and some one of them admits to having a roomer who might be Anne, how are you going to know? Anne might be out. What do we do then? You surely don't think they'd let me into her room to rummage around and make sure, do you? Besides, I ought to be getting over to Bradley's. I don't have any key. I'll be keeping them up . . ."

"It didn't worry Bradley keeping *me* up last night." In the light from the dashboard, I could see the stubborn line of Gale's jaw. "Let him sit up for a change. And if we find anyone who might be Anne, and she's not there, we'll wait until she *does* get there, that's all."

I sighed again. "But if we find out where she's staying, couldn't we let it go until morning? I mean, we'd know where we could find her . . ."

A snort was my answer. "And have the fool landlady tell her we're looking for her? What do you think she'd do then? She'd get out, disappear for good and we'd never know—I'd never know . . ." His voice shook a little.

We'd reached our destination. I put my hand over his, where it lay idle on the wheel.

"You're really afraid for her, aren't you, Gale?"

"I am. Yes. Terribly afraid."

"But why?"

"I'm not sure. Just a hunch. Something's ringing a bell in my head."

There was no answer to that. I said, "Well . . ." and climbed from the car. It looked like a long night.

The automobile camps were easier. For one thing, there was always someone awake in the manager's office. They were helpful, too. It wasn't necessary to tell the story—with improvements—which I'd concocted. Without argument, they let us look at the camp register. Gale went in with me now. It looked better.

Oddly enough, it was at the last camp we visited that we struck pay dirt. It was on the main highway, a half a dozen blocks into the residential section. The cabins were small and white-painted. They stood in a half circle at the top of a little hill and behind them the ground sloped down in a sort of miniature ravine much overgrown with weeds and young trees. There were no houses within half a block.

In the center of the semicircle formed by the cabins, and separated from them by the width of a graveled driveway, there was a large white frame building.

A painted sign, a hand with finger pointing, said *Office* and above the door neon lights flashed an invitation to *Stop and Dine.* Between the cabins the reflectors on the parked cars caught our lights.

The big building was more restaurant than office. A long counter crossed one end. There were the inevitable booths. On a grill at the back, hamburgers sizzled. A juke box beside the door was strident with music.

There was only one person in the room, a woman. She came around the open end of the counter, wiping her hands on her apron. Her little eyes, cold and blue, appraised us.

"You looking for a cabin? I'm sorry, business has been pretty good, this being Festival Week. I've only one left. It's small but, if you can make it do tonight, maybe tomorrow somebody'll move out."

I said, "No, we don't want a cabin. We're trying to locate a—a friend. We think she might be staying here. If we could see your register . . ."

She didn't like that, obviously. She said grudgingly, "Well, I s'pose you can" and went back behind the counter. She took a book from a shelf and opened it. "What's the name?"

I looked at Gale and improvised desperately "I don't know. I mean, she may not be using her own name. You see, she's had a bad shock. Her husband, my brother, was killed in a plane crash overseas and she'd been so sure he was safe and would come back—now that the war is over—that she, well, she went a little crazy, we think. Anyway she left home—just disappeared. Now one of our friends thinks she might be here in Harriston. He thought he saw her on the street today. So he called us and . . . If you'd let me see the book. I'm sure I'd know her handwriting."

It wasn't a proper register, just a school composition book with a pencil on a string attached to one corner. There was a date and a list of names. My eyes skimmed them: Leon Brown and wife, Norris City; Mr. and Mrs. Allen Thornton, Condon; Harold Heustis . . .

"Gale," I said.

I was looking at a name, not the right one but near enough. Annabelle Kane. I heard Gale's long sigh behind me.

The woman heard it, too. "You found her?"

"I think so," I said. "This one."

She studied the name with pursed lips and then glanced over her shoulder at a board on which two single keys hung from, nails. "Number Four—well, she's out tonight. No, there's no good you asking me what she's like. I don't know. I wasn't here when she checked in. Must have been my son. You sure she's the one?"

I looked at Gale. He was staring at the name, black

letters straggling on cheap yellow paper. There was no help there.

"I'm pretty sure. You say she's not here?"

She shrugged. "Her key's here. We're strict about keys. Turn them in when you leave camp—that's the rule."

Gale spoke for the first time. "Did she have a car?"

Her manner implied that we ought to know but she shook her head. "I don't know. My son might."

"Where is your son?"

"Downtown. This is Festival Week." (As though we didn't know!)

"Do you usually rent cabins to people without cars?"

"I rent to those who can pay the rent I ask—in advance. Besides this is Festival Week—the town is crowded. It don't do, being too particular, if you want to make a living."

"She had luggage?"

Again the shrug. "Maybe, maybe not. That's not my business."

We were getting nowhere fast. I said, as though in sudden inspiration, "If she does have luggage, we'd know her clothes. If we could look around the cabin—cabin Number Four . . ."

She said, "No." It was flat and decided. "What do you think I am? You two come here with a fancy story—maybe it's true and maybe not. I got no way of knowing. But so long's she pays her rent and"—she consulted the book again—"she's paid up till the end of the week, it's her cabin and nobody but her gets in."

"You could come, too," I wheedled. "Make sure we didn't touch anything."

"No."

There was no getting past that "no." I turned to Gale whose eyes were blank and blind with some inner pre-occupation. I had a hunch what he was going to say. He said it.

"How late are you open here?"

"All, night. After twelve the big trucks keep stopping. The drivers want to eat."

"We'll wait," Gale said with decision. He looked down at me and he was smiling. "Truck drivers mostly know where they can get good food. Think you could eat a steak, Connie?"

While the woman busied herself behind the counter, we chose a booth from which we could see the cabins, faintly glimmering in the moonlight. Number Four was right opposite our window.

We didn't talk. With the end of our search, the need to talk was over. Gale sat with arms laid along the table edge, his eyes looking past me without seeing. His face was closed, secret. I had the feeling that, should I speak, he would not hear me.

Our steaks came. They were good. Truck drivers *did* know.

I finished my pie, pumpkin, with a snowball of ice cream melting beside it. I lit a cigarette, drank my coffee.

The electric clock stuttered past the hour. It was one o'clock. Gale roused and looked around. There were other people in the restaurant now. Two of the booths were occupied. Three truck drivers in leather jackets were hunched over the counter. "I don't like this," Gale said softly. "I think that old harpy is giving us the run-around. How do we know Anne's not back in that cabin right now? That key story didn't go over with me. There's only one key on that nail and they're sure to have extras."

I agreed reluctantly. Turning in keys at a cabin camp sounded silly. A cabin camp wasn't a hotel . . .

I said, "What are you going to do?"

"I think I'll take a look around," Gale said. "You wait here."

I watched him thread his way between counter and booths and thought nostalgically of my bed. I wondered what Mrs. Bradley would say if I were to stay out all night. I didn't waste any thoughts on Fred Bradley. I hoped Gale would hurry.

He didn't. The hands of the clock jerked along. The original truck drivers finished their coffee and departed amid a great roaring of motor exhausts. A new contingent fed nickels into the juke box. A thick smell of grease and frying onions began to overlay the other odors. At intervals the cash register jingled.

Gale had been gone twenty minutes. I'd smoked all my cigarettes and my throat was tight and dry. I wondered if he had gone, driven away and left me stranded—you think of things like that. I knew it wasn't true. He wouldn't do that to me. More likely he'd found his precious Anne, was in her cabin.

I wasn't the only one wondering. I looked up to see the woman standing at the booth edge. Her eyes were colder than they'd been at first. She said, "Your friend hasn't come back." It wasn't a question it was an accusation.

"No," I said.

"He didn't pay his check," she said and mopped with her apron at a water spot.

"I'll pay it," I said and took out my purse.

She brought back change, slapped it down. "He better not go fooling around them cabins."

I scooped up the money, slid out past the table "I'll tell him. He went to look at his car."

I was glad to be out of doors. It was colder now and the moonlight was brighter. The world was an etching done in black and silver.

Gale's car was gone—that was the first thing I noticed. It was queer, but only a part of all the other queer things. Perhaps he'd left me after all. If he'd found Anne . . .

I hesitated, half angry, not quite certain what to do. Of course I could go back to the cabin office and telephone for a taxi but I didn't want to—not yet. Gale had said he was coming back. No, come to think of it, he hadn't. He'd only said, "Wait here." Well, I hadn't waited . . .

I stood there, on the gravel walk, just outside the office door. I was shivering, more from nerve tension than because I was actually cold. I wondered if anything could have happened to Gale. If he'd been poking around Anne's cabin and someone had seen him . . . He might even have blundered into the wrong cabin,

I considered going back to the cabins myself and then didn't. The woman was suspicious already and she might be watching. Probably was. Perhaps I could get to the cabins from the back. There was the little ravine we'd noticed.

I moved out to the sidewalk, turned slowly down the street. Let her see that if she were watching! It was very still and my footsteps echoed hollowly. A solitary car flashed past, its red lights flickering into distance. The street was quiet again.

I reached the corner, made the turn. Gale's car was there, opposite the ravine, long-bonneted, impossible to mistake. I drew a breath of relief. He hadn't gone then. He was around somewhere. Probably he was as wary as I of the cabin camp manager and had moved his car to divert suspicion. Doubtless he, too, had remembered the ravine and marked it as a means of access to the cabins.

But where was he now? The car was empty; I looked in to make sure. Was he still up at the cabins? He'd been gone a good thirty minutes now—long enough to find Anne if she were there. Unless he was sitting on her doorstep, like Patience on a monument . . .

There was nothing for it—I'd just have to go up myself and see. I didn't relish the prospect but . . .

The ravine was a gash of blackness. I stepped abruptly from brightness into deep shadow. The steepness of its sides and the trees along its rim effectively cut off the moonlight. Dead grass lapped about my ankles. A stiff growth of weeds interspersed with low bushes, rose almost to my waist. Thorny stems clawed at my stockings; the tops of young trees lashed my face. I stumbled over a tree trunk, barely saved myself from falling.

This was all wrong. I stood where I was, peered about. There was a schoolhouse on the rise above the camp. Then, somewhere, if I knew children, there should be a path. If I could find it . . .

I decided to fight my way back to the sidewalk, try again from the other side.

I did. A second time I left the pavement, plunged into underbrush. It was no better. The bushes on this side were stiffer, the trees a little closer grown. The going was treacherous. I stepped into a hole, felt my ankle turn, and came down flatly on hands and knees. Something brushed wraith-like against my face. I sprang up, careless of my wrenched ankle, and stood trembling.

It had been quiet on the street but the ravine was alive with sound—infinitesimal noises; small creakings; the click of a beetle; the whisper of tree leaves faintly stirred; the pattering of small mysterious feet. Off to my right, a bush rustled in the breeze.

It was no good—I just couldn't do it. I'd go back to the car, wait there. Or I'd even go back to the cabin office again. Better that cold-eyed woman than this.

The bush was rustling again. It was the wind, I told myself, only there was no wind. Well, then, a dog perhaps, or some small night animal making its rounds. There was no reason to be afraid. If I stayed perfectly still, it would go away.

The rustlings were closer now, louder. I pressed back into the shadows, held my breath. Green eyes flickered momentarily at my feet. A cat meowed querulously and was gone. I could have shouted aloud for sheer relief.

I was just turning to follow the cat when I saw Gale. He was standing motionless at the ravine's edge, opposite and about fifty yards away. The moonlight powdered his hairy and gleamed whitely on his face. I called to him—"Gale!"—and it was half a sob. Not until I heard my voice had I known how frightened I'd been.

He heard me. I saw him start, look quickly around.

"Anne!" he said. "Is that you, Anne? Where are you?"

Swift anger licked over me. I didn't speak softly. "It's me, Connie," I said. "I'm down in the ravine. I've been looking for a path but I can't find one . . ."

He showed no surprise that I was there. "Over to your right a few feet. Stay where you are. I'll come down."

Bushes crackled as he swung over the edge.

There was sense in staying where I was but I was beyond sense. If there was a path to be found within a few feet of me, I meant to find it myself. Anne indeed! I could do very nicely without Gale Ullman's assistance.

I struck forward at right angles to the way I'd been going. Here were more bushes, shoulder high, bound with creepers of some kind. I couldn't get through; I'd have to go around. I moved cautiously sideways, seeking an opening. A loop of creeper, tough as wire, curled itself about my ankle. I kicked out to free myself, stumbled and went sprawling forward.

Instinctively you protect your face when you are falling. My elbows took the first shock, then my hands. I rolled over, the breath knocked out of me. I tried to sit up, and couldn't. Something was dragging at my arm—a creeper, tendril, I thought, caught upon the buttons of my sleeve. I reached my other hand to free it . . . .

It wasn't a creeper. No creeper ever felt like that. It was fine, silken-soft, tenacious. There was only one thing in the world that felt like that . . .

I lay there, very carefully not moving. I didn't want to move; I didn't dare. Because I knew what that thing was, knew it even without seeing. It was human hair, and the drag upon my arm came because the hair wasn't free, because it was still attached—to a head.

13

I must have blanked out then for the next thing I knew I was sitting in the car, with Gale trying to force the mouth of a brandy flask between my teeth. "Stop it!" I said and sat up. But the very act made me remember and I dropped back with a shudder. "How did you get me free?"

"I had a knife." His voice was a monotone. "I cut you loose."

I considered that—with shut eyes. I didn't want to look at him. I was afraid of what I'd see.

"It was Anne, wasn't it?"

"Yes."

"And she was dead?"

"She is dead."

I put my hand over his. I said, "I'm sorry, Gale. I know that it is terrible for you."

His hand twisted under mine. "Yes, Connie—it's terrible for all of us."

I opened my eyes then and, strangely enough, the world hadn't altered. It was just as I had seen it last, a black and silver etching. Peace lay over the quiet streets. No one would have guessed, by looking, that in that dark and secret hollow . . .

I said, "Gale, how did she die?"

"How?"

"She was murdered, wasn't she?"

"Yes. She was murdered."

"Then . . ."

He shook his head as though to clear away some secret seeing. "You shouldn't know, Connie. I don't want you to know."

"I'll have to. That woman at the cabin camp will talk. When the police come . . . . They'll have to come, Gale."

"I know."

"You didn't call them?"

"No. I couldn't leave you there and it was hard to think what to do."

"But you—saw her?"

"I had my cigarette lighter and some matches. Then, after I got you down here, I went back. With the flash from the car."

"Then—tell me, Gale."

"She was beaten to death, Connie. Choked first, I think, and then . . . He must have snatched up a stone . . . She was smashed. Her face—if I hadn't known it was Anne . . ."

I said, "Let me out! I'm going to be sick . . ."

There was an interlude.

"It's not your fault," I said when I could speak again. "I asked you. Shall I call the police, Gale? Shall I call Bradley?"

He looked at me gratefully. "Do you think you can? All right. I'd better stay here. You can call from the camp office. I'll take you to the corner and watch until you get there. You don't need to be afraid . . ."

There was no one in the cabin office. The woman— Mrs. Meyer, she must be; I saw the name on the door—was dozing. She opened her eyes as I came in. "So you're back! Run off and left you, did he? Well, I'm not surprised. I didn't like his face . . ."

I didn't answer. I shut myself into the telephone booth and called the Bradley number.

It was hard to raise the Bradleys. The phone rang and rang. Finally a sleepy voice said, "Yes—what is it?"

I said, "This is Connie Waring, Mrs. Bradley. May I speak to the chief?"

I heard her say, "It's that Waring girl, Fred. She wants to talk to you," and then Fred Bradley's voice came over the wire.

"Bradley speaking. What is it?"

I said, "Mr. Bradley, I'm at the Meyer Auto Camp. Can you come? A girl's been murdered here."

He said, "Hunh?" and his voice quickened. "Meyer's Auto Camp, you said? You alone there?"

I said, "No. Gale's with me—Mr. Ullman."

"Okay, you stay there. I'll be right out."

I said, "All right" and hung up. Mrs. Meyer was watching me curiously but, much as I'd have liked to have thrown the facts of murder in her face, I didn't. She'd know soon enough—within minutes, actually.

My knees were wobbling as I came out on the gravel again. Queer—they hadn't before. Delayed reaction, I supposed. I could see Gale standing at the corner. He waved to me; then, doubtless seeing how I was weaving over the sidewalk, he came to meet me.

"You're all in," he scolded. "You shouldn't have gone. I shouldn't have let you. Here, have some more brandy."

I pushed it away. "No. We don't want them to think we've been drinking. Gale, what are we going to tell them—the police?"

"What is there to tell them?" he asked bitterly. "The truth."

"It's going to sound awfully queer," I said slowly, "no matter how we tell it. Me wandering around in the ravine without any sensible reason—you leaving me for half an hour . . . That woman in the cabin office thought you'd run out on me. She'll probably remember to the minute how long you were gone."

"Oh, Lord," he said. "It looks as though I'd landed you in a mess, doesn't it?"

"I'm not thinking of myself," I said. "It's you. They're going to . . . Gale!" This was something I had to ask, to know. "You didn't kill her, did you?"

"No, I didn't. You believe that, don't you?"

"Yes," I said. "I believe you. But will the police? Are you going to be able to prove it? How long had she been dead?"

"Not long. Matter of minutes, perhaps."

"As close as that?"

"I think so. I couldn't be sure, but I think so."

I sighed, set myself resolutely toward honesty. "It's going to look bad, Gale. For both of us. First Mandy and now—her; your wife and the girl you were to have married. And I'm mixed up in it, too. And Chief Bradley already thinks it's funny that I was willing to drop my work at the Conservatory and rush off with the band. I'm afraid . . ." I stopped, not quite sure how to say it.

He said it for me. "I get it. You're afraid he'll think it was collusion—that you and I together . . . Oh, hell, that's it! You're afraid he'll get it into his head that I'm in love with you and that these murders came from deliberate planning on my—on our—part."

"He could take it that way."

"Yes, I see that. I'm sorry, Connie. I didn't realize—I shouldn't have brought you with me tonight."

"It's not your fault," I said drearily. "How could you know?"

"One thing," he said. "No woman killed her. Bradley's not a fool. He'll see that."

I shivered.

The police cars came then, three of them. We heard the roar of their motors, saw the wide sweep of their lights. One car swept past, stopped beyond, and then backed until its bumpers touched ours. Another drew up behind. The third was beside us. We were hemmed in. The fools, I thought angrily. If we'd meant to run away, wouldn't we have gone long before this?

They came out of the cars, quiet, grim-faced. I saw Bradley, Murphy, Detective Burns, others whom I hadn't seen before. Gale met them. They talked. Then Bradley's arm beckoned and they moved off toward the ravine.

They must have known I was there in the car but no one suggested that I come with them. I was thankful. I don't think I could have taken that walk again. It was better—much better—to stay where I was and watch.

Or was it? The lights pin-pointed the ravine now. Presently, they converged. Over one spot there was a luminous glow . . .

I hid my eyes.

It was shortly after that Gale came back to lean against the car door, one elbow thrust through my window.

"What are they doing?"

His voice sounded remote and far away. "They're taking pictures. The doctors are there. I don't think it will be long . . . ."

It wasn't. It was only a breath after that he spoke sharply. "Keep your head down, Connie! For God's sake, don't look!"

I didn't. I knew what he meant. They were taking Anne away.

The pressure of his hand decreased. When I raised my head again, there was nothing to see. The car ahead was pulling away from the curb, that was all. Lights, moving now, still starred the ravine. Chief Bradley stood on the sidewalk, talking to two men. Even as I watched, he left them, came toward us.

He opened the car door on my side. "Shove over. We're going downtown."

The Municipal Building was old and dilapidated. Stucco had broken from its gray-painted walls leaving great bare patches. The police station was at one side. The chief led us down a narrow corridor, opened a door at its end. "My office," he said. "Sit down and talk. I'm ready to listen."

I sat, gingerly. "Aren't you going to have a stenographer take down what we say?"

"Nope." He leaned forward, flicked a switch. "Recording machine takes care of that. Ever heard one played back? You can learn plenty sometimes."

I subsided. It was true. They'd made recordings of my voice at the radio station. Playing them over had been—instructive.

"Well, go ahead." The chief was impatient now. "Who talks first?"

I looked at Gale. I heard his long-drawn breath. "I will," he said. "If I go wrong, you can check me, Connie."

The first part of the story—our search for Anne—didn't sound too silly if you weren't too curious about its reason. The chief wasn't—not then. Gale reminded Bradley of the map he'd given him. He produced it, traced our route, house by house. The Meyer Auto Camp was the last place. We hadn't checked it off.

The chief asked his first question then. What time had we arrived there? Gale appealed to me. Somewhere around twelve, he thought. I agreed.

"But Mrs. Meyer can tell you," I said acidly. "She never took her eyes off us."

"Murphy's talking to the Meyer woman right now," the chief assured me. I thought of the preposterous yarn I'd spun for her and shivered.

Gale went on with his story. He told about finding the name "Annabelle Kane" in the camp register and our conviction that it stood for Anne Kent. He told of Mrs. Meyer's refusal to let us go back to the cabin, our decision to wait. "We ordered a dinner and ate it, but still Anne hadn't come. So I thought I'd go out and look around a bit."

The chief cut in again. "When was this?"

"Just past one o'clock," I said eagerly. "I wanted to leave then, but Gale thought we ought to stay—until she came."

The chief's eyes had narrowed. "So you went out? Why?"

"I'm not sure just why," Gale said slowly. "There was my car for one thing. I'd just remembered I'd left it near the drive that led into the camp. It's a conspicuous car and Anne would have known it. I was afraid if she saw it she wouldn't come into the office at all. Then, too, I wasn't sure she would anyway. That woman's story about checking keys in when you left the camp didn't ring true. I've stayed in a few cabin camps myself. I thought Anne might have come in and gone straight to her cabin. I wanted to find out."

"And so-o-o-o?" the chief drawled.

"I went. I moved my car down near the corner. There was a patch of shadow there I hoped would help to hide it. Then I came back to the camp and walked up the drive until I reached the cabins. The woman had said Number Four was Anne's. There was no light but I rapped on the door and listened. There wasn't a sound. Either she wasn't there or, if she was and heard me, she wasn't answering knocks. I hung around for a while. When nothing happened, I started back to the car."

"And then?"

"I walked back around the office. I thought I'd go and sit in the car for a few minutes, think it out, decide what I'd better do. I'd tied my hands pretty badly as far as action went. I had Connie to think about . . .'"

I wanted to protest that. Connie would have called a cab and gone home; she would have been glad to. Or she could have taken the car. There was that vacant cabin—he could have stayed there all night. I wanted to remind him. I wanted to say, "A lot you were thinking of Connie when you stood on the rim of the ravine and called 'Anne—is that you, Anne?' Where were your thoughts of Connie then?"

I didn't.

Gale was going on, slowly as though feeling his way, "I could see the car before I got to the corner. It was in a patch of shadow but it seemed to me there was more shadow than when I'd seen it last. There was one dark spot at the back. And then the spot moved and I saw that it wasn't shadow. It was someone fooling around my car. It made me mad. I'd had a couple of tires slashed in Akron two weeks ago and it's not easy getting tires even now. So I yelled and started to run. He legged it off into the ravine. I followed."

"Wait a minute." The chief was checking again. "What time was this?"

"I'm not sure," Gale began, but I cut in. Something cold seemed to be closing about my heart.

"Why? What difference does it make? What time did she—was she killed?"

The chief surveyed me thoughtfully. "You called me about ten minutes to two. Took a while to get organized and over here—say fifteen minutes. It was five after when we saw the body. Doc's guess is she died not more than three-quarters of an hour or less than half an hour before—probably the first. You figure it out."

It didn't take complicated mathematics. Somewhere between twenty minutes past one and the time I'd found her. And Gale had been alone . . .

I looked at him. I said, "Gale—" imploringly, and he said, "Shut up, Connie, let me tell this. He took that path through the ravine with me after him. You couldn't see much—it was dark as Erebus—but I could hear him plunging ahead. He went up the side of the ravine like a spider and I saw him for a second crouching at the top. I wasn't as good at climbing blind. I fell a couple of times and, when I did get up, there wasn't a sign of him. I looked around among the cabins as well as I could without a light but I didn't find him. So I came back to the ravine to look around those trees. That's when I heard Connie calling. It's her story from then on."

"She'll get a chance to tell it," the chief promised grimly. "It can wait. Right now, let's shape yours up a bit. This car—you say Miss Kent would have known it. Anyone else?"

"How do you mean? The band would. People in Harriston might, too, for all I know. They see it and ask whose it is and then they remember."

"Got any idea what he could have been doing to it?"

"I didn't look. There wasn't time."

"Hmmm. Give me the keys. I'll have the boys look it over. Got to do it anyway."

Gale gave him the keys in silence and the chief dangled them from one finger. "Pretty thin story," he said at last. "The truth often is."

"Uh-huh, maybe. This fellow you were following—you sure it was a man?"

"Yes. I had a pretty good look when he scrambled over the top. Why? Who do you think it was? Connie? Or Anne?"

"Not thinking. Not Connie, though. Might have been the other."

"That's pretty," Gale said grimly. "So you think I chased her, caught her and killed her. Is that right?"

"I didn't say so. Got to consider possibilities. This fellow—where do you think he went?"

"I don't know. I'm not a mountain goat and he had a good lead. He might have dodged back to the road or hidden behind one of the cabins, even gone into the office for all I know."

"I thought Miss Waring was in the office."

"Some time during this she came out." Gale's smile was lopsided. "Take it away, Connie."

My story sounded sillier than I'd thought it would. Even Gale gagged at parts of it; I saw his face getting longer and longer. I didn't blame him. No one in her right mind would flit around a weed-grown canyon in the dark.

I don't know how much the chief believed. His face stayed inscrutable even when I reacted the preposterous climax of my story. "That part I can prove," I told him. I stretched out my arm. "Look! There's still hair caught on the buttons of my sleeve."

The chief looked in silence. Rebuffed, I took my arm back.

"After that, I don't remember. I fainted, I think. Gale cut me free and carried me to the car. Then we—I called you."

The chief said, "Yes," and drummed on the desk. "Let's go back a ways. This rustling you heard—you say it was a cat. Could it have been Ullman?"

"No. The cat ran off to my left. I was just turning to follow it when I saw Gale to my right up above. It was too far— He couldn't possibly . . ."

"Okay," the chief said. "Got that cleared up. Now this girl. You identify her as Anne Kent, a singer who'd been with your band. Yesterday you told me a yarn about her being in town and you wanted to find her so she could sing with you again. That story true?"

Gale shook his head. "Not entirely. I wanted to find her but . . ."

"Thought so!" The chief sounded triumphant. "All right, let's have the real story now."

I don't think Gale skipped a thing. He went back, farther even than I'd heard. He told of his engagement to Anne, his involvement with Mandy, their marriage at her insistence. "It was a gesture that was wasted," he said bitterly. "There wasn't any question of a child—never had been. It was just Mandy's way of getting what she wanted. Anne took it hard. She wouldn't let me explain, wouldn't talk to me even. She'd been queer anyway, ever since that birthday party of Tait's. I never knew why—whether she'd found out about Mandy and me and was punishing me or whether something was wrong . . . I couldn't put my finger on it."

He told the rest of it, then—about Anne's drinking and the night she attacked Mandy with a knife, about leaving her in Dr. Wilson's care. "I had to do something—she was half crazy and I was responsible. Then, after she ran away and they couldn't find her, well, I felt more responsible. That was why, when I found out that she was supposed to be in Harriston, I went about trying to find her. Don't you see . . ."

The chief said he saw and resumed his tap-tapping. "You think it could have been Anne Kent who killed your wife?"

Gale said hotly that he didn't, and I said, "How could it have been Anne? She's dead, too. Why, Mandy's murder was more apt to have been the reason *she* was killed. If she saw anything or anyone in the hotel that day . . ."

They both turned on me then. Gale said, "What the hell are you talking about?" and the chief said, "Wait a minute! *Who* was at the hotel *when?*"

"Anne Kent," I said soberly, "the afternoon Mandy was murdered. She told Johnny so. If the murderer knew that . . ."

Gale said, "Oh, my God, Connie!" and the chief said, "Shut up, Ullman. All right, Miss Waring. I'm considerably confused. Maybe you better tell us where you got all this inside information."

The beginning was in Chicago and it was evident that they were skeptical about it. Johnny's message to me, the night of Mandy's murder, they couldn't disbelieve—they'd been present when it was given. The telephone calls here in Harriston were different. So was the restaurant date. Not being able to disprove, they accepted. The chief listened silently. Gale said only the one thing: "You might have trusted me."

I didn't answer. How could I say the thing that lay between us? She didn't trust you—why should I? But it was there.

The chief was reaching for the telephone. "We'll just bring in this Johnny Davis . . ."

I said, "But he didn't kill Mandy. He was with me that afternoon. Anne wasn't any danger to *him*. Besides, he wasn't the only one who knew Anne was in town. Lots of others did, too."

"Who?"

"Tait Gilmore, Shorty Sims, Dick Travis, myself." Gale was tight-lipped. "Any one of us could have told the others."

"But only one would have a reason for killing her," I said. "It couldn't have been Johnny—it wouldn't have mattered to him what Anne saw in the hotel that day. He was with me. That clears him, doesn't it? And Gale was with me tonight . . ."

"Maybe Davis is out of it—I wouldn't know." The chief's eyes were distinctly unfriendly. "As for Ullman here, well, he could have killed his wife. And Anne Kent's murder wouldn't have taken much of his time. She was a little thing—wouldn't have put up much of a fight. Seems to me Ullman would have had plenty of time to kill her during the half hour or so he's got unaccounted for. I haven't heard anything yet that clears him."

"Maybe I can clear myself," Gale said slowly. "Look, whoever killed Anne would have blood on him, wouldn't he? He could hardly have helped it. That's right, isn't it? Well, do you see any blood on me?" He indicated his gray flannels. He took two handkerchiefs from his pockets, displayed them. "That mean anything?"

The chief shrugged. "Maybe." A second time he reached for the telephone. "I'll take those names again, the ones who knew Anne Kent was in town."

He never made the call. Not then. There was an interruption. The policeman, Murphy, stood at the door. "Look, Chief, here's something Doc Borman thought you'd want to see. Got it out of her hand. This is it."

He dropped it to the desk top. We crowded close. It wasn't much—the fragment of a bracelet, perhaps; one side of the clasp, a latticework of large white stones interset with blue.

I recovered first. "Costume jewelry," I said. "Probably she wore a bracelet and in the struggle it was torn off . . ."

It was Gale who stopped me. There was an expression on his face I'd never seen before. "Costume jewelry, hell! I don't know much about stones but even I know diamonds when I see them!"

The chief gathered it up, held the fragment in his own palm. "Diamonds now—think of that! Well, well. Looks as though maybe we're getting somewhere after all!"

Perhaps we were. But, if we were, I couldn't see it.

14

Things began to hum right away. Murphy was ordered to round up Johnny, Dick Travis, Tait Gilmore and Shorty Sims, and hold them in readiness for questioning. All right—if Murphy needed help, let him call in Burns. He ought to be somewhere around the hotel. In the meantime, Bradley meant to get on with this diamond thing. He put in a call to someone named Mr. Silber—would he come to the police station and bring with him whatever he needed to determine the value of some diamonds? No, it wasn't the middle of the night—not any more. All right, even if it was, this was police business. He hung up with a satisfied jerk of his head.

Gale didn't look nearly so satisfied as he stood by the desk fingering the fragment of bracelet. There was a frown between his brows.

"You didn't need to do that," he said quietly. "These are diamonds. What's more, I think you'll find they're hot." The bracelet made a little tinkle as he flung it from him.

The chief snatched at it. "Hot, huh? How do you know?"

"I don't know," Gale Ullman said and sighed. "I'm just guessing. I think I've seen it before—on a woman's wrist. No," he said quickly as Bradley opened his mouth, "it wasn't Mandy's. I suppose I'd better tell you the story."

177

"I suppose you had," the chief agreed. He moved the fragment closer, scrutinized it again.

"It's not the sort of thing I like to tell," Gale said. "I don't know whether you know much about bands or not, but in a short space of time they cover a lot of territory. Take us. Last year we played a winter engagement in New York." He named the hotel. "In the spring, we went out to California—San Francisco and Hollywood. We played a three-week engagement in Chicago and then flew back to the Coast. We go into the same spot in New York again October first, but in the meantime we've been playing our way across the country. Dances—this sort of thing. Well, just before we started on this road tour, we were in San Francisco . . ."

They'd been playing in the Rose Room of a very, very swank hotel—supper music and dancing. He grimaced a little.

"It's a different racket than the road. You settle down a little, establish roots, and you get a little restless. You're free all day. You sleep comfortably at night and you want to be amused. You don't even rehearse very often. You meet people . . ."

Around hotels, when a band played an engagement, there were always a lot of women who tried to give the boys a play. Some of them were young, a lot were old enough to know better. There was a Mrs. Lorenzo, wife of a war profiteer . . .

"She was about forty-one. My guess was she hadn't had money very long. You know the type—Mrs. Got-rocks with dyed hair and a lot of expensive clothes and hung all over with jewelry. She went nuts about the band. She had the same table every night for the supper dance—up front. She'd sit there, all alone, and give the boys the eye. When the intermission came, she'd buy whoever she could per-suade to come over a drink. Funny thing was, she didn't seem to play any favorites. It was the whole gang—nothing was too good for them. Some of them lapped it up . . ."

A couple of nights before the hotel engagement ended, she'd thrown a big party. She had a suite in the hotel and her husband wasn't there very often, just weekends when he could get down. She couldn't have the party the last night because he'd wired her he was coming and anyway the band was catching a plane as soon as the dance that night was over. It had been a pretty big evening—champagne and a lobster supper . . .

"I looked in for a little while," Gale said, his nose wrinkled in distaste. "It was pretty bad—everybody drinking and Mrs. Lorenzo herself a trifle high. She was showing everybody a bracelet. Her husband had just closed some big deal and told her to get what she wanted to celebrate. What she wanted was the bracelet. It was a flashy thing—diamonds and sapphires set in filigree. Some of the diamonds were big ones, over a carat, and the sapphires started out small and worked up to big ones at the center. It was worth a lot; she told us how much. She had plenty of other stuff on that night—rings, earrings, a pendant—but nothing that compared with this in actual value."

She'd had the bracelet next day. Gale himself had seen it when he passed her table at lunch time. But that night, at the supper dance, her table was unoccupied.

"It was the first time since we'd been there and naturally we asked questions. The headwaiter was cagey but finally, down the line, we found a busboy who'd heard things and, for a consideration, was willing to report that Mrs. Lorenzo's bracelet had disappeared."

But it wasn't until next day that they'd had the full story and then it came from Mrs. Lorenzo herself. She'd worn the bracelet all day—she'd shown it to everyone she'd met. When she went up to her room to dress for dinner that night, she'd left the bracelet on the dressing table while she took her bath. When she came out of the bathroom, the bracelet was gone.

"She went into hysterics, of course," Gale said. "But after a while she quieted down and called the desk and they sent up the house detective. But there wasn't much that she could tell them. Just that the bracelet had been there and then wasn't. She hadn't heard anything but her bath water was running and that might have covered any sound, such as a key being inserted in the lock. The door was locked—she insisted on that."

A chambermaid was under suspicion. It seemed that Mrs. Lorenzo had found the girl handling some of her jewelry one other time. The girl had excused herself with the plea that she loved pretty things and seldom got a chance to see them close. But after that Mrs. Lorenzo had watched. She had thought the girl made errands to enter the suite, had brought fresh towels unnecessarily often. So long as she never actually missed anything . . .

"The girl was arrested," Gale said. "That much was common gossip. What happened to her we never heard. We left on the late plane that night. If I thought anything, I supposed the girl *had* taken it. Now"—he shrugged lightly—"now I don't think she did. I think that's Mrs. Lorenzo's bracelet lying there."

The chief drew in his breath with a hissing sound. His eyes were glowing. "You got the damnedest organization—two murders and now jewel thieves. Who do you think took it? Your wife?"

"Mandy? Good Lord, *no!* What makes you say that?"

The chief shrugged. "Suppose this Anne Kent did see her on Sunday afternoon. Maybe Kent killed her and took the bracelet."

"You're forgetting someone else killed Anne and tried to take the bracelet from her. That he didn't wholly succeed

. . . No, Mandy wouldn't steal. Her idea would be to go out and buy something bigger and better."

"Humph!" Chief Bradley said. "Kent with you on the Coast?"

"Yes."

"Mandy, too?"

"Certainly. But the girls didn't run with Mrs. Lorenzo. It was the boys who interested her. The girls—had other interests."

"The rest of your band the same as then?"

Gale frowned. "Pretty much. Oh, I had to replace a couple of men in Chicago, but in the main it's the same. Why?"

"*She* wasn't with you?"

The frown was a scowl now. "Connie? No, of course not. I told you where I got her and when."

"All right, you don't need to get mad about it. If she didn't know about the bracelet . . ." He turned on me sharply. "You didn't, did you?"

I shook my head. "No. I'm not even very bright, I guess. I'd never have thought they were diamonds. The stones look too big to be real."

Again the chief said, "Humph!" but he seemed pleased. "All right, if Miss Waring didn't know about the bracelet, and it looks as though it might be the king-pin of the whole problem, then I guess she's out of it." He nodded at me. "You got any objection to being searched?"

I hesitated. "Why, no, I suppose not—if it's necessary. But why—"

"The other half of that." The chief indicated the bracelet. "Somebody's got it, the murderer most likely. Or he could have passed it to you."

"I haven't got it," I said and stood up. If this would in any way help to clear Gale . . . "All right, what do I do?"

It seemed there was a police matron. She led me into her private office, stood by while I removed my clothes, fingered them piece by piece, and then returned them. The contents of my purse she spread out on the desk. She looked at my shoes, even ran her fingers through my hair.

"We had a woman in here once," she told me. "Dope fiend. She carried the stuff rolled into the hair at the back of her neck."

I was permitted to dress again, was convoyed back to the chief's office, certified blameless.

The chief nodded to me. "You can go, Miss Waring."

"But I don't want to go," I said and sat down. "In the first place, it's awfully late—or awfully early, whichever way you look at it. I haven't any place to go, except to bed, and I'm not sleepy. I thought that, when you're through with Mr. Ullman, he—we could have breakfast together."

The shadow of a smile touched Gale's mouth but the chief was scowling. "What makes you think Ullman will be buying anyone breakfast from now on? Maybe you better get used to eating alone . . ."

It was a nasty crack. I said, "I know. Because you won't be able to hold him. He didn't kill Mandy—he didn't kill Anne Kent. You're letting me go because I don't have that piece of bracelet. Why don't you search him and see if *he* has it?"

"And how in Hades can we search him with you sitting here?" the chief demanded.

"All right," I said and stood up. "I'll go. There must be other rooms around somewhere. I'll wait."

Gale caught me at the door, brought my hand up to his lips. "For that declaration of faith, little Connie," he said softly, "my eternal gratitude."

All the way down the hall I kept thinking, You fool— you idiot! Bradley shouldn't have seen that! But I felt warm and good just the same.

The only other room I found was the entrance to the police station. It was a big bare place with a sergeant yawning behind a high desk, reading a newspaper. He looked at me speculatively so that I felt moved to explain, "I'm waiting for someone," I said with dignity.

He grinned. "Lady, if your someone's inside there, maybe you got a long wait."

I didn't answer that. There was a row of battered armchairs against the wall, I took one. I suppose I should have been overjoyed at my freedom but I wasn't. At that moment I'd gladly have traded a modicum of it for a chance to sit on in that inner room and learn what happened next. I felt a little like Eve must when she was thrust from the Garden of Eden.

For a long time nothing happened. The sergeant continued to blink behind his newspaper. Occasionally the telephone rang and he carried on a one-sided conversation. "Yeah" and "no" and "okay." I twisted in my chair, yawned in my turn. I wondered if I could smoke, decided against it. I wondered if the girls at the Conservatory knew what had happened to me since I had left them, wondered what they were thinking if they did. "From radio station to dance band to police court." It wasn't funny. It didn't even bear thinking about.

The outer door opened with a groan to admit a rotund individual wearing heavy glasses and a disgruntled expression. He spoke to the desk sergeant. Bradley himself appeared to lead him away. Mr. Silber, I judged.

They'd be evaluating the diamonds now. The diamonds were large, some of them over a carat, Gale had said. I wondered how many there were all together. The ones that were left were set closely. I measured my own wrist, tried to guess. Enough. How much would a diamond that weighed over a carat cost? It would depend on its purity and the cut but—say at least a thousand dollars for each stone. Then, if you counted in the sapphires and the workmanship . . . The whole, by my calculations, made a nice sum. Gale had said they were worth more.

Of course, that was the original price—the dealer to consumer cost. The thief couldn't hope to get as much out of it. The bracelet, in its original form, obviously couldn't be thrown on the market. It would have to be broken up, the stones sold separately. Probably he'd have to take an awful loss but since he'd gotten the thing for free in the first place . . .

I wondered how you'd go about selling an unset diamond. Just walk into a jewelry store and plank it down? But surely jewelers asked questions. Weren't they notified about robberies and urged to be on the lookout for any stones that might have come from them? Well, then, obviously, you'd have to go to someone who wasn't a legitimate jeweler. Probably in New York such a one could be found. No doubt he'd demand a consideration for handling "hot" stuff . . .

I shifted uneasily in my chair. Take off the loss incurred when the stones were broken up, take off the loss necessary to obtain safe handling—it didn't look as though the thief would come out so well. Unless he were desperately in need of money . . .

But if he were that desperate could he have waited? Wouldn't he have tried to dispose of the bracelet right there in San Francisco? Why take it across the country and risk discovery? Unless, of course, he made a sideline of it—stealing jewelry here, there and the other place, and had a regular outlet for it.

I wondered if there had ever been jewelry stolen in any other place the band had been. I decided to ask Gale. He'd know.

Mr. Silber reappeared and hurried away. It hadn't taken him long, I thought. Probably one glance at the diamonds and he'd told them all they wanted to know. I didn't think there was any doubt that they were diamonds. Gale's story had been too convincing.

Nothing more happened. I shifted in my chair and wondered what Gale was doing, what Bradley was doing to him. Asking questions, probably. Maybe he'd ever thought of the "other robberies" angle for himself.

The outer door opened again. Murphy this time, looking pleased with himself. Five of the band were with him— Tait Gilmore, Dick Travis, Morris Levinsky, Shorty Sims and Johnny. They were disheveled, unshaven. They looked cross and half asleep. Tait saw me. He halted, pointed. "For the love of Mike, guys, look who's here! Connie, my little angel . . ."

Murphy silenced him with a scowl. "No talking. Chief's orders."

He hurried them past. I went on waiting. Gradually gray dawn came filtering through the tall glass windows. The lights that burned above the desk began to pale. Morning walked softly along the streets.

Something was happening at last. Murphy had reappeared. The, others came out. This time they didn't look at me. With Murphy behind, they went out the street door.

I sat forward on the edge of my chair. Gale hadn't been with them. Surely he'd be coming, too. When he did . . .

He was coming but Chief Bradley was with him. Now what? I half rose.

Gale saw me. He spoke to Bradley, moved in my direction. He looked tired but he smiled.

"You poor, kid! Rather out of it, aren't you? Well, you can be glad—"

I said, "What's happening? What about Johnny and Tait and the others? Are they arrested? Was it the bracelet—"

He said, "Whoa! You go too fast. No, they're not arrested but Bradley wants to keep them together until we've looked over their stuff. That's what we've got to attend to now."

"For the bracelet? But it won't be at the hotel. Nobody'd be that stupid, not when he knew Anne had part of it in her hand . . ."

He shifted his feet, anxious to be gone. "Maybe not. I'll tell you better later—when we're through."

I said, "Gale, if he's letting you help, that must mean that he doesn't suspect you."

"Does it? I wouldn't know. I've been searched, however. Otherwise, I doubt if the chief would be so willing to let me talk to you. He'd be afraid I was getting rid of the evidence."

I said, "What evidence? Oh, you mean the bracelet. What about the others? Did they—"

"I've got to go, Connie. But they didn't—the bracelet wasn't mentioned. He's keeping that to himself. It was all alibis and what they knew about Anne. I'll tell you later." He turned away from me as Bradley moved purposefully in our direction. "Chief, how's about giving Connie a ride to the hotel? We may have that breakfast together yet."

When we arrived at the hotel, the big wall clock above the desk showed a few minutes to eight. The hotel was stirring into life. From the coffee shop came the tinkle of silver and china, the heartening smells of toast and bacon. At the cashier's desk Gale bought me cigarettes, the morning paper. He gave me a pat on the shoulder. "Now, read that—until I get back."

I didn't read it. One glance at the headline was enough. *Girl's body found near cabin camp* . . .

That didn't mean any girl. That was Anne—Anne Kent.

I didn't have to wait long. Not more than ten or fifteen minutes had gone by—the clock vouched for that—when the elevator door opened and Bradley and Gale reappeared. I thought, Why, it didn't take long. That's queer. Six people's

things—you'd think . . . I stopped, then, knowing why it
hadn't taken long. There was only the one reason. Because
they'd found what they were looking for. They'd found the
bracelet.

They talked briefly, separated. Gale came toward me.
"Let's eat," he said. I followed him into the coffee shop.
We found ourselves a booth at the back. I was bursting
with questions but a waitress bore down on us before I
could open my mouth. Gale lit a cigarette. We ordered.

The waitress left at last. I put my hands on the table
edge, gripped it hard. "You found it, didn't you? Whose—
where—"

He nodded. There was a nerve jumping beside his
mouth.

"Yes, we found it. I wish we hadn't. Damn it, Connie, I
feel like hell! Those guys—I've known them for years. I'd
have trusted them with my life. And yet, poor devil, I can't
even blame him. I know some of his story. There's a big
family; the father's dead—has been for years. Almost every
cent he gets goes home. There's one brother who wants to
be a doctor—you know what medical training costs. He
even does his own laundry—most of it. I've seen him—in
hotel washbasins . . ."

I couldn't stand it any longer. If he didn't tell me soon,
I was going to scream. I said, "Gale, for mercy's sake, tell
me! Who was it?"

Pain was dull in his eyes. "It was Morrie—Morrie
Levinsky. We found the rest of the bracelet in the toe of
one of his socks, a pair of socks I'd seen him darn myself."

15

I said, "I don't believe it!" and Gale's glance was grateful.

He said, "It was there—I saw it," and then the waitress slapped our plates down. I waited until she'd gone before I spoke again.

"Any of the others, yes—I'd make myself believe—but not Morris Levinsky."

"If he weren't so darn hard up all the time," Gale said. "Then, there's something else. He has an uncle or a cousin who's a pawnbroker. He might be able to dispose of the stones for him."

I thought of Morrie's dark, somber eyes, his bitter mouth. "I still don't believe it," I said stubbornly.

Gale stabbed at his scrambled eggs. "He's had a hell of a hard time all his life. Ever heard him play? Brilliance, technique—everything except the thing that makes pianists great. He knows it, too, poor devil. His family scraped up enough money to give him his chance. He had a concert at Town Hall, but the critics were lukewarm. Morrie went the way of a lot of other young artists, only he was luckier than most. He got a job he could do and one that paid decently. And he needed it. The family didn't have a cent. Now there's a brother who wants to be a doctor and another who's a cripple. There's some big surgeon who's interested in him. He'll do the operation for nothing but there'd be hospital expenses and care for a year or two after. I've heard Morrie tell about it."

"The bracelet," I said, "could be the operation."

Gale sighed. "Yes. I've thought of that."

"Was he with Mrs. Lorenzo much?"

"Not any more than the others. I'd have said Tait had the inside track there."

"Tait!" I pounced on it. "Is *he* hard up?"

"Not that I know of. Tait gets top pay here."

"How about the rest?"

"How do you expect me to know? How many do you think there are in the band?"

"I don't mean all of the band," I said impatiently. "It rather looks as though most of them were out of it. I meant Johnny and Dick Travis and Shorty Sims."

Gale shrugged. "Shorty's his own best confident. I've known him for six years and I don't know a thing about him. He's close-mouthed but he's also loyal, efficient and honest—in his dealings with me."

"He could be honest with you and still be dishonest with someone else, couldn't he?"

"Not for my book, he couldn't."

"All right, what about the others? Johnny?"

"I like Johnny," Gale said slowly. "He plays a damn fine piano. He gets a good salary and throws it around. No reason he shouldn't. His family have money and he's not married. He liked Anne pretty well . . ."

"They all did, didn't they?" I asked hopelessly.

"That's true enough. She was likable. After I married Mandy they were—sorry for her."

"Dick Travis?"

"Even Dick. He's a pretty queer fish, you know, Connie—nervous, erratic. He's in this business solely for the money and he makes no secret of it. He wants to be an architect and he saves every cent he can get his hands on. Says he's making hay while the sun shines for crooners."

I was only half listening. "You say they all liked Anne and nobody liked Mandy. But somebody killed both of them—Mandy first and then Anne. And Anne had a piece of bracelet in her hand when she was killed. But the bracelet had been stolen a long time before."

"If you want to know how I figure it," Gale began, "I think Mandy knew who stole the bracelet. Don't ask me how—she had her little ways. I think she tried to cut herself in on the profits. I said I didn't think she'd steal and I don't. But her scruples would only go so far. If she knew something was stolen and no suspicion attached, she'd see no reason why she shouldn't receive some recompense for keeping quiet about it. I think she tried to put the heat on that Sunday and was killed for her trouble."

"But where'd Anne come into it? Mandy surely wouldn't have told *her* about the bracelet or what she suspected. And where'd Anne get the bracelet?"

"You ask too many questions. How would I know?"

"There'll be a lot more asking questions," I reminded him. "I can see why Anne would have to be killed if she had the chance to talk to Mandy Sunday afternoon or if she had been in the hotel and happened to see someone in the hall or coming out of Mandy's room. But I don't see where the bracelet comes into it. Unless Mandy had the bracelet and gave it to Anne—for safety."

"She wouldn't," Gale said decisively. "If Mandy had the bracelet, she'd hang on to it, safety or no safety. Suppose someone else gave it to Anne—to keep for him."

"I don't think so. Wouldn't that make her an accessory?"

"Not if she didn't know what she had. Look, Connie, that's not such a bad notion. Musicians are always broke— it goes with the job. Gil Morris has a watch I bet's been in every hock shop in the country. Some of the fellows get Shorty to hold out a percentage of their pay each week until they need it. If one of them gave Anne a package to keep for him, she'd keep it, and not think anything about it."

"Maybe," I said dubiously. I hadn't known Anne. "Then how'd the bracelet get out of the package and into her hand?"

"Woman's curiosity—there is such a thing, isn't there? She might have opened it. Then when she found what she had, she confronted him."

"I don't like it," I said. "If she knew she had stolen goods and had a grain of sense, she'd have gone straight to the police. *I* would. And, besides, how does that tie in with Mandy? Unless Mandy *knew* Anne had the bracelet . . ."

"That could be it!" Gale's hand came down hard, upon the table. "Perhaps Mandy *did* know and told Anne Sunday afternoon. Perhaps they *did* meet up there in Room 320. That would explain a lot, wouldn't it? Why Mandy wasn't dressed, I mean. If the visitor she expected was another girl . . ."

I said, "Huh!" I wasn't sure I was convinced. "But what if Mandy were dead when Anne got there? She couldn't have told her anything then. And I don't suppose the murderer just left the bracelet lying around for her to find. Unless, of course, you think Anne was the murderer."

"I don't." Gale sounded miserable. "I don't see how she could be now. He rather slipped there, didn't he? If he could have staged a suicide for Anne the case would be closed right now."

"Not with part of that bracelet clutched in Anne's hand," I said grimly. "No, I think that was why she had to be killed—the bracelet. But why she'd have it with her at night or how *he* would know . . . Of course, there's one thing. If she did have it, if she were keeping it for someone, it could explain why she was here in Harriston. He'd have been keeping track of her and he'd have her address. He could have written her to meet him here. Then when she did meet him and handed over the bracelet, he killed her. That doesn't make sense, does it?"

Gale shook his head. "Not an awful lot. Oh, the facts are all right but I think we're putting them together wrong."

"There's this," I said slowly. "Perhaps she didn't have the bracelet but she *did* see someone in the hall near Room 320 that day—someone she knew. If he saw her, too, he might have tried to use the bracelet to buy her silence."

"And it didn't work!" Gale burst out. "She wouldn't buy! Connie, that could be it! He made a date with her for last night and tried to keep her quiet by offering her part of the proceeds from the bracelet. Then when she wouldn't play along, he killed her. That would fit—although why anyone in her right mind would go out to meet a murderer is past me."

"Do you think she'd know he was a murderer?" I asked. "Mandy's death had been pretty well hushed up. I mean, people know that she died but the way it was given out, it could have been from natural causes. Unless she were in touch with someone who knew . . ."

"She was. We know that."

"Johnny?" I asked dubiously. "Yes, but if he were the murderer, he wouldn't have told that, would he?"

"Don't ask me. Perhaps—if he were smart enough."

"So that we'd think he wasn't? Well, but it wasn't Johnny she was making dates with—it was me."

"She wasn't making dates with you, Connie," Gale said soberly. "She didn't want to see you. If she had, she'd have kept that date. I knew Anne. No, that was camouflage of a sort."

"I might believe that," I said, "if I didn't know better. Because she *did* want to see me, Gale. She proved that in Chicago—when she asked for me at the hotel."

Gale scowled, considering it. "Well, maybe," he said dubiously. "She might have—oh, Lord, I don't know! But one thing's certain, Connie, even though she did try to see you in Chicago, it couldn't have had anything to do with Mandy's murder."

"Then what did she want? Why—"

"I don't know," he said for the umpty-fifth time. "Perhaps we never will."

I could believe that. Anyway it was over. What was the good of talking about it? Anne Kent wouldn't be making any more dates—not ever . . .

I sighed, said, "Well, what happens next?"

Gale said, "I wish I knew. We'll just have to wait and see."

We waited.

Not long—for almost at once there were newsboys on the street, in the hotel lobby, crying papers. It was a later edition than the one I'd seen and the headlines screamed. No secrecy now. Anne's death, Mandy's, even the fragment of bracelet got brief notice. As a clue upon which the police were silent.

The papers were going like hot cakes. Everybody in the hotel lobby had one. I was conscious of sidelong glances . . .

Gale slapped his paper together. "Well, it's all here," he said glumly, "out in the open for anyone to read. I'm going to wire my lawyer."

He left me abruptly, came back. "Connie, we're all marked men now. It's not going to be pleasant. I think if I were you—"

"I know," I said. "I'll go out to Bradley's."

The streets were crowded. I edged along, hearing the newsboys' raucous shouting: "Girl murdered—read all about it!" I pulled down my hat protectively, fled to a quieter street.

There were voices in the Bradley kitchen—women's voices. I tiptoed up the stairs, shut my room door and threw myself on the bed. So far, so good. I wanted to think.

I couldn't. Perhaps my brain wasn't the right kind—not analytical enough. Goodness knows I had plenty of facts to work with, but apparently they weren't the right ones. Put together they just didn't make sense.

Anne Kent had tried to see me in Chicago. She had tried again in Harriston—I had Johnny's word for that. Through Johnny again, she had made a date to meet me yesterday in the restaurant. She hadn't kept it. Now she was dead.

Why? Because, in the hotel, she'd seen someone in suspicious proximity to my room, the room in which Mandy lay murdered? But how had she gotten into the hotel in the first place? Not through the lobby, certainly. She wouldn't have risked that, not if, as Johnny had insisted, she didn't want the band to know she was in town. The service stairs, then. But in that case, she could have been the one who stole the chef's knife. She could have been Mandy's murderer.

Only, I didn't think she was. The fact that she'd been killed, too, brutally beaten and smashed, a fragment of jewelry clutched in her hand, disclaimed it. No, Anne, like Mandy, had been a victim.

All right, I was as far as the bracelet and now where was I? The bracelet had belonged to a Mrs. Lorenzo of San Francisco. It had been stolen from her hotel room by one of the band. The bracelet had been hidden, unsuspected, until part of it had showed up in Anne's dead hand.

It was no use. I wasn't getting anywhere. The whole thing, as I saw it, hinged on that bracelet. Who had stolen it and, since the two need not be synonymous, in whose possession had it been? How did it get into Anne's hand? And why had her murderer brought the fragment back to the hotel? Why not get rid of it—damaging evidence as it was—in some less easily discovered place? The smart thing, surely, would have been to leave it with the rest. Why, then, cling to it? Cupidity—greed? The diamonds were worth a lot, even out of their setting. All right, the risk had been taken and the laborer was worthy of his hire—or the thief of his booty. Then, why in the name of all reason, hide it away in the toe of a pair of socks? Contempt of the police and their ability to discover it? Or for another reason? Did someone hate Morrie Levinsky—for not in my wildest dreams could I imagine him as thief and murderer—enough to endeavor to cast suspicion on him?

I didn't know. I was all mixed up. All I had were a lot of questions and no answers. The sensible thing was to forget it. It wasn't my problem to work out. Let the police handle it.

I must have slept then, for the next thing I knew it was half dark and Mrs. Bradley was rapping on the door. It was the telephone, she told me. Someone wanted me.

It was Johnny and he wanted me to come downtown and have dinner with him. I hesitated; I wasn't trusting anyone this time. I said, "Well, I don't know. I wouldn't be very good company . . ."

Johnny said, "Oh, come on! You won't have to talk if you don't want to. But you've got to eat somewhere, haven't you?"

That was true. I said, "Ye-es . . ."

He resorted to coaxing. "Come on. Why not? What's the matter?"

I went all honest then—with myself, with him. I said, "Johnny, I'm—afraid."

There was a silence. "I suppose you are," he said at last. "I don't know that I blame you. Shall I come out for you?"

I said, "No!" and it was a cry of protest. I was shaking, all out of control, hanging to the telephone for dear life.

Another silence. Then he spoke dryly, "I get it. You're off me, too. Is that it? Well . . . Hold on a minute, will you?"

I held on. Faintly I could hear some sort of a colloquy at the other end of the wire and then Johnny's voice came through, buoyant, normal. "All set. Murphy's here—you remember him? The policeman. He says he'll go for you in the police car. How's that?"

I said, helplessly, that it would be fine. I didn't know whether it would be or not, but the alternative—the lonely walk through yawning silent streets—made me shiver. I could never do it—not alone.

Johnny met us at the entrance to the hotel coffee shop. He said, "Thanks, Murph" and "Hi, Connie" and then, quickly and softly, "Afraid of me, you little idiot? You don't need to be—ever. I wouldn't hurt you, don't you know it?" At the moment it seemed true. I made myself smile.

There was a table at the back of the coffee shop. We went there. It was set for five. Three men rose as we approached—Tait Gilmore, Dick Travis, Shorty Sims. Johnny pulled out my chair. We sat down.

Tait Gilmore saluted me with a wave of his cigarette. "Welcome to the leper colony! Sorry you're forced to associate with us but we've been told to stick together. And just to see that we do . . ." He glanced over his shoulder to where Burns, the hotel detective, watched us from glassy eyes.

I said, "Oh! You mean . . ."

Tait ground out his cigarette with vicious force. "Turned us out of our room, by God! Until the police are done with their search. They're up there now, going through our stuff."

I felt better, relaxed. I said, "Well, it happened to me. I lived through it."

"I don't like it," Dick Travis said. The whites of his eyes were very prominent. "They found that damned bracelet in Morrie's stuff, didn't they? Do you think Morrie stole it, or knew anything about it? Do you? Or you? Or you?" His finger stabbed about the table.

I said, "Where Is Morrie?"

Tait answered me, shortly. "In the clink—where do you suppose? Go on, Dick, what are you getting at?"

"I'm getting at this." Dick's voice rose high and thin. "If Morrie didn't take that bracelet, how'd it get into his socks, tell me that! It was a plant, wasn't it? Our murderer must have put it there. Then how do we know what else he planted up there, in your stuff or mine?"

There was a second's quiet and then Tait began to swear softly. Beside him, Dick had slumped down, spent, his bolt shot. Shorty Sims was studying his linked fingers. Johnny's hand drummed steadily upon the table top.

"Someone," I said, "put the knife that killed Mandy into my suitcase."

They hadn't known. I told them about it. They listened in silence but I was conscious of quick looks that passed between them. I said, "What is it? What's wrong?"

They'd forgotten me. Their eyes were for themselves. Shorty Sims' fingers had clenched. He said in a thick voice, "Jesus God, that raincoat! You think that Gale . . ."

Something closed like ice about my heart. "What about Gale?" I asked sharply. "What are you talking about? Where is he?"

They looked at me then but they weren't seeing me. Shorty said, "He's all right. Bradley's got him down at the station. But we got a lawyer and Forrester's flying in. He'll be here tomorrow."

"Why is he at the station?" My voice was going shrill. I couldn't stop it. "What—"

"I'll tell her," Johnny said. "Listen, Connie, it's like this. The police think that whoever killed Anne couldn't have escaped getting blood on him somewhere. It would have splashed. They went over our clothes but they couldn't find anything. Then Bradley thought of Gale's car. There was a raincoat stuffed in the trunk. There was blood on it. So they took Gale down to the station."

"But he didn't do it!" I said. "And even if he had, he'd have had more sense—anyone would!—than to leave the coat there for the police to find!" I stopped then, remembering that Gale wouldn't have had a chance to remove it. Bradley had taken the car away from him.

"Sure," Tait said gloomily. "That's the point. It's another plant, that's all. Somebody's getting too damned smart. You and Morrie and Gale . . . I wonder who the hell is next?"

Beside him, Dick Travis made a strangled sound. "I'm getting out! I can't stay here. I don't want any dinner . . . I—"

"Sit down!" Shorty Sims ordered crisply. "There's no place to go, and anyway you gotta eat. Forget about our wiseguy killer. One of these times he'll overstep himself—get a little too smart—and then . . ."

"And then?" It was Tait. He was leaning forward, an odd sardonic smile on his lips., "What happens then?"

"Then," said Shorty Sims with smacked-lip satisfaction, "*then* we'll have him!"

16

We sat and ate our dinner. As Tait put it, you had to eat.
We didn't talk; we had too much to think about. Once I
said, "What happens to the show?" and Tait showed his
teeth at me.

"It goes on—what do you think? There's nothing sweet-
er in the ears of these yokels than music, the music of the
cash register."

Shorty Sims nodded. "Yeah. Murder or no murder, we
pack 'em in tonight."

He was right. When we reached the Harvest Hall—with
escort; Burns was about two feet in the rear—there, was a
block-long line before the ticket office and inside, a dis-
tracted member of the Festival committee was dusting off
the SRO sign.

"They'll be standing in the aisles tonight," Tait proph-
esied. "We'll be lucky if they're not sitting on the stage."

An air of tension pervaded backstage. Beside the alley
door, Murphy sat on a tilted chair. Fred Bradley lounged
in the corridor that led to the dressing rooms. I saw other
men, strangers.

There was a clatter of conversation in the dressing
room. Some of it died when I walked in, but not enough.
A synthetic redhead was slapping powder on an already
made-up face and declaiming, "They say Ullman won't be

201

here tonight. You wait till I see Bergner! I'm gonna ask him what's the idea, sending me out with a bunch of lousy murderers! There oughta be a law!"

The blond bicycle rider was watching me. "I don't think it was Ullman," she said and then made direct appeal. "Do you?"

I shook my head. I had my housecoat on now and was seated before the mirror. "No," I said, deliberately loud, "I do not. And what's more, I don't want to talk about it or hear about it—not tonight."

There was a moment of silence. Then somebody laughed. Someone said, "Well, that's telling us!" and a general titter filled the room. No one spoke to me again, but the whispered conversations resumed, in groups of twos and threes. I finished my make-up with hands that shook a little.

I put on the blush-rose dress. I fastened the silken roses in my hair. The mirror showed me a pallid face—Ophelia with her posies. Furiously I dabbed on more rouge, scraped a lipstick across my drooping mouth. Now I looked like a clown. More powder.

It was no use. The sibilance of whispers rose around me. If I were out of this, I thought, they could talk in comfort. Why shouldn't they? It was their right. Given other circumstances, with no personal involvement, I would have been talking, too.

I left the dressing room, closed the door softly behind me. The long corridor was quiet, but from the stage came the sound of instruments being warmed up—single sustained tones, the quick ripple of a scale, a snatch of melody. Cutting sharply above the other more muted sounds, Tait Gilmore's horn rose in staccato brilliance, stopped, raced upward again.

There were footsteps behind me. I leaned against the wall, tried to look as though it were a favorite lounging place. The fat drummer and the tenor sax man hurried past. The drummer was saying, "Tait's feeling high tonight."

I heard the tenor sax's laugh. "Why not? If the boss is out . . ." The drummer's answer came in a raucous cackle. "Gale may be down but he's not out—not yet. Don't ever think it! Tait could be counting his chickens too soon."

They were gone. Up the steps into the brightness that was the stage.

Another door opened, the door opposite. Gale Ullman came out. His eyes were somber but he smiled at me, a grave smile gone almost before I was sure I'd seen it. He said, "Hi, Connie" and was gone.

At least he was *here,* I comforted myself. They hadn't held him . . .

The corridor was chill. I wondered if there were some law for builders that backstage and onstage must always be cold. I wanted a wrap but my cape was in the dressing room and I lacked the courage to go for it. I hugged my bare arms and shivered.

Fred Bradley spoke softly at my shoulder. "You'll freeze out here, girl. Where's your coat?"

I indicated the dressing room door. "But I'm not going in there for it. They talk too much."

He surveyed me dubiously. "Guess maybe that's one place where even a police chief and a married man would lay off. Never mind, we'll borrow Ullman's place for a bit. Got something to show you."

Gale's dressing room was small but it was warm. There was a couch, a straight chair. I sat on the couch. The chief stood.

He fumbled in his pocket, produced a folded yellow paper. "Here, see what you make of that."

I didn't make anything of it, the first reading. It wasn't sense. It couldn't be. It was sent from San Francisco and it was signed by Bertha Lorenzo. In between were words. *Do not understand query. Bracelet stolen by floor maid has been recovered. No member of Ullman's band implicated.*

I gave back the telegram. "I don't understand it."

The chief shrugged, replacing it in his pocket. "Looks like Ullman's been feeding us some fairy tales."

I didn't like that. "What do you mean?"

The chief was patient. "Who mentioned that bracelet in the first place? Ullman. Who identified it? Ullman. Who told a long rigmarole about how it could have been stolen—"

"Don't tell me, let me guess," I said bitterly. "It was Ullman. Are you really trying to tell me that it couldn't have been true? Perhaps he really thought it was Mrs. Lorenzo's bracelet . . ."

"Yes, and right there," Bradley said ruefully, "is where I should have smelled a mouse. I might have known, with a bracelet that valuable, the Frisco police wouldn't have let the band go off into thin air. I certainly wouldn't have myself."

"But Gale mightn't have known," I argued hotly. "I don't suppose he really ever had a good look at the bracelet—held it in his hand or anything like that. And a man wouldn't be so apt to notice little details as a woman would. You don't think Gale would *like* telling you that story, do you? He's proud of his band. Accusing one of them of being a thief—"

"Little matter of murder goes along with it," the chief said.

"I know. But even so . . . Doesn't the fact that he told you all about the bracelet, without coercion, mean anything? Doesn't it prove that he couldn't have had anything to do with it?"

The chief cut me off. "Can't say that it does," he drawled. "Me—I don't trust the Greeks bringing gifts. Learned that back in high school and I've been finding places to apply it to ever since. People aren't altruistic by nature and when they get helpful in a murder case, watch out. Usually means they've got some sort of axe to grind."

I was only half listening. "But who does the bracelet belong to?"

The chief's mouth was a steel trap. "Don't know—yet."

"I never knew Anne Kent," I said slowly, "but I don't think it would be hers. It looks more like Mandy's."

The chief pricked up his ears. "She have a bracelet?"

"I don't mean that; meant she was—oh, flamboyant, spectacular. She'd like wearing diamonds to show off."

"If it was hers, why didn't Ullman recognize it? Of course, maybe he did and that was why he spun that other yarn."

"He mightn't have known Mandy had a bracelet," I said. "They'd only been married a little over a week. She could have had it before—bought it, and not told him. Do you remember what he said—that Mandy wouldn't steal; she'd go out and buy a bracelet bigger and better. Perhaps that's what she did."

"Maybe," the chief conceded. "Kind of looks right now as if that was what she did. But even if Ullman didn't know she had it, someone else could have. Could be that was why she was killed."

"To get the bracelet," I said. "I wonder where she'd get the money to buy it. It was valuable, wasn't it?"

"Close to twenty thousand, Silber made it, and Silber's what I call a conservative guesser. You know if she had any other jewelry?"

"She had a wrist watch, gold and diamonds," I said, "and a lot of earrings and pins, but I think they were just for show. Her wedding ring was a band of diamonds . . ."

"We got all that. Thought she might have been bragging, showing off her stuff. You know anything about her personally? Where she came from? She ever tell you?"

"No. Gale . . ."

"He claims he can't tell us much. Says Martin was her right name and all her family's dead. Came from Minnesota originally. Says those cousins over at Somerset she didn't go to visit were the only ones left. The cousins say the same thing. Say she was an only child and her father and mother were killed in a train wreck when she was about eight. An old aunt brought her up, but she's been dead for some years. Sam Martin—he's the cousin—says she married a farmer who died of pneumonia about six years back. He didn't have any family either. Sam says he thinks Mandy sold the farm and went East. Ullman says she was in New York when he hired her. Sam says she used to sing in the Lutheran church choir after she was married."

I tried, without success, to imagine Mandy singing in a church choir. I said, "Perhaps that's where she got the money for the bracelet—from the sale of the farm."

The chief said it could be, though without enthusiasm. "Guess they'll bury her tomorrow. Martin's got a plot over at Somerset. Says she can be buried there as well as not, and Ullman agrees. That'll be in the afternoon. Inquest's in the morning."

"Inquest! But—"

"Got to have one, according to law. We delayed it once but there's no point holding up things now, not with two of them to handle."

"Will I have to go?"

"Yes. Now, don't go getting upset, it won't be much more than a formality. Anne Kent now—that may be different. Her brother's coming. Ought to get in tonight."

"Her brother. Then you found out something about her?"

"Uh-huh. It wasn't hard. Funny, nobody had a word to say about Mrs. Ullman. When it came to Anne Kent, everybody knew something and was willing to tell it."

"Anne must have talked first then," I said. "Some people talk a lot about themselves and their background, others don't. Mandy never said a word to me. Then, too, they all liked Anne."

"Seemed to," the chief agreed. "Might be they overestimated her. Some of these people who talk a lot are one person on the surface and somebody else deep down inside. Often takes a smart man to figure them out."

"What do you mean?"

He didn't answer for a minute. When he did, what he said sounded irrelevant. "Ever hear of a fellow named Joseph Glanzer?"

Wordless, I shook my head.

"Didn't suppose you had. I've got a hunch it's somebody's dark secret. Lots of name-changing in this business, isn't there?"

"I suppose there is," I said. "I didn't change my name but if it had been Sadie Schultz, for example, I might have. Did Anne Kent?"

"No." The chief lit a cigarette, drew on it heavily. "Only so far as she changed her name by marriage."

"Marriage!" I fairly yelped it. "She was *married?*"

"Looks like it. Certificate and wedding ring put away among her things. Married this Glanzer last July, over in Reno."

"But," I said. "But—" I stopped then. I didn't have anything to say and I couldn't sputter on indefinitely. "But she was going to marry Gale!"

"So he said. Of course, if we could prove Glanzer was Ullman's right name, we'd have considerable of a motive. Bigamy's an ugly thing."

I said, "But he married Mandy! Didn't she have a wedding certificate? Didn't you find it?"

Bradley nodded. "We found it. All correct. Hubert G. Ullman—Amanda Martin."

"Then Ullman's his right name," I said. "No one would ever deliberately choose a name like Hubert. And anyway, if he were married to both, then why kill Mandy? Why not

Anne? She would have been the first, the one he supposedly wanted to get rid of."

"Might depend on which he wanted to stay married to,"
the chief said dryly.

"But Anne's dead, too."

"Then it could be he's changed his mind again."

I gaped at him.

"You been seeing quite a bit of Ullman lately." The
chief's little eyes were cold. "Yes, I know you only met
Ullman last week. Maybe he's a fast worker. Or—could be
you're a faster one."

I said, "Why—why—"

The chief raised his hand. "Now, don't bother getting
insulted. We got to figure all angles on a thing like this.
Could be we're all wrong and this Glanzer fellow is someone else."

"But can't you check on it? On Anne's marriage?"

"We're checking. Trouble is, in a place like Reno,
there's a lot of marrying goes on. You can't expect a jus-
tice to remember all about every couple he marries—not
when months have gone by. But we're trying it. The bracelet, too. Got the police of New York, Chicago and Frisco
working. Trying to find out who bought it and where.
Maybe we'll find out, maybe not. Have to wait and see."

I said, "Have you asked Gale about Joseph Glanzer?
Does he know Anne was married?"

Bradley shook his head. "You're the only one who
knows—yet."

I was the only one who knew! I liked that. I loved it. I
said, "For pity sakes, why tell me? I didn't want to know."

"*I* wanted you to know," Bradley said calmly. "I thought
perhaps you could find out a few things I couldn't, you being on the inside as it were, new to the band and a woman,
curious. When I ask questions, the whole bunch freezes
up. But you . . ."

I liked it less. "You want me to ask questions, to find out who Joseph Glanzer is and about Anne's marriage and report back to you, like a spy? Well, I won't do it! It's too much like looking for trouble!"

The chief shrugged. "Okay, have it your way. Only, well, murder's not exactly the same as some other things—stealing a bracelet, for instance. Murder means that some-one who ought to be living has been cut down, so to speak, sooner than he or his friends had a right to expect. Murder goes against man's law and against God's. No lawful per-son wants a murderer walking around loose. The law's got a right to deputize citizens—"

"You can't deputize me," I said stubbornly.

He shrugged again and walked to the door. "Nothing was farther from my mind, Miss Waring. I thought maybe you could find out something that would give us an end to unravel this tangle. If you don't think you can, all right. Only I think there's something you're maybe forgetting. Two girls are dead—murdered; two girls who used to be-long to this band. Ever think that maybe there'll be a third and that one you?" He waited a second. "Better think it over, hadn't you?" he asked softly and was gone.

I stood there, in the center of Gale's dressing room, and I shook. At first I thought it was with anger—I was angry enough, God knows. Later on I knew that I was wrong and that it was fear that had set me shaking. The chief had made me afraid, afraid of being murdered. But why should I be murdered? There was no reason for it. Yet had there been reason for Anne's death or Mandy's? Per-haps a murderer didn't need reason. Perhaps *this* murder-er didn't. There were pathological killers—the history of crime was filled with them—men who killed for the sheer love of killing. If our murderer were one of those . . .

I couldn't go on like this. There were cigarettes on the make-up shelf and I took one, lit it. Gradually my nerves steadied and some of my panic died—but not my anger. I hated everyone and everything—the band, Chief Bradley, Gale Ullman, myself most of all.

So I was seeing a lot of Gale Ullman, was I? So much that others noticed and commented. Very well. I wouldn't again. I'd stay out of his way. I didn't like him anyway—not very much. I didn't care if I never saw him again, outside of rehearsals and the show, of course. It didn't have to be Gale; there were others I could go around with, always supposing my own company wasn't enough and I needed someone to go around with. There was Johnny Davis . . .

I felt better, thinking of Johnny. Johnny wasn't in it any more than I. The telephone calls from Anne—they didn't mean anything. He hadn't *seen* Anne. And when Mandy was killed, like myself, he'd been far out in the country. You couldn't kill people from long distance, not the way Mandy was killed. Gale . . . Now Gale was different. He'd been in the hotel the afternoon of Mandy's murder. He was in the neighborhood of the auto camp when Anne died. A blood-stained raincoat had been found in his car. Mandy had been his wife, Anne his sweetheart. Only, where in time did the bracelet come in? Gale wouldn't have killed because of that. *He* wasn't hard up . . . Or was he? Bands often went in the red. He must be carrying tremendous overhead . . .

I stubbed out my cigarette. Well, if he was, what of it? It was nothing to me. I was done with personal interests; I'd better be. Hadn't I made that same resolution when I first came with the band? And look what had happened to me because I hadn't stuck to it! Okay, this time I would stick. I'd be the cat-who-walked-by-herself in very truth.

It was a beautiful decision, a wise one, but even while I, so to speak, stood and admired it, a little imp of common sense kept nagging at me. If I were done with Gale Ullman in very truth, then what was I doing hanging about in his

dressing room? If I meant all the things I'd been so com-
placently telling myself, I'd better get out—and fast.

I did. I would have had to in any event. The show was
about to start.

17

Everything went wrong with the show that night. There were blue notes in plenty. Dick Travis went blank in the middle of one of his choruses and was forced to finish it up with "Ta-doo, ata-doodle-de-ay" or sounds to that effect. I missed a cue with the result that I came in singing from the wings, scarcely to be heard until I reached center stage and the microphone, which picked up my voice and magnified it in a sudden and disproportionate blare. There was none of the smoothness of the opening night. Gale's forehead was puckered in a perpetual frown.

Nor was this the worst. The girl assistant to the knife thrower, standing spread-eagled against the throwing board, took half a dozen knives, sweetly smiling, and then, without warning, threw up her hands and screamed on a shrill high note. Almost before we had heard it clearly, Tait Gilmore had caught the note and was throwing it upward, tossing it, catching it again. Gale brought the orchestra in in quick crescendo and the act ended with the startled knife thrower bowing and smiling in center stage and the throwee stumbling off into the wings where the lady bicyclist and I dosed her with brandy, supplied by the synthetic redhead. The music altered to a slow swinging waltz and the roller skaters hustled on.

It took a lot of brandy to calm the throwee, whose name was Ida. Stan, she explained through hursts of sobs, was her husband and he had been casting eyes in the direction of the platinum blond roller skater who was also one of her own best friends. She'd never been afraid before but some how tonight—those murders and all—she kept thinking how easy it would be, if Stan wanted to get rid of her, to let a knife slip. "Every time he threw one I thought about it and at last I couldn't stand it any longer. I just opened my mouth and yelled!"

She was getting a little maudlin, what with brandy and self pity, when I left the dressing room again. I passed Stan, sulking in a corner, and went to stand in the wings. The roller skaters were off. Grippa the Great was whirling, to a swift drum roll, on the parallel bars. Just as I arrived, he missed a hold, scrabbled desperately for another, and came down on the point of his collarbone with a sickening crunch. Pandemonium again. The lights went out, the curtains came together. Grippa was carried, moaning, from the stage and an ambulance summoned.

The show went on, uneasily, with many a hitch. There were no more open slips, however. The final, the breathtaking climaxes were cut from a few acts or modified out of danger, but the great mass of the audience seemed neither to notice nor care. They had come, after all, less for entertainment than out of curiosity. They had wanted to see, and with their own eyes, those who were by way of being principals in a horror that had hitherto been, to them, unexperienced. Murder, per se, seldom touched Harriston and this was murder—or murders—on the grand scale. Wherefore they gloated, making the most of opportunity.

The weight of their eyes, the insistence of their demanding, reached across the footlights and pressed upon

us. There was no getting through. The spark, the customary rapport with the audience, was not there. It had never
existed, never been allowed.

We were all wrecks by the time the show was over and
the band had played them out. The difficulty was that
they didn't go. They had no intention of going. So far as
they were concerned, the show wasn't over. It wouldn't be
until every actor was gone and there remained no further
targets for their prying eyes.

They lingered in the aisles, loitered in the lobby. They
stood in the street outside. They waited. The alley leading
to the stage door was clogged with humanity. When the
stage door opened, faces pushed forward, hostile and staring. I wondered if I had the courage to pass those faces. I
knew I didn't. Not alone.

Make-up removed, back in suit and hat again, I stood
forlornly in the corridor. Members of some of the acts
went by—in twos and threes—and, always when the door
was opened, you were conscious of movement outside, of
the shifting of feet, unseen, to let them pass. It was a
gauntlet I knew I'd never run. Sooner than that, I'd spend
the night in the Harvest Hall.

There was no sign of Chief Bradley or his men, and
most of the band, I suspected, had already gone. It was
getting quiet backstage. Only Murphy, on guard at the
door, remained. I looked at the width of his shoulders and
was comforted. None should get by him . . .

Gale had not appeared. That was all right—I was done
with Gale. If I never saw him again . . .

It wasn't so. I knew it. I wanted him, wanted him badly.
He could get me past, get me out of range of those avid,
seeking eyes. By sheer force of personality, he could do
it, the right of the leader born to command all kinds and
conditions of men.

But Gale didn't come. Instead, the door of the men's dressing room opened. I heard footsteps, voices, the scratch of a match. I turned eagerly. Was this rescue?

It was. Johnny Davis's smile flashed at me. He said, "Hi!" The smile died. He spoke soberly. "What's wrong, Connie?"

I said, "I'm scared."

"Again?" His eyebrows rose. Then he glanced through the door's glass, burlesqued a shiver. "I don't know that I blame you. Hi, Murph! What goes on?"

Murphy swung around, grinning. "Kind of a crowd out there. Guess the lady don't like the idea of bucking it."

"Neither do I." Tait Gilmore flung his cigarette to the floor, trod it out. Where the hell's Burns? Maybe if we put Connie in the middle and you two ran interference . . ."

But Murphy shook his head. "Nope. I got orders to stay here. The chief says you fellows are on your own now."

"On our own, are we?" Johnny whistled softly. "Ain't that nice? You trail us around when we don't need you and when we do—phooey!—you bow out. Well, nothing doing, Mr. Policeman. What's the matter with giving us a little protection for a change? Where's Bradley anyway? If he thinks he's only playing this game one way, he's got another think coming!"

Murphy's neck was reddening. Shorty Sims said, "Shut up!" and I tugged at Johnny's arm. "There might be another door . . ."

There was. Murphy explained its whereabouts eagerly. If we'd go into the body of the auditorium and cross toward the west, we'd find some big rolling doors they used when they had auto shows. Over in the corner there was another smaller door. Its night latch would be on but we could open it all right. That would let us out on a side street.

The side street was dimly lit and quiet. We could see the edges of the crowd that milled before the entrance doors, but we were able to cross the street unseen and flee down an alley.

Back on the midway, we made a little huddle at the corner of a fortuneteller's booth.

I said, "Now I'm lost again. I'll have to go back to the hotel and start from there to find Bradley's."

"We'll take you," Johnny promised, and, at my look of doubt, "All of us. Won't we, fellows? No more twosomes, for Connie."

Dick Travis spoke loudly. "I want a steak! After that, okay, we'll see Connie home. But first—I'm hungry!"

"Pipe down, will you?" Shorty Sims groaned. "Want to get that pack after us again?"

Tait said soothingly, "We all want a steak, even Connie. How about it?"

I started to say that I didn't in the least want a steak, and, then reconsidered. Perhaps Bradley was right and there *were* things I could find out—without too much difficulty or danger to myself. I could try. I said I believed I was hungry at that and a steak would taste good.

"Well, come on!" Dick ordered belligerently. "What are we waiting for? There's a taxi place a block over. Let's see if we can grab a cab."

There was some argument on the way as to our ultimate destination, Dick Travis holding out for the auto camp at which Anne had been killed. Someone had told him they had super steaks there. The others voted him down ruthlessly. Where, Shorty demanded with acid emphasis, did he think the crowd would be heading for, if their curiosity hadn't been sated at the Harvest Hall? Some of them would be sure to remember the camp and go out there. For all we knew, there might be some ugly customers among them. Had Dick ever seen a mob in action? Harriston's civic pride had been badly wounded by these murders spang in the middle of their festival season and we wanted to remember we didn't have Murphy or Burns on call any longer. Three or four drinks under the belts of some of the town's riffraff and only God knew what might happen.

For like reasons, he wrote off all the downtown cafés. The band was in a nasty enough spot without looking for trouble.

They heard him through and agreed, Dick a little sullenly. Johnny suggested the eating place we'd discovered as being quiet and off the beaten track. We went there.

There were plenty of people in the restaurant—a neighborhood crowd, I thought; nice and quiet and uninterested. No one looked up as we wandered in. Johnny found a back booth that was empty. We took it.

We all ordered steaks, French fries, pie à la mode. Tait and Dick and Shorty had beer, Johnny coffee, and I tea. I hoped it would be strong tea, black and bitter. I needed it.

We'd have to wait about twenty minutes, the waitress told us, for the steaks. That was all right, Dick assured her, but for God's sake bring the beer *now!*

She brought it. Under its influence, tongues loosened, irritability vanished. They began to speculate.

What, Tait wanted to know, did Bradley mean by calling off his dogs like that?

Shorty shrugged. "That's easy—give us rope. He figures he'll hang us quicker. Well, we can check that. If we stick together—all of us—*all* the time, we call his hand. We have alibis all the time. Get it?"

"Maybe," Johnny said doubtfully. "Of course, he's got Morrie and maybe he thinks he's got Gale, too—on that raincoat thing. Could be he figured he didn't need us any more."

"Could be," Tait agreed, "but I've a hunch it's more than that. You got any ideas, Connie? You talked to Bradley tonight."

They were all waiting expectantly and I decided to offer them a nickel's worth of news. "It's the bracelet," I said. "It wasn't that Lorenzo woman's after all. The chief had a wire tonight saying hers was found."

There was a moment's silence and then Tait said slowly, "Not Mrs. Lorenzo's? Then whose was it—Mandy's?"

Johnny opened his mouth but Shorty got in first. "Not a chance! That gal oughta been on Wall Street. She didn't go in for glitter. She stacked her dough away where neither moth nor rust—what's the rest of it? She was worth money when she died and don't forget it. Unless she made a will that cuts him out, Gale's going to come into a nice little piece of stuff."

Tait eyed him thoughtfully. "How come you know so much?"

"Same guy handled my wad. Mandy fixed it up for me. What I got ain't so much, but, brother, one of these days I'm quitting—for keeps. No more traveling one-night stands, no more fighting with hotels and booking offices, no more—"

Tait said, "Oh, dry up, will you?" but Dick Travis looked from one to the other anxiously. His face looked pinched and queer.

"You suppose that's straight—that Mandy left a wad? Does Gale know?"

"How the hell would I know?" Shorty asked sullenly.

Tait shrugged, drawing a circle in the moisture that beaded his glass. "Well, he married her, didn't he? There must have been a reason!"

Johnny scowled at him. "Don't kid yourself, Gale never thought that far ahead in his life."

Shorty snapped abruptly from his sulks. "I'm not so sure. Gale's been pretty hard up lately. Sure, he makes big money but . . . You don't think he likes playing this sort of racket, do you? But what's he going to do? You gotta keep out of the red . . ."

I began to wonder if the question of money had had anything to do with my being hired for the band. He hadn't wanted to take the time for auditioning, Gale had told me, but he'd also said that Anne Kent's salary had been greater than mine. Had he saved pennies then—with me?

Tait was glowering into his beer. "The whole set-up's crazy," he pronounced. "But what can you do about it? You're a kid and one day you get hold of a horn and fool around with it and after that you're good for nothing else. You don't even care. All you want to do is fool around with the horn. You think music, dream music, play music. You get together a crowd of other guys who feel the same way and you click and first thing you know you're playing the sort of music you've always wanted to. You're good and you know it. But you're grown up now and you got to eat and music's the only thing you know. So you try to eat on your music, only there's no money in the kind of music you like to play. The guys with the bankrolls want waltzes and Guy Lombardo and crooners with adenoids. But you try to break in somewhere—anywhere—and you can't. No-body'll take a chance on you and the big names, like Ull-man, have it all sewed up. But you get along somehow and then you meet a girl and first thing you know you've married her and then she's got to eat, too. So you go over to the big boys—you got a reputation now and they know you—and you take their money and it's a lot and you know you can always get more. But the music you want to play is gone and so you sit on the stand night after night and eat your heart out and you know it's all over. You've sold yourself, you're nothing but a hack musician now—"

He flung out his hand and the beer bottle tottered. Johnny caught it. "Cut it out, will you? So you've troubles, have you? Well, so maybe have the rest of us—even Gale."

It was high time for a diversion. I offered one. "Mandy's funeral is tomorrow," I said into the momentary quiet.

It was a diversion, all right. Tait eyed me without favor. "Well, well," he said nastily. "So little Connie's got all the answers. How'd you get your direct line into headquarters, baby, or shouldn't I ask?"

Dick Travis said, "Tomorrow? You mean they're going to bury her here? Oh, those cousins—I forgot them."

Shorty said, "Hell, that means somebody's got to see about flowers and where are you going to get flowers in a place like this? Not even a florist shop . . ."

Johnny said, "What about Anne?"

It was Johnny I answered. I said, "I don't know. Her brother comes tonight. He'll probably take charge. Unless, of course"—I dropped this delicately and with a prayer; I wasn't at all sure it was what the chief had meant me to do—"her husband chooses to claim her."

I'd dropped a bombshell. I tried to see all their faces at the same time and failed. So far as I could tell, they all looked the same—shocked and blank and unbelieving. It was Tait who found his voice first. "Anne *married?* You're crazy!"

I said, "Oh, I'm sorry—perhaps I shouldn't have mentioned it. But Chief Bradley said . . ." I stopped in simulated confusion.

Tait appealed to Shorty Sims. "You know anything about this?"

Shorty shook his head. He looked dazed. "I thought she and Gale were set. You mean she married Gale before he married Mandy?"

It was my turn to shake my head. "It wasn't Gale. It was someone else. I don't remember the name."

That was a lie. I knew it as well as my own.

"I don't believe it!" This was Dick Travis. "Bradley's just having you on. Anne was crazy about Gale. She wouldn't marry anyone else. God, I ought to know! I—"

"Wait a minute." Tait's eyes had narrowed. "Let's get this straight. Anne was married, you say. When was it supposed to have taken place—this marriage?"

There was no good in playing innocent. I'd gone so far, I'd have to go on. I might be spilling all the cherished secrets of the police department, but I couldn't help myself. "In July, I think the chief said."

"Where?"

"Reno."

"How'd he find out? She have a certificate or something?"

I nodded. "And a ring."

"Did he tell you the guy's name?"

"Yes." I spoke carefully now. "But it didn't mean a thing to me. I'd never heard it before. I'm sorry, perhaps I should have paid better attention but—you can ask the chief, can't you?"

"Sure." The answer came pat. "Sure we can ask." Quick glances went around the table.

Then Johnny said gruffly, "It wasn't a name you'd heard before? It wasn't anyone in the band?"

"I don't think so. I'm sure I would have recognized it."

They seemed satisfied. Again quick glances crossed the table. Then Tait yawned, deliberately. "No one in the band, huh? Well, that's all to the good. Must have been someone she picked up at the hotel then."

Shorty frowned. "July—we were in Frisco then. Any of you remember who Anne was running around with?"

Dick Travis barked a laugh. "Who? Say, that's a hot one! Who didn't she? Little Annie played the field!"

"Listen, you big lug—" Johnny began furiously, but I put my hand on his arm.

"Don't," I said. I looked at Dick Travis. "I don't understand. You just said she was crazy about Gale."

He turned to me eagerly. "Well, she was. So long as Gale was around, the rest of us didn't count. But he wasn't always there and then anybody'd do. That's how it was, wasn't it, Shorty?"

"Near enough," Shorty mumbled around the cigarette he was lighting.

"You see? Anne was a sweet kid but she took a lot of babying, petting. We all took turns—one time or the other. God knows I didn't want to get married—can't afford it—and yet, I'd have married Anne if I'd thought I had a chance. She sort of got you—all of us—Johnny, too; even Tait."

"You can leave me out of it," Tait said sourly. "I've one wife and she'll do me!"

But Johnny spoke soberly, "Yes. I was crazy about Anne." He left it there.

I said, "But even so . . . You say she was in love with Gale, you say she had no time for anyone else when he was around. They were engaged. But she married someone else. Why?" I appealed to Tait, perhaps as to the only one there who was married. "Why should she do that?"

Tait shrugged. "Why ask me? Maybe she quarreled with Gale and the other guy got her on the rebound. If she was sore, she'd drink, and with a few drinks down her, you could talk her into anything. Then, next day, when she sobered up and knew what she'd done, she—threw the other guy overboard and kept her mouth shut. Because it was Gale always—first, last and all of the time—with Anne. At any fate, that's how I'd figure it."

"Sounds okay," Shorty grunted. He had his neck craned around the edge of the booth and was looking kitchenwards. "Where's that waitress and where the hell's my steak?"

Tait said, "Aw, forget your steak. Let's stay with this. Maybe the guy was drunk, too, when it happened. Maybe afterwards they were both willing to let it fizzle out. And then, of course, Anne couldn't marry Gale, and she couldn't get a divorce on the quiet, racketing around the country the way we were. So there wasn't anything she could do but play Gale along slow and easy. But Gale doesn't play well that way and so Anne lost out. Mandy cut in. Yeah, that's about the way it must have been!"

The others were silent. Shorty had forgotten the waitress to listen. Dick Travis's mouth was a little open. Johnny was gazing down at his hands, folded upon the table.

I said, "I can understand why Anne wouldn't want Gale to know she was married, but what about the husband? There was no reason for him to keep quiet. Why didn't *he* talk?"

Johnny spoke then with a bitter sting in his words.

"Perhaps the poor fool loved her. Perhaps what she wanted meant more to him than what he wanted himself. Perhaps it was enough for him that once she needed him and was willing to look his way . . ."

He looked up then, caught our goggling glances, and a swift anger flushed his face. "Don't look like that—it's true. There'll always be men like that, so long as there are girls like Anne. You laugh at Gale, you sneer at him, but let me tell you, he's a better man than I am, or Dick or Shorty—or you either, Tait Gilmore!—because he made Anne love him!"

It was a good thing our steaks arrived just then. I think we were all thankful we didn't have to talk. Johnny's words had put an abrupt end to anything we might have meant to say, but, with the waitress trying to find room to put down dishes for five on a table meant for four, the bad moment passed and we returned to normalcy again.

But we didn't mention the murders, or Mandy, or Anne Kent again. Instead, someone, I think it was Tait, began to talk about the evening's show and presently we were all laughing over Stan and Ida and sympathizing with Grippa the Great. "Poor guy!" Tait said. "That puts him on the shelf for the rest of the season and maybe he'll never regain his nerve enough to go on."

It was almost twelve o'clock when we left the restaurant. It was so nice a night that we decided to walk to Bradley's. Johnny, who seemed to have the geography of Harriston at his fingertips, said the Bradley house was only a few blocks due north. I walked beside Johnny. The others, after lighting cigarettes, trailed behind.

At the Bradley house I was all ready to say thank you and good night, but Johnny's hand remained firm upon my arm. Over my head, he spoke to the others, "I'm going in with Connie—you fellows go on. I'll be along."

They were only blurs in the darkness. I heard their muffled laughter, their chorus of "good nights." Then they were gone.

I kept silent, walking to the porch, but at the door I shook off Johnny's arm and turned on him. "I don't like this," I said. "It's not necessary. There's no reason why you should come in with me. Do you think I want those others to start talking about me?" I nearly said "as they do about Anne" but I bit it off in time. "I'm not the least bit interested in you—"

"Nor I in you. Period." In the faint light that seeped through the stained glass of the outer door I could see his smile, faint and bitter. "As a matter of fact, it's Bradley I want to see. You see, Connie, nothing you told us this evening was news to me. I knew Anne had been married—I even knew the guy she was married to. That's why I want to see Bradley. I think it's time some of this got cleared up."

I felt a little dizzy. "You mean you sat there and kept quiet and all the time you knew who Joseph Glanzer was?"

He said, "Sure I do" and turned me gently toward the door. "Haven't you guessed it yet, honey? *I'm* the guy Anne Kent married. *I'm* Joe Glanzer!"

18

Chief Bradley was there. So were Gale and the District Attorney. The air of the little parlor was thick with smoke. They weren't talking. It was more as though they were waiting. I wondered for what.

Johnny surveyed them with sardonic eye. "What is this, a pinch? Okay—get on with it. I'm here."

I thought the chief looked uncomfortable, Gale worried. The District Attorney interlaced his fingers, contemplated them. "If you'll give me a reason, Mr. Davis," he suggested, "why we should want to—er—pinch you . . ."

"I'll do that, too," Johnny said. He was standing very straight. "For the reason that I'm Joe Glanzer, Anne Kent's husband."

The chief grunted. "That's what we thought. Been trying to get it out of him"—he indicated Gale—"with no luck. Figured that a man in his position should know."

Gale smiled faintly. "I come across a lot of things in my business, Chief, that I don't consider the public's." He looked at Johnny. "I didn't know you two were married, kid."

Johnny sat down suddenly, as though the stuffing had gone out of him. "It didn't mean anything—it was just a gesture. She was mad, she wanted to get even with you. I didn't know it then. She—she fooled me, too."

Gale nodded. "I thought it was something like that. It was that party, wasn't it? I made a fool of myself that night. Mandy was—something extra and I . . . I suppose I thought Anne wouldn't notice. I'd drunk too much and the stuff went to my head. I didn't know what I was doing. And Anne wasn't there . . ."

"She was there long enough to see what was going on," Johnny said. "She'd had a couple of drinks herself and then she said she had a headache and got out. She went down to the bar. That's where I found her. She was drinking brandy and crying into it. I couldn't leave her there. Remember that sort of a park across the street? Well, I coaxed her over there and we sat on a bench and she cried on my shoulder. She said she couldn't stand it any longer—that if it wasn't Mandy, it would be someone else with you. Any new face . . ."

Gale said, "God!" very quietly.

"I couldn't stand it either." Johnny was speaking quickly now. "I'd always thought that Anne . . . I'd held it back before but that night I let go. I kissed her and told her that I loved her and she let me. And then, all of a sudden, she sat up and she stopped crying. She looked at me and she said, 'Do you really mean that?' and I said I did. Then she said, 'All right, if you really feel like that, let's get married! Let's get married right away!'

"We didn't stop to think; I didn't want to. It was too much like having a dream you'd dreamed for a long time come true. We rushed out to the airport, chartered a plane, flew to Reno, and were married. Then we flew back. We decided to tell the rest of you in the morning. Anne was all in and she went to her room and I—I was so damned happy I walked the streets the rest of the night. When morning came and the stores opened, I bought that bracelet."

The chief said, "Ah—the bracelet!" and Gale said. "*You* bought it!" Goodwin, the District Attorney, didn't say anything. He just hunched forward in his chair as though afraid he'd miss something.

"I was lucky over the bracelet," Johnny said. "I wanted something wonderful for Anne and there it was. There was a salesman in at one of the big stores. This was one of his samples. I called the hotel and had them certify my check."

"Wait a minute," the chief said. "Why should the hotel certify your check? Must have been a big one. Hotels aren't generally that accommodating."

"I thought you knew," Johnny said evenly. "It was one of the Glanzer hotels. I'm that Glanzer."

I heard the hiss of Goodwin's breath and then Johnny was going on. "When I got back to the hotel, Anne wouldn't see me, and when she did she'd been crying. She told me it was all off—that she couldn't be married to me. She loved Gale, she'd never love anyone else. She was half crazy—afraid I'd told someone. I tried to calm her down. I promised to keep silent. I even swore it on a Bible she dug up somewhere. But I made her promise to wait a week, to think it over, and tell me then. Just before I left her, I gave her the bracelet. It was all wrapped up, just as I'd taken it from the store. If I hadn't given it to her, she'd be alive today."

"You sound mighty sure of that." It was the chief.

Johnny nodded. "Yes. I'm sure. I know now. I didn't guess then. She took her week and she didn't change her mind. She told me it would always be Gale with her—she couldn't help it She was afraid you'd find out and be off her for good." He had turned to Gale now. "I swore again I'd keep silent. I even offered to quit the band and get a divorce myself, but she wouldn't hear of it. She said she'd work something out. She didn't mention the bracelet. I didn't know why then. I found out later."

"What do you mean, you found out later?" It was the chief again, his eyes bright with interest. "What did you find out?"

But Johnny was looking at Gale. "Tait's birthday party was the eighth, remember? It was that night we were married. I'd given Anne a week—that brought it to the fifteenth. Remember what happened the fifteenth?"

Gale was scowling with the effort of thinking backward. "We played a dance at some lake hotel—Tahoe, wasn't it?"

"We had to stay overnight and it was something like it is here—overcrowded. The girls shared a room. When Mandy got a chance, she went through Anne's things. Don't ask me why. She was like that. She wanted to know everything about everybody. She found the wedding certificate—and the bracelet."

"Anne had them with her?" Gale's voice was a cry of anguish. "Oh, the fool, the pitiable little fool!"

"She had Anne right where she wanted her then. All she had to do was threaten to tell you. Thank God, the significance of the Glanzer name escaped her. But she did know diamonds when she saw them. Anne cried and prayed and in the end Mandy promised to keep quiet. But she kept the bracelet as—oh, I don't know—surety for her silence, perhaps. If Anne tried to get the bracelet back, she'd tell you."

"Any of this make sense to you?" The chief appealed to the room in general.

"It does to me," Gale groaned. "But then I knew them both. Johnny, Mandy wore that bracelet, didn't she?"

"Every night. She flaunted it. Oh, not too obviously—she mixed it in with a lot of flash stuff—but I saw it and Anne did. So did someone else." Johnny's lips were tight. "Her murderer."

The chief hitched his chair a little forward. "Seems to me you're doing some good qualifying for that post yourself, young man. It was your bracelet—you'd given it to your girl. If your story's straight, Mrs. Ullman took it away from her . . ."

"No." There was a sadness to Johnny's words that made you know them to be the truth, as he believed it. "Anne was never my girl. She belonged to Gale, to no one else but Gale. I made a bad mistake. I never should have married her."

"That why you kept still?" It was the chief again.

Johnny turned toward him. "Partly—but mostly because I'd promised Anne. I was out of it. It was her show and I owed her the privilege of running it."

The chief grunted. "She tell you about the bracelet?"

"The next night, the sixteenth, Mandy wore the bracelet. I saw it. I went to Anne. She told me what had happened. She said she'd get the bracelet back for me somehow. She might even tell Gale herself—they were going around together again. I said that the bracelet was hers—I didn't want it—to get it back for herself."

"Hunh!" There was the faintest of sneers underlying Goodwin's voice. "Mighty open-handed, aren't you? Twenty thousand bucks—just like that. Money doesn't mean a thing to you, does it?"

"Not a thing," Johnny said quietly. "I've plenty."

There was a little silence—each of us, I suppose, contemplating the wonder of a man who had "plenty"—and then the District Attorney exploded into action. He jumped to his feet and shook the stub of his cigar under Johnny's nose.

"And, let me tell you, young man, you're maybe going to need that money! If I ever saw anyone heading for a murder rap—"

"Wait," Johnny said. "I'm not finished. I didn't see much of Anne after that. She stayed out of my way. But I noticed that Mandy stopped wearing the bracelet. I wondered if she'd given it back to Anne but I never got a chance to talk to her. She saw to that. She was with Gale again . . ."

"But it wasn't the same," Gale said slowly. "I couldn't get close to her. She wouldn't even let me kiss her. Before, we'd made all sorts of silly plans but she was half-hearted about them now. And she'd stopped wearing my ring. She'd forgotten it, or it was in her room, or in her other purse—she always had some excuse."

"I know," Johnny said. "There was talk—I guess you heard some of it. Well, it went on like that. Anne kept getting thinner and she was doing more drinking. I began to wonder if we couldn't get our marriage annulled somewhere, quietly. I was just going to suggest it when you married Mandy.

"I don't think you've any idea what that did to Anne. I was with her afterwards—that night. It wasn't nice. She couldn't understand and the fact that she'd married someone else herself made no difference. Her marriage was a mistake—yours treason."

"She wouldn't even talk to me," Gale said softly. "I tried to see her, to explain. God knows I had a reason for marrying Mandy. I thought I could make her understand."

"No one could have explained to her," Johnny said. "Not in the mood she was in. She was half crazy and she was all set for an explosion. It came—the night she went after Mandy with a knife."

"You there?" This was the chief.

"We all were. It happened over at Inwood Lake during an intermission. The hotel had turned its lounge over to us and we were all in and out."

"Know who had the knife?"

"It was Shorty's knife," Johnny said slowly. "He always carried it. It was one of those big clasp knives with a bone handle and it was sharp. He sharpened it himself. We used to kid him about it."

"But Shorty wasn't using the knife," Gale said. "Someone borrowed it—to sharpen a pencil. I've tried to remember who it was, but I can't."

"It was Dick Travis," Johnny said quietly. "He was writing a letter over in one corner and his pen went dry. He tried to borrow another pen but no one had one. Then, after a while, he dug up this stub of a pencil and said if it was sharpened he could finish his letter. That was when Shorty chucked him the knife."

"That's right," Gale said. "I remember. And Dick sharpened his pencil but he didn't give the knife back. He just threw it down on the table. We were all standing around—Dick and Shorty, Mandy and I and Tait—when Anne came over. We were kidding about the knife. Tait called it a toad stabber and said it looked as though it would be equally good for mumbly peg or slitting a throat. He tossed it over to Anne and she stood there, weighing it. Then Shorty said it was a valuable knife and he wouldn't take a hundred dollars for it, and Tait told Anne to give it back quick if it was that valuable. That was when Mandy chimed in with something about Anne being notoriously careless with valuables, and Anne went for her. I got in the way and the knife went into my wrist and when Anne saw that she went to pieces. That was when we sent for Dr. Wilson. I told him to look after her for a week and I meant to get in touch with her family, but before I did she'd run away. I didn't do anything then— Wilson said she seemed entirely rational again, and I didn't want to get the police after her."

"It would have been better if you had," the chief said sternly. "Maybe she'd be alive now. Well, that brings us pretty much up to date and sheds some light on a few dark corners. Next thing she's in Chicago, according to Miss Waring. She get in touch with either of you there?"

Gale shook his head and Johnny said no, the first he'd heard was when Anne called him at the hotel Sunday night. "It must have been around eight o'clock—before we knew Mandy'd been murdered. She was pretty excited. She said she had the bracelet, that she'd seen Mandy that afternoon and Mandy had given it to her. She said even Mandy could see she had no legitimate reason for keeping it now and that Gale might make trouble if he saw it. I asked jokingly if she'd left Mandy in one piece, and she laughed and said they'd both acted civilized. She said, 'I've grown up a lot in the last few days, Johnny. I know I've made a mess of my life and maybe of yours. I know that traveling with a band isn't for me. I'm not big enough, I guess. After I get the bracelet back to you, I'm going back to Reno and get a divorce. I'll start all over again.' I told her again to keep the damn bracelet but she wouldn't listen. She wouldn't meet me either, she said she didn't want to see me or any of the band. I told her to mail it then but she wouldn't— she said it was too valuable to trust to the mails. I got mad and asked her how the hell she expected to get it to me then and she said perhaps Miss Waring would meet her and take it to me. She said she'd have it all wrapped up and it would just be a package and Connie needn't know what was in it. I said I guessed that would be all right so she told me to ask Connie and she'd call me next day at the Harvest Hall. Then she hung up. Next thing, the police were hauling me downstairs on suspicion of Mandy's murder. You were there when I got the message through to Connie."

Gale said, "Suppose Anne *was* at the hotel—how'd she get in? There were a bunch of us in the lobby—I was there myself. And if she saw Mandy alive, it must have been just before Connie came in at noon or just after she left for her walk."

"I asked her," Johnny said. "She'd heard about Mandy and she was pretty scared Monday when she called. She said she was sure no one saw her, that she'd come up the back way. I asked her how she knew Mandy's room and she said that was easy—she'd just called the hotel and asked to be connected. When she heard the switchboard girl say Room 320, she hung up."

"You ask her what time she was there?"

"Yes," Johnny said reluctantly. "She said it was about two-thirty. It must have been right after Connie left."

"And Mrs. Ullman was alive when she left?"

"She said so."

The chief said, "Hmm."

I said, "But if she came up the back stairs after I did, when the chef was at the telephone, she could have been the one who took the knife!"

Both Johnny and Gale jumped on me. "But she didn't! Anne wouldn't kill. It would never occur to her—"

I managed to insert, "What about the time she did go for Mandy with a knife?" before the chief stopped me.

"She tell you if she saw anyone on the way down?" he asked.

"She said she didn't."

Chief Bradley walked across the room and back. "Must have been considerable traffic on those back stairs. Let's see—it's a concrete stairway opening on the various floors through fireproof doors. Open stairwell, though. Anyone on one level could look up or down as the case might be. Hmm. Any of you know who first brought Anne Kent's name into this murder?"

Johnny looked at me and I looked at Gale. "Well, Johnny knew and I did," I began slowly. "But it was Tait who actually said he'd seen her in Harriston."

The chief wasn't pleased. "Humph! Would be the only one claiming an alibi."

Gale said, "Has Tait an alibi?" and the chief said he did.

"Spent last night up until three this morning over at Father Kelley's. Seems the father was once head of a school Gilmore attended. He's out so far as the Kent murder is concerned."

I asked about the rest of them—did they have alibis? The chief said they weren't any better off than Gale or I except that they hadn't been found at the scene of the crime. "Travis claims he rented a car and drove over to a dance at Somerset. Nobody there remembers seeing him but there was a crowd and a lot of strangers. Travis says the dance was no good so he left. He turned in the car about two-thirty and, according to him, went to bed. Sims and Davis here just wandered around—not together. Seven blocks of midway and they didn't pass each other once. Sims says he played Bingo and has a blanket to prove it. Davis isn't so definite. He . . ."

"I did a little shooting at one of the galleries," Johnny said. "But my eye was out and I was worried about Anne. One of the girls at a milk depot across the street gave me the addresses of some boarding houses. I checked them. I never thought of the cabin camps or I'd have gone there, too."

He'd checked rooming houses—my sainted aunt! After Gale and I, probably. I wondered what his reception had been and what the rooming house keepers had thought.

"Levinsky was the only one who said he went to bed after the show and he can't prove it. But he does tell a queer yarn about waking up in the night and hearing someone panting and fumbling in the pile of suitcases across the room. Didn't investigate though. Turned over and stuck his head under the covers. If the story's true, that could have been when the bracelet piece was planted."

Planted, I thought. That must mean he's stopped suspecting Morrie. Then who . . . Was Gale, by virtue of that raincoat, elected?

I couldn't tell by the chief's face. It was blank and still. I looked at the others. Goodwin was chewing at his cigar. It had gone out but he didn't seem to mind. Johnny was leaning back in his chair, relaxed now that his story was told. I couldn't look at Gale. It would hurt too much.

But they weren't getting anywhere, I thought hopelessly. They kept secrets like conspirators, and when they did decide to talk, nothing they said made sense. Any of them told a good story, made himself innocent. But there was more to solving a murder than that. You had to dig deep below the surface. It was there you found the hidden unpleasantnesses—the frustrations, abnormalities, the twisted mentalities . . .

Twisted mentalities! It hit me like an electric shock. Something that Tait had said and I'd almost forgotten. Marihuana—that was it. Marihuana distorted people's minds. I looked at the chief. I said, "Did Tait ever tell you he thought Anne might have been given marihuana before she attacked Mandy with that knife?"

Gale looked at me reproachfully but the chief's bellow of rage brought Mrs. Bradley to stand, wide-eyed, between the eucalyptus portieres. "Marihuana—good God, we got everything else! Now you haul that in, too!" He appealed to Gale. "All right, Ullman, you know if any of your men smoke marihuana?"

"Not if know it," Gale said grimly. "I know it's done in some bands but not in mine. Tait was talking through his hat."

He explained Tait's theory and the chief snorted. "Don't know much about the stuff myself except its bad. You think it could be possible?"

"I don't know," Gale said wearily. "I can't picture Anne smoking reefers if she knew it and they're something you have to know about *to* smoke. They're not like other tobacco and there's a special technique about smoking them."

The chief stood up. "Okay, maybe we'd better talk to Gilmore right away and see what's on his mind. You two come along. We'll get some of that story down for the records and while we're going down, you, Mr. John Davis-Joe Glanzer, can explain how come you changed your name in the first place."

I had considerable curiosity of my own regarding that. Without thinking I, too, was on my feet. The chief saw me and scowled. "You sit down, Connie Waring. This is one time you stay at home. You go to bed!"

I went. It seemed the part of wisdom to obey.

19

Mrs. Bradley and the telephone awakened me at eight the next morning. My caller was Tait Gilmore and he sounded brisk and business-like and everything else that I wasn't. He said, "Come on down and have breakfast with me, Connie. I want to talk."

I hedged. "What about? I've had about all the talking I can stand."

"This talking," said Tait with meaning, "is going to be different."

All the time I was dressing, I was conscious of a feeling of unease. I told myself that it was silly, there was neither need nor occasion for nerves. It was only Tait. He hadn't killed anyone—certainly not Anne. You had to take the word of a priest . . .

Tait didn't pretend to talk until our orders had been placed before his. Then he looked at me with sober intentness. "Connie, do you believe in hunches?"

I laid down my fork and sighed. Hunches—if that were all it was . . . "Not in a murder case, I don't," I said firmly.

"I'm not so sure. Look, it's like this. The police aren't getting anywhere and God knows it's not their fault. Give them a murder case in their own territory among the kind of people they know and they'd handle it all right. But they've been lifted out of their territory. We're all strangers to them and what they find out about us they have to get from us. Oh, maybe they could find out some more if they checked back but that would take time and time's what they haven't got. Now me, I'm different. I'm in my own territory and there's darn little about the band I don't know."

I challenged that. "You don't know anything about me."

He patted my hand. "I don't need to. You're a nice girl, that's all. It sticks out all over."

I said, "Thanks," not too gratefully. "If you know so darn much, why don't you try helping out the police?"

"What's the good? They wouldn't believe me. Old Bradley hauled me out last night just to have the fun of pooh-poohing my marihuana theory. Okay, maybe he's right and I'm crazy, but I don't think so."

He sounded so positive that I was impressed. "But I should think—if, you really know something . . ."

"And give him a chance to talk me down again? No, thanks. The chief's still running around looking for a motive in Mandy's and Anne's deaths. Good Lord, the motive's staring him in the face and he won't see it. Somebody wanted that bracelet bad enough to kill for it, that's all. All right, even the chief sees some sense in that, but he's overlooking the crux of the thing—how the murderer found out that Anne had the bracelet and how he got in touch with her. Neither Johnny nor Gale knew where she was—or say they didn't. Now I don't think either one of them killed her. Johnny certainly didn't, and as for Gale, well, it could have been pretty smart to get around to that cabin camp when he did." He lapsed into thought for a second, shook himself out of it. "Nope. Gale's not that smart. Okay, where was I?"

"You were telling me how you were going to 'try and catch the murderer,'" I said spitefully.

"How I'm *going* to catch the murderer, you mean. Look, Connie, I had a long talk with Johnny last night. He said he got two telephone calls from Anne. That the way you understood it?"

I nodded.

"Well, what would you say if I told you there were *three* calls made for our Mr. Davis?"

I forgot to be spiteful. "Tait!" I said. "You don't mean— How did you find out?"

"The way the police didn't. Johnny said two calls—one to the Harvest Hall and one to the hotel. All right, I cuddled up to the switchboard operator at the hotel, gave her a pair of the nylons I've been buying for my wife, and she came through with that extra call. The police hadn't asked her. It came into the hotel around four o'clock Monday afternoon. She rang the room and no one answered so she had him paged."

"I know," I said excitedly. "I was there—in the coffee shop with Gale. I heard the boy paging him. But, Tait, Johnny wasn't even in the hotel that afternoon. He was out with Bradley, checking over the walk we'd taken Sunday."

"Yeah, I know. Johnny never got the call but someone did."

I considered. "Well, then, the bellboy ought to be able to identify whoever it was, shouldn't he?"

"It's not that simple. The bellboy never saw the man. I told you she rang Room 420 and then she had him paged— in the lobby, the coffee shop, et cetera. Finally someone cut in on a line and said he was Davis. So she completed the call."

"And it was Anne who called?"

"Could have been. She thinks it was a woman's voice."

I was beginning to regard Tait with awe. "And the girl doesn't know who took the call?"

"How could she? He took it from the house phone on the mezzanine. She never had a chance to see. She thought of course it was Johnny—anyone would."

"But why would anyone take another person's call? And don't you think it's considerable of a coincidence that the call happened to be from Anne?"

"I'll admit the coincidence," Tait said slowly, "and I think it was an accident that the murderer got that particular call, but I think, too, that there was a perfectly logical reason for him taking it. If you can't see it, all right—skip it."

I didn't stop to ponder over that. I was busy pursuing another train of thought. "Wouldn't Anne know it wasn't Johnny?"

"Not necessarily. She probably did most of the talking. I think she must have given herself and the fact that she had the bracelet away in her first sentence. Something like, 'Johnny, I've got the bracelet and I'll give it to you myself if you'll meet me after the show tonight.' That would be enough. He'd make the date—and keep it."

I shivered a little. "Tait, it's horrible."

"Of course it is," he said quietly. "That's why I want to end it—before he gets anyone else."

"How?"

"I'll tell you later."

"Later, why? You mean you've more to tell me? What more?"

"Odds and ends. I checked on the money angle for one thing—Shorty saying that Mandy left Gale a pile. I didn't like that. But Gale says it was a pipedream, that Mandy had had some money but that she lost it on the grain market. She was selling rye short—then when the market went up, she lost all she had. He said if Shorty'd been in on it and got out with any money, he was either lucky or smart.

Gale didn't know whether or not anyone else in the band had been caught."

Anyone else in the band—I caught my breath. "That could be it, then."

"I think so. If you'd managed to save a little money and you gave it to someone who was going to, well, say double it for you, and something went wrong and you lost what you had—and if you'd seen the person you gave it to wearing diamonds worth a lot, you might get it into your head that the diamonds had been bought with your money and really belonged to you."

"I see," I said slowly. I broke off a piece of roll, put it down again. "Tait, what is it you want? You didn't get me down here just to tell me all this. I know it. You're planning something—and I'm in it. What?"

"I want your help," he said soberly. "It's this marihuana thing. I wasn't joking when I brought it up and I wasn't waving red herrings around either, the way the chief thinks. There's been marihuana used in the band—not so much when we're on tour as when we're stuck in a big place and come in contact with other bands. Gale may not know it but I do. I've been on a few of the parties myself, and the guy I've got my eye on has been there, too. So I'm giving a little party myself tonight—small and select. Just you and I and—one other."

I sat up. "If you think I'm going to smoke marihuana—"

"I'm not asking you to. You won't even be there except for a split-second appearance. I want to dress you up like Anne Kent."

"Dress me up like Anne Kent!" I pushed back from the table and regarded him with horror. "Tait, what in God's name are you planning to do?"

He reached over and took my hand. "Nothing to hurt you, honey. I just want to get him high and then confront him with Anne Kent in the flesh. I think he'd break then."

Anyone would, I thought. "And if he doesn't?"

"He will. He'll think you're a ghost come back to haunt him."

"And what if he goes for me and tries to kill me the second time?"

"I'll be there. Nothing will happen to you—I promise that. Maybe I won't even have you in the room—just let you look in through a window."

"A window! Where?"

"Meyer's Auto Camp. I've rented a cabin for tonight."

"Not Anne's?"

"Nope. That's locked up. I got another."

"And if he doesn't come?"

"He will. He likes parties."

"Tait, tell me who."

"And have you give it away every time you look at him? Not a chance. Come on, Connie, you know you want this thing ended—before anyone else gets killed. Maybe this will do it. It's worth taking a chance on, isn't it?"

It was that "before anyone else gets killed" that finished me. Anyone else could be Gale or Johnny or even me. What was it the chief had said—"How do you know there won't be a third girl murdered and that one you?" Reason for it or not, it wouldn't make any difference. Once you'd killed, a second murder didn't mean much. Neither would a third . . ."

I wavered. "But I don't look like Anne . . ."

"You will when I get through with you," Tait said confidently. "I'm a whizz on make-up. There's a costumer's down the street a ways. I'll get a blond wig there. Then with a little shadow here and here—" His fingers dabbed at my chin. "Anne's face was heart-shaped, did you know? Besides it'll be dark and he'll be woozy . . ."

I didn't like it—I was afraid even then—but I agreed at last. We talked a long time, our heads almost touching across the table. The toast grew cold, the eggs shriveled on our plates. We ordered second pots of coffee, thirds.

There was little for me to do but. listen. Tait's plans were made, complete to the last detail. I was to do this—and this. He'd make me up himself, get me out there. There were two rooms in the cabin. I was to stay hidden in the bedroom until he gave me the signal to come out; he'd tell me what it was to be later. I was to stand in the doorway for a second, that was all. I wouldn't need to be afraid. He was tipping off the police. They'd be there, too.

"You're taking an awful risk," I told him.

He shrugged. "Perhaps. But if it comes off . . ."

We left it like that.

The day sped by so fast that the hours blurred, one into the other. It was nine and ten and eleven and there'd been nothing in between.

The inquests were held. I was there, like the others, by request. They were private, mere formalities that satisfied the law and left us no wiser than we'd been before.

At three o'clock we got into rented cars and drove over to Somerset, to the little church upon a hill from which Mandy was to be buried. It was a dreary funeral. The cemetery was small and ill-kept. Grass grew high at its edges. Straggling cedars, rusty from the summer's heat, held precarious foothold against the churchyard wall. Over fresh-turned sod, an American flag waved forlornly.

The sun was slanting low into the west when we drove back to Harriston. I rode with Gale and Johnny. We didn't talk. There was nothing to say.

They let me out at Bradley's. The house was quiet. I climbed the stairs to my room and lay on the bed. I didn't let myself think. I was afraid to.

When it was time to go down to the Harvest Hall, I dressed. I put on my gray suit because Anne had worn gray. I didn't bother with a hat—Tait had promised to find one, red. Anne had worn red shoes and I had none, but Tait had said that wouldn't matter—that my feet wouldn't show. It was the hat and the suit and the wig that counted.

I stood in front of the mirror for a long time before I finally left the house. I studied my face, pale in its frame of paving dark hair. Anne's face had been heart-shaped, Tait had said. Mine was oval. With shadow here and here—my own fingers touched the places his had dabbed—would I look like her? I didn't know. It seemed impossible . . .

There was another record crowd at the Harvest Hall. I scarcely saw them—I didn't let myself. I stayed in the dressing room, came out only when my numbers were due. The other girls watched me curiously. I didn't care. When Tait came for me, I was ready.

He had a car; the Drive-Yourself place was doing big business since the band had come to town. We went directly to the cabin camp. It was a dark night, moonless, and a stiff wind was scattering the leaves from the tall old maples that lined the streets. Upon the ravine's rim, the growth of trees writhed in steady motion. I turned my face from them.

He left the car in the street and hurried me along the gravel. "Keep quiet," he cautioned. "If the old girl sees you . . ."

I was quiet. I didn't want to be seen.

The cabin was the center one of the three closest to the ravine. It was small and shabby. There was a tiny sitting room, a slightly larger bedroom, and infinitesimal kitchen. Tait gave me little time to look around, however. He shoved me into a chair, pulled jars and boxes from his pockets.

"Got to hurry," he told me. "Here, hold your head still. I'm going to work and talk at the same time. You know what you're supposed to be—Anne's spirit coming out of the ravine. That'll be my build-up. First I thought maybe I'd have you appear at the window but there's no second door and you can hardly perch outside on a rock for an hour or two. So it'll have to be the bedroom—Tip your head back, will you? Remember, all you've got to do is open the door when you hear my signal. I'll whistle a bar or two of something—what'll it be? *Coming Through the Rye,* how's that? You open the door and stand there for a second—that'll be enough."

I must have shivered, under his hand, for he stopped working at my face and held my shoulders tightly. "Don't be afraid, honey, nothing's going to happen to you. I won't be smoking—I'll handle him. Look, there's a window in there. Would you feel better if I slipped the screen off when I go so you'd have a way out? Then, after you've looked in here, you can climb out and beat it for the office. How'll that be?"

I said it would be all right but my voice sounded listless and uncertain. Tait frowned as he fitted the blond wig to my head and stepped back. He said, "God, that's a job! You look like Anne—damn it, you *are* Anne! Want to see? There's a mirror inside . . ."

I shook my head. I didn't want to look into the mirror and when I did I wanted it to be myself whom I saw.

Tait was sweeping bottles and jars into the table drawer. He took a last look around. "Good enough. Now you've got it straight—what you're to do? Stay in the bedroom until you hear me whistle, then open the door and stand there for a second. After that, you can shut the door and beat it as fast as you like. The window's low, you won't have any trouble. Make sure it's open, that's all. Sorry I can't leave you a light, baby, but you're better without." He came closer, touched my chin with a finger. "Good luck, Connie—happy ending!"

I said good-by. At the door, he paused with his hand on the light switch. "I'll see about the screen right now." Then he was gone.

Without light or moon, the cabin was very dark. I felt my way into the bedroom, closed its door securely. I could see Tait's shadow as he fumbled at the screen. Presently he lifted it down and I could push open the window. A wind, chill with autumn, swept in to stir the sleazy curtains. I felt better.

Tait's footsteps receded along the gravel drive. I heard the car stir into motion, attack the long grind of the hill. Then everything was still again.

I crossed to the bed and sat on its edge. Springs creaked. I stood up again. Too noisy—I'd better find a chair, get myself settled before they came . . .

Before they came . . . Well, they *were* coming, weren't they? Tait had said so . . .

But why believe Tait? He might have lied to me. What if Tait himself were the murderer?

Panic took me then. How did I know Tait's story had been true? How did I know I could trust him? His story had been good and I'd swallowed it. I'd been a fool— oh, such a fool. No one knew I'd gone with Tait, no one knew where I'd gone. Even movie heroines were smarter than that. They left notes or messages so the heroes could rescue them in time. I'd done nothing. Why hadn't I? It would have been so simple, so easy to leave a note.

What if Tait came back alone? He could be the murder- er, Father Kelley or no Father Kelley. How did I know there hadn't been time—*before* he went to the priest's house— to murder Anne? Tait knew all about that telephone call, too, and I'd admitted being in the hotel when it came in. Suppose he'd been there, suppose he'd been the one who'd taken it. He might have thought I'd seen—been fishing to find out. If he were afraid I'd remember and talk, he might consider it reason enough to kill me.

Why was I so certain he'd come back? How did I know he'd ever gone? He could have moved the car, come back softly to the cabin. I might not hear him. The door was locked—I'd heard him turn the key—but there was the window. He'd made it ready. What would I do if he appeared suddenly at the window? I braced myself, stared hard at the grayed opening. I'd see his shoulders first . . .

But no shoulders loomed against the grayness, no fingers I fumbled over the sill. Nothing entered save the wind. Time went by and gradually my taut nerves relaxed. Once again I was able to wait.

Not long. There were footsteps on the gravel, a rattle at the door. I heard Tait's voice, easy and assured. "Hold it, we want a lamp here." A thread of light crept softly below the door. Something bumped the table as though packages had been laid down. Feet passed the bedroom door and I heard Tait's voice again. "Make yourself comfortable, I'll just be a sec." Water ran in the tiny kitchen—ordinary, everyday sounds; nothing to fear in them.

Tait was speaking again, softly—I couldn't hear what he said. If the other answered, I didn't hear him. Perhaps I wouldn't. The wig was tight about my head, thick and hot over my ears. Its coarse hair fretted my neck. If I were closer to the door . . . I slipped off my shoes, tiptoed cautiously across the floor.

I still heard nothing from the other. A grunt or two— that might be he. Tait returned from the kitchen. A chair scraped on the floor; then silence.

I began to be aware of an odor, weedy, pungent, penetrating. It drifted faintly through the loosely fitting door frame to tickle my nose with unexpected sharpness. The marihuana, I thought, and drew back, a little, from the door. Could you get high on marihuana without inhaling? I didn't know. As a precaution, I held my handkerchief across my nose.

The persistence of the silence baffled me. Somehow I'd expected a reefer party to be gay, noisy with laughter and singing and all the sounds uninhibited emotion could devise. But the room beyond remained still and quiet—as quiet as death.

I don't know how long it was before I heard the giggle. It was a soft, silly little giggle, and after it a voice that wasn't Tait's, a voice that was thick and blurred and throaty, spoke.

"Wanna drink. I'm dry."

"Inna kitchen. Help y'self." This was Tait and his voice, too, was thick and different.

Movement now. Water running. A thump as though a chair had overturned. The first voice spoke again. "Anything to eat?"

"Package of stuff. Onna table."

A rattling of paper. "Where's a knife?"

"No knife. Forgot the knife."

Silence again. I pressed closer to the door. The keyhole was dark. The key must be on the other side. If I could only see . . .

A yawn. Tait's voice again. "Kinda scare-y here."

The other voice sharpened a little. "Wha' you mean, scare-y?"

"I dunno. Jus' scary. You believe in ghosts?"

"Me? Naw!" There was scorn, ineffable, in the monosyllable. "You?"

"I dunno. Maybe. This'd be a good place for ghosts."

"You think so? What kinda ghosts?"

"Anne Kent's ghost."

This was it I thought. This was it.

"Anne Kent's dead. Somebody killed her. Down inna ravine. You didn' know?"

"*I* know." Tait sounded smugly wise. "Her ghost's not dead."

"How'd you know?"

"Everybody's gotta ghost. People die—ghosts don't."

There was a little silence before the other voice spoke again. "What's she gotta ghost for?"

"I dunno. Maybe she's gonna haunt the guy who killed her."

Another silence. Then the voice rose triumphantly. "She ain't gonna haunt *me!*"

"How'd you know? Ghosts always haunt the person who kills them."

"Who said I killed her?"

"You said so—jus' now."

"Naw, I didn't." The voice lowered, turned cunning. "What makes you think she's haunting me? You see any ghost around?"

"Give her time. Ghosts gotta have time."

"Look, you see a ghost around—maybe I killed her. I don't say . . . You don't see a ghost . . . What'sa matter? What you looking at?" The voice shot upward to a screech. "Christ Almighty, you see a ghost?"

"Naw, I guess not." Some of the blurred quality was gone from Tait's voice. "I just thought maybe I saw the door opening."

"What door? You crazy! Ghosts don' open doors."

"How'd you know what ghosts do?"

"Ghosts can't open doors," the other voice said stubbornly.

He had something there, I thought, even as Tait's chair squawked backward. "Okay, have it your way. I'm just telling you the door was opening . . ."

Footsteps moved lightly across the floor. I heard the tag-end of a whistle. *If a body meet a body . . .*

I took a long breath and turned the doorknob—soundlessly. I had luck there. The door came toward me. I stepped back, noiseless in my stocking feet, and let its own weight swing it back. It passed me. Slowly I moved toward the opening, paused in it, remembering to stand within the shadows . . .

I heard the long sibilant hiss of fear.

My eyes were dazzled. I had been in the dark too long. I was aware of the room, of Tait taut beside the table, of his voice: "It's Anne—my God, it's Anne, I tell you! You *did* kill her—she's come back . . ."—of a figure that crouched forward in its chair, its eyes gleaming with the madness of fear . . .

It held like that for an instant. Then, with a low growl, the figure sprang.

I couldn't move fast enough to swing the door between us. My fingers slipped wetly on its edge. I heard Tait's yell—"Look out! For God's sake, look out!" and saw him lunge forward. I heard my own voice screaming . . .

Hands were holding my arms, pushing upward toward my throat. There was a voice in my ears. It said over and over again the same words, horrible, ugly words fraught with terrible meaning. "Haunt me, will you? You can't haunt me, damn you! I'll fix that. You can't haunt me, understand? You're dead—I killed you once—I'll kill you again—I'll kill you again—I'll kill you again . . ."

I tore madly at the fingers. They were too strong. I tried to scream and couldn't—I had no breath. Red darkness was splintering my eyeballs, roaring in my ears. I felt myself falling—falling . . .

Then—nothingness.

20

I had gone down into red darkness. I came back through white light, incandescent and burning. It stabbed at my eyeballs. I put up a hand to ward it off. I said, "Don't!" and it was a croak.

Something clicked and the light was gone. Someone said, "She's out of it. She'll be all right now, thank God!"

I heard with interest. Incredibly I was still alive.

I didn't move or open my eyes. I didn't want to. It was enough just to lie there and contemplate the miracle of it. I'd been choked into insensibility; my throat's ache testified to that. I'd fallen and bumped my head—a whole bees' nest buzzed around inside it—but I was alive. Wonder of wonders, I was *alive!*

An arm slid under my head. A voice said, "Maybe if I can get some brandy down her . . ."

I knew that voice, I knew that brandy flask. I pushed it aside, struggled to sit up.

Gale said, "Here, wait a minute—take it easy. Lean against me."

I opened my eyes.

It was still the cabin's shabby sitting room but now people were in it. I was sitting on the couch, Gale's shoulder steady under mine. Shorty Sims stood in front of us,

a basin of water in his hands. Johnny leaned against the
table. Tait . . .

"Where's Tait?" It was my own voice but I hardly recognized it.

"Right here," Tait said sourly. "All set for the medal
ceremony. Your hero!"

It was an effort to turn my head but I managed. He was
lying back in a big chair. There was a turkish towel ban-
dage about his head.

"You," I said reproachfully, "were the one who wasn't
going to let anything happen to me. I'd be perfectly safe—
you could handle him . . ."

As much as I could see of his face winced. "Lay off,
Connie. I made a fool of myself. Think I don't know it? I
went for him all right, football fashion, but my feet must
have slipped or I misjudged the distance. I went wham
into the door frame and knocked myself out. I never even
knew it when the marines landed."

"And none too soon either," Johnny said with a shiver.
"I thought Connie was a goner, all right."

I did a little shivering myself. After all, I was the Connie
who'd been almost a goner. I said, "It was Dick, wasn't it?"

There was a little silence, and then Shorty said, "Yeah.
It was Dick. It was Dick, all right."

Tait said, "Didn't you know?" incredulously. "Didn't
you see him?"

"The light blinded me," I explained. "All I saw was
somebody with eyes—horrible eyes. But after he grabbed
me and started to choke me, I—oh, well, I suppose I had
a sort of mental flashback. All of a sudden I knew exactly
what you'd meant when you said that telephone call was a
coincidence and that the murderer getting it at all was an
accident but that there was a perfectly logical reason why
he did get it. And because I knew what the reason was, I
knew *who* he was."

Shorty said, "The kid's nuts!" and Johnny said, "Telephone call! What telephone call? What are you talking about?"

I started to shake my head at Shorty, but the shaking set off too many fireworks. I said, "I'm not crazy, really I'm not. Johnny, that afternoon I was supposed to meet Anne, I was in the hotel coffee shop with Gale. A bellboy came through paging you. Tait thinks it was a call from Anne to tell you she'd changed her mind and would meet you herself. Only Dick got the call instead of you."

"Dick got the call instead of me? How? I don't get it."

"It's your names," I said. "Davis—Travis. You know how the boys page you—they just keep saying 'Mr. Davis —Mr. Davis' over and over. If you say it often enough, it could sound like Travis. That's what Tait meant when he said there was a perfectly logical reason why he might have taken it. And then, of course, if Anne said who she was right away and mentioned the bracelet . . ."

"He had a car that night," Johnny groaned. "Poor kid, she didn't have a chance. Once he had her in it . . ."

"But she did what she wanted to do, Johnny," I said. "She hung on tight to the bracelet. Even though it broke, she kept hold of it—for you. And it was the bracelet that tripped him. Although that was mostly his own fault. I can't see why he'd hide the piece he did get in such an obvious place as Morrie's sock."

"He was reefer-happy that night," Tait said. "I'd bet on it. He was smoking tea pretty consistently—we all knew it if you didn't, Gale. And you know how marihuana distorts values. He probably thought the toe of Morrie's sock was a brilliant hiding place and one the police would never find. At that, if they hadn't been on their toes . . ."

"But why did he want it?" Johnny burst out. "He could have had it. I'd have given it to him gladly—to keep Anne alive."

"We figured that out, too," Tait told him. "Gilmore and Waring, master detectives. Shorty, the other night you gave out with the news that Mandy'd helped you make a lot of money on the stock market. Was Dick in on that, too?"

"He might have been," Shorty said cautiously. "Why?"

"You also announced that she'd left Gale a packet. That was a lie. If you made any money, you were lucky. Mandy lost her shirt and, I think, Dick's."

"And he'd seen Mandy wear the bracelet," Johnny said, "so he killed her to get it. Only Anne had it and so he had to kill her . . ."

"He killed Mandy because she didn't have the bracelet," Gale said grimly. "If she'd had it, she'd have handed it over fast enough. She wouldn't have risked her skin for some-one else's property—I knew Mandy."

"Do you suppose she told him who had the bracelet?" I said. "If she did, Anne wouldn't have had to mention it, even."

"I don't know," Tait said. "Maybe when Bradley gets back, we'll know. Dick was sure spilling his guts when they took him away. I think Bradley's sore at me," Tait added pensively.

"I don't see why," I said. "You caught his murderer for him, didn't you?"

"Yeah, but he thought he should have been in on it, I think he likes you, Connie. He said I'd taken unwarranted risks with your life."

"But he did know about it! You said . . . Tait, didn't he?"

Tait shook his head. "I told you I'd played the fool. That story was just to make you feel good."

The bottom of my stomach dropped. "Then how . . ."

"I told you—the marines." He waved his hand at Shorty and Gale and Johnny. "They always get there in time."

"We ran it pretty fine this time," Gale said soberly. "You see, Connie, we've been keeping a pretty good eye on you lately, the mortality rate on singers with the band being high. It was Shorty who saw you go off with Tait and he thought Tait was just taking you out to Bradley's. He told Johnny and Johnny, being a cautious soul, checked and you weren't there. So he told me and we routed out Bradley. He didn't want another murder either so he coop-erated—fast. But we wasted a lot of time checking eating places. I don't know who first suggested the cabin camp but we got out here just in time to hear you scream and to find Tait out cold on the floor and Dick doing his best to finish you off. If Tait here hadn't thought he was Super-man . . . Next time, fella, let someone else in. Your help may come too late."

"How'd I know you weren't in it yourself?" Tait de-manded, unabashed. "I thought it was Dick. But if it hadn't been, it could have been anyone of you fellows. And so far as Bradley goes—poof! I'm in the clear. It's not my fault if the guy I invite out for a bottle of beer and a bite to eat gets high on reefers he brings along himself, I didn't smoke any, I didn't do a damn thing—"

"Except stage a resurrection from the dead," I mur-mured.

Tait surveyed me from wide, innocent eyes. "I don't know what you're talking about."

"Tait! What about that make-up? What about that wig?"

"Wig? What wig? Any of you fellows see a wig around here?"

Solemnly they shook their heads.

I hesitated, between tears and laughter. "But my face—that make-up—"

"Nothing wrong with your face," Tait said. "It's clean. What do you think Shorty had that water for?"

I gave it up, partly because my head hurt too much and partly because there was a rap at the door. It was Dr. Borman and he said Bradley'd sent him "to look over the Casualties."

I got off easily enough. He looked at my throat, rubbed his hand over the bump on my head, and assured me I'd be all right. Oh, my throat would be sore for a while but after a good night's sleep . . . To insure the sleep, he gave me half a dozen little yellow pills with instructions to take two and then, if they didn't work, two more.

Tait didn't do so well. There was a nasty cut on his temple that required two stitches to close. "I won't say you'll have a scar," Dr. Borman told him. "But I do say you're going to have a nasty headache for a few days. Next time kick the door—don't try to butt it."

"If a sore head's all he's got, he comes out lucky," said a new voice, the chief's. He had come in quietly and was now standing just within the door. Our heads turned toward him like sunflowers to the sun. It was to me he spoke. "You all right?"

"Yes, thanks," I said meekly, "I think so."

"Huh! Guess you're lucky, too. Now, wait, I don't want to hear any explanations of this evening's performance. I don't want to know how it was done or why. We've got our man and we're grateful within limits, but we don't want to take official notice of a lot of illegal acts. So far's any of you go, none of this ever happened."

"Maybe that's what you think," I said with a reminiscent hand to my throat. "It was real enough for me."

"You don't come into it," the chief informed me. "It's dead women we're interested in, not live ones. Now, take it easy, the whole lot of you. I know what you want and you're going to get it, to the best of my ability. Anything you don't understand, you can ask about later. Maybe I won't have all the answers yet, but what I do have . . ." With a wide gesture, he left it open.

"Travis was your murderer, all right," he went on. "He's admitted it. Told us quite an interesting story. I guess, though, from what Sims and Davis told me, coming out here, that Gilmore had it pretty well figured out why he did the killing. It was just Mandy Martin's—Mrs. Ullman's—bad luck that she started to make money on the grain market and let Sims in on it. But Sims was smarter than she was. He got out when he'd made his pile. Only he'd talked and Travis had heard him. Travis wanted money pretty badly—he'd saved some but it wasn't enough for what he wanted. This looked like a chance to cut in on something pretty good, and so he went to Mandy.

"Mandy took his money—she was getting in pretty deep by then—and the money came in handy. She threw it into her own account to save it and the break never came. She lost her money and Travis's, too. She had to tell him.

"Must have been a bad shock at that—the news. Travis isn't what I'd call a very stable citizen and he'd counted on that money to get him out of band life which he hated. Knowing it was gone, he brooded and the more he brooded, the more he blamed Mandy, especially since Sims had come out with a stake. Then, just as he was feeling the lowest, Mandy started wearing that bracelet.

"Ullman wasn't the only one who knew diamonds when he saw them, and Travis got it into his head that Mandy had lied to him—that the money hadn't been lost, that the bracelet represented part of the profits and that, morally, he was entitled to a share in it. He tried to see her—accuse her—but Mandy was keeping pretty much to herself those days. He never got a chance at her.

"He got his chance when you came to Harriston. He was always watching for an opportunity to talk to her and

he was watching that Sunday afternoon. He saw Mandy
and Ullman come into the hotel lobby, saw them separate
and Mandy go up to her room. He was going to try and
catch her then and there, but Connie came in and spoiled
it. So he waited and watched some more. Ullman didn't
leave the lobby, Mandy didn't reappear. But he saw Connie
come down again. Yes," he said in answer to my questioning look, "he was on the mezzanine. He watched you from
a distance, saw you stop and speak to the maid and then
go toward the service stairs. He followed you—still at a
distance—clear out to the alley, to make certain that you
didn't intend to return. That's when he got the knife. The
knives were on the kitchen table and no one was in the
room, the chef being at the telephone. On his return trip,
it was a simple thing to reach in and take one.

"He says he didn't intend to kill Mandy then—he only
meant to frighten her a little, to force her to give up what
he considered rightfully his. But he was only halfway to
her door when he heard other steps coming up the stairs,
so he retreated around a corner of the hall. He saw Anne
Kent knock on Mandy's door, saw the door opened to her.
He watched her come out again in about five minutes, saw
her go back the way she'd come. He didn't wait any longer
then. He didn't want to knock and warn Mandy. He tried
the door and it was locked. He says he had a hunch then
that his own key might fit. He tried it and it worked. He
went in.

"He says she told him to get out but he didn't pay any
attention. He demanded his money—or the bracelet—and
she laughed at him. His money was gone, she said, and
as for the bracelet, it never had belonged to her and she
didn't have it now. He didn't believe her. He saw red, he
says, and before he quite knew what was happening, she
was dead. He'd stabbed her.

"He didn't get much blood on him, only a little on his hands. He wiped that off on a damp towel he found on the floor in the bathroom. The knife he hid in Connie's bag. Then he went through Mandy's things, still looking for the bracelet. He didn't find it.

"He was afraid to take too much time for his search, afraid, too, to try his luck on the back stairs again. He climbed the flight to the fourth floor. There was no one in his room and he lay down for a while, He was pretty badly shaken up. When Sims came in later, he made a point of leaving the hotel in his company.

"He would have liked to bring Anne Kent into it, after the murder was discovered, throw suspicion her way. But he was afraid. The claim that he'd seen her in the hotel hall would automatically turn attention to himself. He couldn't have that. So he kept quiet.

"But he thought about her a good deal. He began to wonder if she could have the bracelet, if Mandy'd given it to her for safekeeping. Why she'd do that, he didn't stop to think. So far as he was concerned, the bracelet was his; it had been purchased with his money and Mandy had lied to him. He meant to have it at any cost. Then, Monday afternoon, Anne Kent made that telephone call and he got it.

"He says he really thought the call was meant for him and that may be. Davis and Travis don't sound unalike as they're pronounced around here. Only the call was from Anne Kent and the first thing she said was, 'Johnny, I've changed my mind. I want to give you the bracelet myself!'

"He did some quick thinking then and when he spoke he tried to sound as much like Davis as he could. He suggested that he meet her, arranged to pick her up on the corner near Meyer's camp after the show. He said he'd have a car.

"It was around eleven when he finally picked her up— it had taken him a while to get the car. He had a little trouble with her after she was in the car and saw he wasn't Davis. But he managed to keep her quiet and in the car until he drove a little way into the country—so they could talk.

"He didn't know how long they talked. Quite a while, he thinks. Anne told him the bracelet wasn't hers or Mandy's—it belonged to Davis. He told her she lied.

"He says it was about a quarter to one when she finally agreed to give him the bracelet. But she insisted she didn't have it with her, that she'd left it in the cabin. He thought she was stalling but he knew he could handle her there. So he drove to the camp.

"They left the car on the other side of the block from camp, and walked down past the ravine. He kept tight hold of her arm as a warning not to try any tricks, but she saw Ullman's car parked near the corner of the ravine. They both recognized it and she wrenched free and began to run. He caught her without too much trouble but it gave him a nasty minute or two and he was angry. She would have screamed but he got his hands about her throat and choked her a little and then he was able to drag her back toward the ravine. Nobody had heard their little fracas; the street was deserted.

"He says he only choked her a little but he knew he'd have to finish the job. She knew too much. For his own safety he couldn't let her go free. But first he wanted the bracelet. He let her down to the ground and went through her purse but the bracelet wasn't there. It wasn't in her pockets either. He decided to try and revive her and force her to tell him where it was and he lit a match to make sure she still breathed. That was when he caught the gleam of something bright in one of her clenched hands. He tried to pull it free and couldn't. Her grip was too tight. There was a stone at his feet . . ."

The chief drew a long breath. "We needn't go into that. But even then he couldn't get the bracelet, not all of it. Her dead hand held it too tightly. And he couldn't wait to pry her fingers apart; it was too risky. He was afraid Ullman might appear.

"There was blood on his hands and, without thinking, he wiped them down the coat he was wearing. Then he did think and he knew he'd have to get rid of the coat somewhere, somehow. It wasn't until he'd taken the coat off entirely that he discovered it wasn't his coat. He knew whose it was."

"And that," said Gale bitterly, "was my own damn carelessness. A lot of us have light rainproofs and we usually just dump them in a pile wherever it's convenient. It looked like rain that night, remember? He must have grabbed the wrong coat, that's all. I wasn't wearing mine that night."

"He had yours, all right," the chief said grimly. "And when he found it out he knew what he was going to do. You were careless with your car—he was pretty sure he'd find the trunk unlocked. The way he figured it, anything that threw suspicion upon somebody else made him that much safer.

"He had just shut the trunk when he heard you coming down the street. He thought at first that you wouldn't see him but when you did, there was nothing for it but to run. He got away through the ravine and back behind the cabins until he could cut over to the cross street where he'd left the car. It was at the top of a hill and he let it coast until the motor caught. Then he drove back to the garage and left the car and then went to the hotel. You know the rest."

"But we don't," I said. "Not all of it. Why did he hide the bracelet in Morrie's sock? Why Morrie's?"

"No particular reason," the chief said. "It was anybody's sock so far as he was concerned. He had to get rid of it quick, that was all. He just shoved it into the first suitcase handy and trusted to luck that it wouldn't be found until he could get it again and dispose of it in some safer place. Anything else?"

"Thanks, no," Gale said. There was a white line about his mouth. "I think we've heard enough."

Tait opened his eyes. "Speak for yourself," he drawled. "How about my marihuana theory now, Chief? Get anything on that?"

The chief surveyed hint without favor. "You still talking about that attack Anne Kent made on Mrs. Ullman? We haven't had time to go into all the details yet but Travis has admitted to smoking marihuana and giving some to Miss Kent. You can draw your own conclusions."

"I already have," Tait said cheerfully, "and a lucky thing for you it was that I did." He stood up gingerly. "Ouch! My head feels as though a mountain had fallen on it! I'm going to bed. Who's driving me into town? At present I'm not trusting my precious life to myself."

"I'll drive you," Shorty said, and the chief looked at me.

"How about you, Connie? Want to ride in with me?" He smiled a little. "Better take me up—may be your last chance to ride in a police car."

I opened my mouth to accept but Gale was ahead of me, "*I'm* driving Connie in."

So they went and the cabin was quiet again. There were only Gale and Johnny and me left. We didn't talk. They just sat in silence, watching me, until I put a conscious hand up to my head. What with wigs and being mauled about, my hair had suffered. "I'm a mess," I said.

"You look all right," Johnny said gruffly, and Gale agreed.

"Lord, yes! When I think what Tait put you through, I could murder him myself. Connie, you know I'm sorry? About all this. When I asked you to come with the band that day in the radio station, I didn't have any idea it was going to—end like this." His voice trailed off, flat and dispirited.

I let my hands fall. "End like this . . . What do you mean?"

He refused to meet my eyes. "Two girls have been murdered, a member of my band has been proven their murderer, you've been put through hell by no fault of your own. It's not nice to think about, to remember. I know it. That's why I'm trying to tell you this—that I won't blame you if you feel you can't go on. I'll release you, as of right now. You don't owe me anything. The debt's on my side. I—"

I took a careful breath, interrupted. "What if I don't want to be released?"

His head came up. His voice was unbelieving. "You can't mean that you're not through—that you don't want to quit the band?"

There was the beginning of a lump in my throat. I had to swallow hard to get over it. "Of course I don't," I said crossly. "Me quit now, before I've had even one pay check? If you'd told me that a couple of days ago, I don't know—I might have taken you up and gone—but not now. Why, you need me now, more than ever before! And I'm not afraid. It's all over. There's nothing to be afraid of now . . ."

"You won't need to be afraid," Gale said quickly. "Not ever again. I promise you that, Connie. I'll see to that. I'll take care of you . . ."

"We'll both take care of you," Johnny cut in firmly.

They were sitting on the davenport, one on either side of me. They were nice. I liked them. It was possible, just then, that I liked Gale a little better, but there was

something solid and rock-like about Johnny, something
you instinctively knew you could trust. The time might
come when I'd be forced to choose between them, but that
time was far in the future, I hoped. I didn't need to choose
now . . .

I stretched out a hand to each. I said, "I'm staying."

Additional classic detective fiction, suspense thrillers, and police procedurals can be found at:

CoachwhipBooks.com
(print)

Coachwhip.com
(epub)

No Face to
MURDER

EDITH HOWIE

CRY MURDER

EDITH HOWIE

VIRGINIA RATH

DEATH AT
DAYTON'S FOLLY

CRIME IN
CORN-WEATHER

MARY MEIGS ATWATER

MURDER
IN A WALLED TOWN
KATHERINE WOODS

THE STRAWSTACK
MURDER CASE
KIRKE
MECHEM